Music for Leaving

A novel by

ERIKA RANDALL

This is a work of fiction. All incidents, organizations, events and dialogue, and all characters with the exception of some well-known historical figures, are products of the author's imagination and are not meant to be construed as real.

www.erikarandall.com

Interior designed by Tim Grassley.
Exterior designed by Kylie Clarke. | www.kylieclarke.com
Cover sketch by Rachel Suter.
Edited by Tim Grassley.

Library of Congress Cataloging-in-Publication Data
Names: Randall, Erika, author.
Title: Music for Leaving : a novel / Erika Randall
Description: First Edition.
Identifiers: LCCN 2025904242 | ISBN 9798992796407 (hardcover)

Music for Leaving may be purchased in bulk for promotional, educational, or business use. Please contact your local bookseller or visit IngramSpark.

A portion of the proceeds will go to support the Julie Bonasera Fund for ALS and neuromuscular disease. Please visit and consider giving: https://giveto.osu.edu/makeagift/details/315770

First Edition: 2025

In memory

of my mother, Barbara (aka Tink),

and her beloved sister Julie.

Two wild strawberries.

To crave and to have are as like as a thing and its shadow. For when does a berry break upon the tongue as sweetly as when one longs to taste it, and when is the taste refracted into so many hues and savors of ripeness and earth, and when do our senses know any thing so utterly as when we lack it? And here again is a foreshadowing – the world will be made whole. For to wish for a hand on one's hair is all but to feel it. So whatever we may lose, very craving gives it back to us again. Though we dream and hardly know it, longing, like an angel, fosters us, smooths our hair, and brings us wild strawberries.

MARILYNNE ROBINSON
Housekeeping

You'd be surprised, but it takes a long time to break something properly.

MARJORIE STEIN
An Atlas of Lost Causes

Nostalgia

I am a bit of a relic. There's not much place for me anymore, but oh, what power this fine magnetic strip holds when unleashed. Luckily, Eleanor still listens to me in the old truck—had a tape deck installed in the '80s. But now, even that seems like a forever ago. The deck doesn't like to hurry itself—no fast-forward, only rewind. If Eleanor has a specific song she wants to hear, she has to slide me in on the opposite side of the track, hit the back arrow, flip me over, and hope she gets what she's looking for. Going backward to go forward. A tedious process but it has its merits.

Sometimes a track comes up that knocks her on her ass. Never seems to fail. There it is. The last few bars of the past that she just didn't want to hear. Is it live … or is it memory? The older I get, the more I know my power—a mix tape is not to be taken lightly. I come from a tradition that transcends dimensions. I am a shamanic time machine. BOOM. Back in time. And place. And pulse. A good mix tape will fuck you up. And take you home. Don't get me wrong, I hate making Eleanor cry, but I think it just might be my job to crack the old girl open every once in a while.

They say I'm built to last, and last I have. No matter the year, I am forever in a loop of autumn 1971, before she met him and lost herself. I am proof that she existed and a reminder that she can come on back anytime.

Kidnapping

Eleanor knew she needed each of them alive and healthy until they reached their ultimate demise—no pathetic-looking wounded to stare her down and make her rethink her misplaced atrocities. As she eased the fifty-nine innocents into their vintage, snug, and squeaky forms, Eleanor wondered if they remembered their Styrofoam homes. Eleanor thought far too much about things that weren't supposed to feel, often rendering herself helpless when it came time to clean out a jewelry drawer of unpaired earrings or to throw out the ends of yarn that would never be woven into anything. She couldn't start over-thinking and over-feeling now.

The act of re-wombing the little porcelain statuettes was such an intimate one that she started to soften and considered calling the whole thing off—until a startling realization about *The Boxes* held her to her plan. She never imagined Walter moving his precious from the custom curio cabinet he had ordered as a part of a screen between the entrance hall and the living room. There they had shone for years under lighted display for all to see. It seemed to her now that Walter had never treated her with that much care. As she was wrapping up Tiny Cowboy, it hit her. The Boxes, pristinely stored in the garage attic over the unused workshop, were the only clue that *he* just might leave *her*. They were the signpost that said, "Don't think I won't slowly and meticulously repack every one of these delicate objects, carefully place them in the back seat of my car, gingerly drive away, and leave you." If she were the one who was left after all she had endured—if she wasn't the one to do the leaving—well then, that was a failure she could not carry.

"Sleep with the fishes," she said in her best gangster voice, bungee-cording the black tarp down over the truck bed. Eleanor walked around the rusty blue Dodge truck and climbed into the cab. Riding shotgun was her small overnight bag, a shoebox full of cassette tapes, and her beloved Olivetti typewriter. She cranked down the window and gave her old life the finger as she screeched out of the driveway, down the street, and out of town.

Jeremy, the hula girl on the dash, nodded merrily at the gesture. Looking back at the miles they had covered together, she appeared to take everything in stride, completely unaware of what might lie ahead.

The Inglorious Coffer

Isabel had never forgiven Eleanor for abandoning her with their mother and two years left of high school in Dayton, Ohio. Eleanor knew this because: a) Her sister never went back on her word, and b) Those words were plainly stated in the first letter she had received when she got to her new boarding school in the woods her senior year. The letter unmistakably bore Bel's handwriting, although there was no signature or return address. Writ simply in the middle of the white page were five words: "I will never forgive you." Why Eleanor had kept the letter, she had no idea. Folded into thirds, the letter resided in the bottom drawer of a jewelry box filled with other devastating objects. A promise ring from her seventh-grade boyfriend, both ring and promise broken within two months of their receipt. A small velvet bag, discovered in her mother's make-up drawer, containing her baby teeth. A rejection letter from the only conservatory she dared apply to—she was not invited to audition. A blue ribbon from her favorite doll's ponytail after Bel gave poor Rosie an unflattering pixie cut, swearing it would grow back. A Polaroid photograph of Eleanor and her dad napping in front of the fire on Thanksgiving, circa 1953. A brass key. Rose petals from the first funeral El had ever attended—a neighbor's. El did not remember her name. A small stone taken from the lake on the boy's side of campus the night El and her high school boyfriend, Lee, got caught sneaking out. It was her first strike, so she was dormed. It was his fifth, so he was expelled.

If this jewelry box were a music box it would play in E minor. If this box had a ballerina, she would be missing a leg. If this box were a chocolate box, each piece would be half eaten. This was an inglorious coffer, one full of the stuff of dashed dreams. It was the perfect place for Eleanor's engagement ring, and the bottom of her favorite lake in Michigan was the perfect place for the box to find its eternal rest. But before heading north, she had to first get it from her mother's house.

Her mother lived on the other side of town in the same home

Eleanor had grown up in. For years now they were only eleven miles apart, but her mother's dementia made the distance feel like a lifetime. Colleen Doyle Page existed in the year of her Most Beautiful—June of 1946, to be exact. Frozen in the moment of her heyday, Colleen went about her present life as a tempestuous beauty queen, recently crowned, not yet engaged, certainly not married, and absolutely without children. In her wearied mind's eye, she rode the hamster wheel of her competition as Miss Dayton during the "Miss Ohio Festival Week" in Mansfield, Ohio. It was, as she was fond of saying, the most profound week of her life—making everything that happened afterward dim in comparison. If it weren't for Ruth Howell of Apple Creek, Ohio and her dramatic re-enactment of both Gwendolen Fairfax and Cecily Cardew from *The Importance of Being Earnest*, Colleen Doyle would have continued her reign onto the national stage.

The loss at the end of Festival Week played over and over again in Colleen's dementia cycle, torturing her in a Mobius Knot of tragedy. No matter how many times she replayed each moment of the pageant, even sometimes breaking the cycle and trying a new talent, she always came up short to Ruth. It was upon losing the crown that week in 1946 that she saw her prospects as limited and, backstage at the Renaissance Theatre, a bested and disheartened Colleen

Doyle finally accepted Frederic Page's proposal. He had been waiting almost two weeks for an answer.

Eleanor's mother now had a live-in nurse who attended to her every need and made it possible for her to stay in the family home. If their mother had been difficult before, dementia made her a tyrannical hellcat. She had a passion for throwing plates and would then yell at Angie, her nurse, for breaking them. Angie wasn't human. To put up with the daily firestorms, there's no way she could have been anything other than a saint or part machine, especially considering how much she was paid.

Colleen had lived well for years off of her inheritance from her father's savvy wartime industrial contracts, stretching his fortune through her frugality. Suffice it to say, she was not a generous woman, and as a mother, she had withheld more than her family's fortune. Hugs were doled out at birthdays, successful performances, and when serious injuries occurred. Yet, her children, especially Eleanor and Danny, grew up entranced by her. Living with a self-proclaimed town legend can have that effect. Colleen had a knack for being outrageous in the way that makes one seem mythical to small children. That magic, which went undiagnosed as bi-polar disorder until a doctor treating her dementia realized there were other variables at play, was lost on Isabel. When Eleanor left for school, Bel began to plan her own escape with a vow to never return or forgive Eleanor for getting out.

Eleanor, though the first to go, was the last to stay. She visited her once a week, knowing her mother had no idea who she was. On good days, she believed Eleanor to be a pageant judge and was on her best behavior. On others, Colleen thought El to be her own mother, and treated her more like a maid than a matriarch. One night, Eleanor came with flowers, and Colleen mistook her for Ruth Howell herself. Colleen ripped the bouquet of roses from her hands, bloodying her fingers on the thorns, and screamed, "Get out of my house, you floozy slut! I know who you are! My first impressions of people are never wrong," ironically quoting Gwendolen Fairfax in her assault.

The jewelry box was upstairs in El's old room, across the hall from her mother's. She was hoping she could sneak in unnoticed, grab the box, and escape unseen. As dull as her mother's mind was these days, her ears were as sharp as ever. She had barely turned the knob of the front door when she heard her mother's voice call out, "Is that you, darling?"

Intrigued by who "darling" was, Eleanor stepped boldly into the foyer. There was her mother, dressed in her rhinestone encrusted competition gown from 1946, hair high to the heavens, tiara in place, looking as if she had just stepped out of one of the portraits that lined the staircase behind her. Colleen's face fell when she saw her daughter. One thing was clear, Eleanor was not the "darling" she was hoping for.

"Hiya," Eleanor tried sheepishly.

"Hiya?" Colleen questioned, venom searing her tongue. "Hiya?! Is that anyway to greet a lady?"

"No Ma'am." Eleanor shrank five sizes.

"You'll start with the upstairs today. I'm expecting company in the drawing room, and I won't be disturbed," Colleen seethed.

So, she was "the help" today. Fine, if it could get her up the stairs and out of the house.

"Yes, ma'am," Eleanor said and slid past her, careful not to step on her gown.

She raced to her old room, grabbed the box from underneath her too-small childhood bed, and had just reached the landing at the top of the stairs when her mother's voice called up to her.

"Do you think he will find me beautiful?" she asked, sounding more like a little girl than the diva she was just a moment ago.

Eleanor had no idea who "he" was, but it was easy to answer truthfully. Her mother was still the most beautiful woman in the world. All of a sudden, it dawned on her that she was leaving, that she might never come home again. The house suddenly began to flood with memories, most of them sad. So quickly was the rise of the tide that she was afraid they both might be washed away. This house was her mother's box of disappointments and she had locked herself inside of it for years. This was the coffin that would carry her mother and her artifacts of failure to the other side. Eleanor imagined picking it up and chucking the whole thing into the Great Miami. She saw her mother released, sparkling chiffon gown swirling around her, floating like a debutante Ophelia, out to sea.

She walked down to her slowly, kissed her on her powdery cheek, looked into her eyes, and said, "Yes."

Her mother remained frozen on the stairs, smiling radiantly, looking after the wake of her daughter as the door closed.

Guilt

God, I'm lucky she has a thing for the past. Nostalgic, that one. She keeps her hair as it has always been, pencil holding it in-place as her fingers fly, her nails just so (a perfect tap tap tapping to my keys), her sweet voice humming melodically with my contrapuntal percussive beat as she goes. Always the same tune.

I wasn't sure I would make the ride. She's traveling light these days. An empty box of might-be words isn't always the first thing you grab from a fire or for the road. It feels good to be chosen amongst all the things.

If I'm being more honest than humble, there is something special about the slick slide of my carriage. Sometimes she is rough with me e e e e, especially with that damn sticky e. Serviced twice this last year. I worry my time of usefulness is running out. But not yet. Not today.

I have given her voice all these years. It will take more than a laptop and an iPhone to replace me.

Who am I, you ask? Who am I *to say such things? An instrument of love. A thing of torture. I am both megaphone and whisper. I am her Olivetti Underwood Studio 44, olive green, with one red pimento of a tab key.*

I was given first to song lyrics—mostly of love, a few of heartbreak. My favorite I've, we've, *ever written, "My knuckles graze your flesh, now turned to stone and brick and mortar. My heart scrapped and bloodied by the wall that keeps me far as you lean toward her." She played me like her guitar when she wrote those lines. And then she fell in love and her love songs turned to letters.*

> *Dear Walter,*
> *My Walt,*
> *Dearest Man,*
> *Sweet Mister,*
> *Your, Eleanor*
> *Forever, Nor*
> *Forever and Always, Mrs. Walter Murphy*
> *With all my heart, Mrs. Eleanor Darlene Page Murphy*
> *And sometimes, just quickly:*
> *to: W.M. x, EPM*

The time of letters was quick and furious. And then came a new language. Didactic, clipped, and "catchy." Here on my keys meant for love and melody, came words that felt like sermons, speeches from on high. She was his writer now and she had little time for proper poetry. His voice came out of her and through me—I felt I was going mad. Years passed. Her hands got heavier, slow on the hammers of my heart. Vitriolic hate speech, softened by humor, and rallied by dogma. This voice was not hers, not ours, but his. I wanted to push back, stop her in her tracks. It was somewhere during the last campaign when I developed the sticky e, a symptom of my disdain, I suppose. Especially when the words started raging against her Jillian. Rhetoric, not fit speak for one so open and kind. And there I was, taking it all down, inking his party politics, pressing onto white paper the black-stained beliefs that both she and I did not share. Guilt—I am wracked by it. How I long to write a letter, a song, anything that will cleanse the palette of the last years and words and actions. I wonder if she feels this wanting, too. Sometimes, when she releases my clip and slips in that fresh new piece of possibility, I think, "This is it! Our letter to the world!" Her hands hover. And then? Nothing. Perhaps one night, half-asleep but more awake than ever, she will come to me by candlelight, take to my keys, release herself from her falsities, and we will find absolution.

License to Leave

On Eleanor's sixteenth birthday, it was Isabel who was ecstatic. Bel had been talking about this birthday for years, co-opting it as her own since Eleanor would be the first to legally get a license—and her grandfather's new Dodge truck that he could no longer drive after mowing over the row of grocery carts last spring at the IGA. Now Bel could get rides anywhere without her mother questioning her every turn. They had wheels, freedom, the road. Such was Isabel's excitement that no one had even thought to ask Eleanor what she wanted for her sixteenth birthday (the chestnut Guild guitar that had just come into the Music Shop last month, if anyone had cared to know). It was just assumed that she would want her license and the truck. El knew what this day would mean. It would mean secret parties on the other side of town for Bel and soccer practice for Danny. It would mean, "Can you run to the store for milk?" at 9 p.m. and "Can you pick-up your brother on your way home?" It would mean more work, not more freedom, and El was dreading the day. She knew she couldn't let Isabel down, so she practiced her excited face in the mirror for weeks, just as she practiced parallel parking and three-point-turns. She practiced "Happy." She practiced "Surprised." She practiced "Eager" and "Grateful." Little did she know that she was really practicing how to be a politician's wife, grooming herself for the faking-it to come.

El had never failed anything, and though she had considering throwing the test to get herself off the hook, she passed with a perfect score. Despite her earlier anguish over the whole driving thing, she came home proud, new ID preceding her through the door. The girl in the photo looked more beautiful than El had ever felt. Her hair was wild, her smile giddy, and her eyes shone brightly through the laminated plastic. Bel had been right. This was exactly what Eleanor wanted for her birthday.

This same, sixteen-year-old sense of freedom filled her now as she crossed the Montgomery County line out of Dayton. She inhaled it deeply, exhaling the anger and shame that had come along for the ride. Today was the day she left her husband. Sometime in the future, this would be the day she looked back on as The Turning Point. But today, it was still impossible, even as she was doing it. She tried to stay with the small details of the moment, so as not to be swallowed up by the day's actual size.

Today was just Tuesday, June 3, 2008, and she was out for a drive.

El looked down at her arm resting on the windowsill of the truck to check the time and realized she had left her watch behind. Constellations of freckles came into startling view—when did she get so many freckles? It's funny what you notice when you really look. She hadn't looked, really looked, at herself for a while. She felt a bit like that T-shirt you once called white that was now decidedly yellow. So many things were different than she had imagined they were, so many things that she had not opened her eyes to see. The universe sure has a hell of a way of making us look, El thought. Some things snuck into focus, like smile lines and old white T-shirts. Others, like husbands and naked interns, smacked you upside your retinas, demanding your attention NOW.

The rhythm of the road quickly worked its trance magic on El, and by the time she reached the Ohio-Michigan border, she found herself tuned into the mystic state that one can only reach through road tripping. Both relaxed and refined, El's mind felt alive and open. The constancy of driving turned the reels of her memory. As the frames of her life flickered faster and faster onto the windshield in front of her, the hula dancer bobbed in and out of focus, surfing the waves of her nostalgic sea. A million stories had been written on this route, a hundred road trips taken since she was a child. Now the road ahead became the perfect palimpsest for the past. Home movies, taken without a camera, projected both before and within her.

Over the miles of flatland, Eleanor sifted through images of all the things and people she was driving away from and those she was racing towards. Behind her? Walter and her mother, both of whom had left her in their own ways long ago. She knew there would be cleaning up to do with Walter—papers to sign, divisions to be made. But for now, she savored the wild notion that he existed literally in another state, separate from her being. Before her? Jillian and Isabel. There was so much to say to both—her daughter, whom she had abandoned in word if not action, and her sister Isabel, dear, dear Isabel, whom she knew she would never, ever leave, no matter how far apart they were cartographically. Anxious as she was to get to them out West, there were a few things she needed to do along the way. There was no cruise control in the old truck, but with the steady rhythm of the road, Eleanor floated easily into autopilot and let her mind have a journey all its own.

Peach Teacher

Riordon didn't have his R's. Every time he said his own name it came out "Weirdon," a dangerous mispronunciation for middle school, which was coming in exactly six months, one week, and four days. That February, Eleanor was well aware of their deadline when she agreed to take him on as a private student.

El had been working with him in the speech trailer outside the elementary school for the past three years. Every Monday, Wednesday, and Friday, Riordon was ready for battle, armed to the teeth with his practice pages. There was a litany of letters to attack in their hour together. S's, L's (when following hard K's and C's and after F's), and, of course, the dastardly and mischievous R. It seemed to hide everywhere, in every word.

One night after watching an episode of Wheel of Fortune on the couch with Walter, El broke down in tears. R was inevitably guessed early and, almost always, had a place in the puzzle, its tyranny unavoidable. Walt looked at her like she was crazy, sobbing away, thinking of her student, as Vanna White flipped R after R after R.

Compared to the other kids in the trailer who typically felt forced into speech therapy, Riordon was the consummate student. He worked hard, reveled in small successes (S's with no lingering lisp at the end of words—he was still working on the beginning sounds), and brought her odd but thoughtful gifts. The first in the collection was a broken watch face, the hands stopped on 8:02, Eleanor's birthday. Another favorite—a mollusk shell—Riordon told her this was a model of the one that held the world. The best gift by far was the hula dancer that Riordon named Jeremy and El placed proudly on her truck's dash. Riordon presented this gift to her the day after she brought her ukulele into the trailer and, through singing, Riordon nailed two S's and a soft C in the first line of "Somewhere Over the Rainbow."

Eleanor showed up at Riordon's house, a beautiful old Victorian that had been updated to look like the inside of a Dwell magazine, at twelve o'clock sharp. She was greeted by his mother, Susan, a freelance writer who was more than a little horrified by her only child's missing letters. Here in this house, words were everywhere. The embossed wallpaper in the foyer seemed to be made of a calligraphed alphabet. Thesauruses and dictionaries stood in for flower vases on every table. Framed poetry replaced landscapes and family portraits.

Susan offered Eleanor coffee, water, tea, all of which El declined. Her "drinking problem" over the last few weeks caused her mouth to go slightly numb time to time, her lips and throat failed to step up to their task of holding onto liquid and getting it down. She would go see her doctor about it soon enough but having likened the sensation to Novocain after a filling, she assumed it would pass.

Eleanor and Riordon worked in the library, a sunlit room whose majestic stacks seemed ominous to El, considering the task at hand. Volume after volume of letters and words held dominion over the space, their dotted I's watching, listening, judging.

Somehow, Riordon seemed undaunted by their stares and settled comfortably into his favorite Le Corbusier chaise lounge, pencil and notebook in hand, determined to seek and to conquer. His indelible spirit was astounding and softened both her concern for him and the spines of the hardbacks that had, only moments ago, seemed rigid and militant.

"Now, where were we?" Riordon eagerly asked in his best British accent. He had discovered that the W/R combination came better when elevated by a "royal" tongue. El laughed and covered her mouth as she sucked in an escaped drip of saliva.

"We were working with poetry," Eleanor said. "Shel Silverstein." Riordon looked up as Eleanor's V softened to an F. El wiped her mouth again. "Let's start with 'Sarah Cynthia Sylvia Stout.'" There was that fluffy V again, never making it down from behind her two front teeth to vibrate her bottom lip.

"Are you making fun of me?" he enunciated perfectly with no affect on the R. This was not the time to praise him and El quickly rushed to apologize. "Oh no, god no, Riordon, I would never!" But the V fell away from its fulcrum at the center of the word "never," destabilizing El's promise and breaking Riordon's heart.

"I thought you were the one person who didn't hate me because of how I talked. I thought you were the one person who understood." Riordon's voice rose higher and mightier. "I'm so sorry, Riordon." All of her consonants blurred, each dropped combination, a stick and a stone thrown in his direction.

"I hate you! I hate you, Miss Eleanor!" The angrier he got, the clearer his voice became. He nailed all of the S's and rounded off the end of her name with the precision of Henry Higgins himself. Somehow, through tears and anger, Riordon had found perfect diction. Eleanor scooped him up as if he were her own. And there, in his snot-filled screaming he heard his voice, his enunciated voice, and he puddled into Eleanor's embrace.

After his little leaf of a body stopped shaking in her arms, he looked up at her and smiled. "Did you do that on purpose to get me mad so I could talk?" In his quiet voice, his R was not as tight, but it was noticeably more refined. Eleanor barely trusted herself to speak and so she bit her nails as she responded. "I'd like to say that was my evil genius plan all along, but I could never, not even to find your R's, treat you like that on purpose."

"Then what's wrong, Miss Eleanor?" Riordon scooted back from her lap and looked her dead in the eye. "What's wrong with your voice?"

"Nothing, Riordon. It's nothing," El wasn't convincing anyone at this point.

It was as if Riordon had put on a lab coat and aged forty years. Grabbing his pencil and pad of paper he asked, "How long has this been going on? How long have you been dropping?"

"Dropping" was the verb he and Eleanor used to describe unclear letters and sounds. As she rolled the question over in her mind, "dropping" took on a much more generalized accuracy. She had not only been dropping letters and sounds, but thoughts, and food, and pounds. She was dropping off in the middle of the day, exhausted, and worn all the time. Emotionally, she was dropping into shadowy places that felt scary to her, words like "depression" and "anxiety" started to stand out and address her personally when watching commercials and flipping through magazine ads. How long had she been dropping? If she were honest, it had been quite some time.

"Don't worry about me, little man, I will be fine." Eleanor tried Riordon's British accent trick and found it helpful in hiding her slippages. "Remember, the rain in Spain stays mainly in the plain."

Riordon giggled at the phonetic—it was one they had used for years and sung together over a hundred times. "I did good today, didn't I?"

"You did well," Eleanor smiled.

Riordon dug into the front pocket of his almost too short blue jeans and produced what appeared to be a stone or a nut. "For you, my speech teacher," he said proudly.

This was the first time he had called her what she was, a speech teacher. For years he had referred to her as his "peach teacher," a moniker she had come to enjoy. She wondered if he heard the difference and the joke inside the mistake. Eleanor took the small oval object in her hand. Upon closer examination, she could see that it was a peach pit, worn smooth and shiny. He had understood everything all along. Riordon's eyes twinkled like new stars. "I have been carrying this in my pocket, every day for every lesson. I held onto it as I practiced. And now that I have found my S and P's, I am giving it to you to help with yours." Eleanor took the seed and pressed it hard into her palm as if she were planting it inside herself. She would call the doctor when she got home.

Possibility

Flesh. As the stone of a fruit, I have known two kinds: that of a Peach and that of a Boy. Both have carried me tightly in their palms—one sweet with juice, the other salty with sweat. My job has always been the same, to help them hold on. I am the solid thing at the center. I am that which helps them grow.

The Peach and I matured together, my fissured pathways a conduit for the flow of nutrients from the tree to her fruit. The gnarled rivers of my woodiness ensured her perfect weight, color, and taste. After four months, we were plucked from our bough, one twist and the cord was cut. Dumped into a bushel of others, the perfume stink of us all was nauseating. During The Passage, all I could think of was how much I missed the sound of birds.

After a long and bumpy journey, we were taken to a harsh, fluorescent place and almost drowned. Strange, masked people, so different from those in the fields, put us through The Works. Run through huge metal machines, we endured things you wouldn't believe. Hundreds, thousands of us tender beings survived The Scrubbing, The Rinsing, and The Drying, only to see the conveyors split into two lines. It was time. The Sorting was ominous. You could smell the rot in the air. It was clear; there was one path you did not want to be sent down. We were lucky. Unbruised, we passed through to The Packaging and found ourselves North in a Kroger in the land of Ohio. And then, after one day among the other beautiful fruit, I was plucked up by my Boy.

The Peach gave herself to him fully, her juices running down his chin, her flesh becoming his. I watched from the inside, staring down the dark hollow of his mouth, wondering what destiny held next for me. It was both terrifying and beautiful to see her go. After The Eating, I was so exposed. She had lived up to her possibility, but now, what of me?

And then it happened.

I was given a second chance.

Picked clean by teeth, I was nestled into the dark of the Boy's hand and held again. For a time far longer than I had known my fruit, I stayed at the center of the Boy. From hand to pocket to hand, I moved with him. Sometimes his fingers worked me anxiously, threatening my grooves. I wondered if I would be worn smooth as a stone. He began to settle at my touch, his fingers lighter, his need less and less fervent. As the Boy ripened, I sensed my season with him was coming to a close.

And now, here I am, chosen again for new flesh.

They say that I contain a poison, just enough cyanide to kill a man—if joined with fifteen of my compatriots. What a thing to hold the possibility of both life and death inside you.

There are always two paths on every journey.

Chasing the Line

The strip of blue that ran down the center of each swim lane was twelve tiles wide and 900 hundred tiles long. El hadn't counted them lengthwise, but she figured that with each lap length measured at twenty-five meters and each tile at about one inch, 900 was a pretty good guesstimation. 10,800 tiles total, end-to-end. El wasn't much for math but as she swam, counting laps, strokes, and kicks was the closest she got to meditation. The numbers quieted the noise of needless words until only the clearest of thoughts could surface. This is where she came to do her best thinking—not a coffee shop or a library, but the pool. As she pushed off the wall from her flip turn, the rush of bubbles through her fingertips softened the edges of her creativity, making her more porous and open to new ideas.

She had written many of Walter's words in the water and had found that speechwriting was a lot like songwriting—find a solid hook, a good chorus worth repeating, and you were golden. Since she had traded in her dive bars and guitars for Walt's make-shift parking lot podiums over thirty years ago, Eleanor had found some of his strongest catchphrases here in lane three, "chasing the line" as she called it. Whatever stroke she was swimming, she tried her best to center herself over the blue strip, working to maintain a symmetry that felt important to the process of creativity. In backstroke she was fastest, but wavered off-center. In freestyle, she tended to breathe to the right, throwing the balance off immediately. Butterfly took all of her concentration just to coordinate her upper and lower halves.

It was in breaststroke, the least taxing and most generous of the strokes, that Eleanor thought best. She could focus on the tile pathway, balance her sides, see both in front and below. By aligning the variables, Eleanor believed she came into her center and was able to get to her most untapped ideas. With no pen or paper at her disposal in this underwater think tank, El metabolized her best lines, repeating them at every turn. Slogans and take-aways piled up on her until she had to jump out of the pool, dry off hastily, and scribble down her thoughts before they got away. Most of her notes looked like love letters found in outcast bottles, so smudged and weathered were their ramblings. But the good ones always stuck, like her "Dollars and Sense" speech for City Commissioner and her "Putting 'Us' back in the U.S." acceptance speech after securing the senate seat for a second term.

Her work as a speechwriter began because of bad wording. After ending her music "career" and going to graduate school in Columbus, El moved back home and listed her services as a private speech therapist in the Dayton Daily News. Deep in student loan debt, El used as few words as possible. "Speech Therapist. Call 937.441.2178." Walter Murphy saw the ad and was certain she was just the thing he was looking for. Ambitious and bright, Walter was starting out in public service and knew that one of the keys to the proverbial castle was oratorical skill. As a young lawyer, he caught the attention of some folks in city government who started grooming him immediately. Walter loved the limelight and began mapping out his sixteen-year plan. His first stop on the political train towards a U.S. Senate seat was to land a position as City Attorney. He had been advised by his higher-ups that this post would give him legal chops and street cred, something that a kid from a lower-middle class family had to earn, not buy. He had no problem speaking in front of crowds; he just wasn't a one-line man. A speech therapist to doctor his statements and slogans was exactly what he needed. He called the number and set up a time and place.

They met at a coffee shop in the basement of the old Rike's department store.

Eleanor spent the entire conversation trying to figure out his impediment. His Rs were perfect, his Ss crystalline, and his Ls rolled off his tongue like honey. She spent so much time staring at his mouth that Walter, with his unending confidence, mistook her cues and leaned in to kiss her by the end of their meeting. The kiss was a good one.

Eleanor could feel the power of this man, and though she had never been attracted to men like him in her past (men with ambition and decisiveness), she felt herself give over to it. Whether it was the taint of recent failure in Nashville or her uncertainty about the future or both, from the moment of that first kiss, Eleanor Darlene Page was Walter Murphy's girl. And his speechwriter.

She had always been told she "had a pretty stroke," a compliment that followed her back and forth across the miles in the swimming pool. It was funny how much it pleased her, especially since it was here, between the shallow and the deep end, that she lost herself most completely and gratefully.

Back at the pool on this day, however, El could not get clean.

She had already swum a mile when she pushed off the wall into her breaststroke. Her hands and legs circled out and in like a frog's; her head bobbed up and back under, her rhythm steady and even. She was swimming away from her fears as fast as possible, chasing the line for quiet and clarity. On lap fifty-three, she noticed her hands. As they drew in from her outside edges they came together at the center of her chest for the briefest of prayers. On she swam, silence drowning out worry, prayer after prayer pulling her forward.

Empty

There was a vintage filling station off I-69 on the way from Dayton to Kalamazoo in Sherwood, Michigan that still served gas and had not yet become a petrol museum. Not many people claim to know Sherwood, population 324, but Eleanor's dad loved to stop there and get ice cold pops. Even though it was only an hour away from his folks, this was a requisite roadside destination. Every last Wednesday of November, Freddy Page would drive up to the building that looked like a miniature Alamo, and the proprietor would come running out to greet the green station wagon. "Coming or going?" he would ask as a way of saying hello, and Mr. Page would smile and say, "Depends on which end you look at it from."

"I'm Glenn Miller," the filling station man would say every time. "Like the jazz conductor." And their father would play the first bars of "The A Train" on an air trumpet and slap Glenn on the back as if they were old friends. The two men would laugh, share a handshake, and Glenn would offer Freddy a cigarette. They lit up in the face of danger, inhaling easily, as if smoking next to a gas tank was the most natural thing in the world. It was the only time El's father would smoke all year and she loved the sight of him there—leaning casually against the car like James Dean, the last of the fall leaves at his feet, smoke circling his head like a halo. El thought the world of her father, was every bit a daddy's girl, and never forgave her mother for her parents' divorce.

The fastest route up to her old music camp was I-75 all the way from Dayton, but she couldn't resist going through the old filling station one last time. As she pulled in under the overhang, now freshly painted yellow, deep blue, and russet red, she wondered if it would still be Glenn who greeted her. How old would he be now? It wasn't the math on Glenn she found herself calculating, but that of her father's. Ninety-one. Ninety-one last January. She wished she had him here to see her through this mess.

El pulled up just as her father had fifty years ago, and there, as the nametag still proudly stated, was Glenn. His approach was slower but still as inviting. There was a spring to his step that said, "The customer comes first!" He wore the same uniform he had donned back in the day, and it fit him as well now as it had then.

"May I?" said the eager, older version of the man she remembered from her childhood.

El, used to doing things for herself, was already out of the car. "I got it. But thank you."

Glenn leaned against the pump and lit a cigarette. El closed her eyes and inhaled the first moment of the burn. She had always loved the smell of the initial lighting up. Not the smoke that came afterward but just that first hit. Suddenly it was her dad against the pump, not Glenn, and her eyes filled instantly with tears. It had been seven years since he'd gone, and she now realized that he was the only man who had ever really loved her.

"I'm Glenn Miller, like the jazz conductor." El heard the "A Train" pass through her mind but wouldn't let it stop. "We used to be full service. Such a nicer way to run a business. Meeting people, coming, going, stopping by, passing through. Which are you?" Unable to speak, El pointed her finger like a gun and shot in the direction of North.

"Ah. Passing through," Glenn nodded. "Coming or going?"

"Going," El said definitively.

Glenn had a gift for small talk. "Nice day for it."

El smiled and looked to the sky. Glenn followed her focus as if their eyes were in conversation together instead of their words. After a moment looking to the clouds, they turned simultaneously to the pump. The numbers spun like cherries and lemons on a slot machine.

"You sure were on empty, weren't you?" Glenn asked earnestly.

"In more ways than most," El laughed.

"When I was a kid, twelve or thirteen, I stole a car," Glenn began. "Drove it until it ran out of gas. Just wanted to see what it felt like to hit empty. Would she stall out and putter to a stop? Or would she just quit and go quiet? It was the middle of the night, I'd been driving for hours, and the thrill I felt pushing it, passing gas stations, taking her to the edge, was more exciting than stealing that car to begin with."

El imagined this younger Glenn on his adventure and her younger dad. Her father had always been her father—he could never be otherwise, and he already seemed "old" as early as she remembered him. Now, she conjured her dad up at fifteen, gangly, disquieted, and hungry for life. She pictured him the first time he heard jazz. She saw him in love with the red-headed girl who broke his heart so badly he could only choose an imitation of love the next time around.

"How'd she die?" was all El could think to ask.

"I don't remember," Glenn answered with a laugh. "Funny. All I remember after all this time was that walk back in the dark towards the dawn, hoping to God I made it home before the sun come up. Hmph. I've never told anyone that before. You won't turn me in now, will ya?"

Who would she tell? If she could, she would call her dad and say, "Dad! Remember that guy at the filling station, the jazz conductor? He's a car thief! To think, all those years he could have robbed us blind!"

"Glenn?" her dad would have said, his name uttered like an old friend. "Glenn would never steal a cookie." They would both laugh, as a trumpet solo whispered behind them.

"I'll take it to my grave," El promised.

"Lemme get your windows."

El hopped into the cab while Glenn squeegeed back and forth, erasing the road from her windshield. As he zigzagged, tears streaked her face like the water running down the glass. El moved over to sit shotgun, making way for her father's ghost in the driver's seat, only an ice-filled Coke and miles and miles of road between them. Her tank, for the moment, was full.

Road Trip

Every spring break, until her parents split up in 1963, the Page family took a two-day road trip from Dayton to Florida and visited Nana Page. In the almost forgotten era before cup-holders and the unimaginable moment in time before TV's were installed in the back seats of minivans, road trips were a time when families sang together, played the license plate game, and passed plastic bags of salty snacks while balancing bottles of sweating soda pops between their legs. Although Eleanor's family could hardly get through a meal together at home without an argument, the team of five could spend nineteen hours in a six-by-six-foot space harmonizing like the Von Trapp Family Singers. Even her mother would release her manicured grip on the household, letting each kid take a turn riding shotgun while she played back seat bingo or French-braided the girls' hair like she was one of them.

Eleanor cherished her time up front as co-pilot. The worlds of the fore and aft were so different that as soon as El entered the seat next to her dad, they might as well have been in a cockpit with a curtain hanging between them and the rest of the family stuck in coach. While the back seat reeked of pre-teen sweat and corn nuts, the front smelled of coffee, car polish, and the lingering remnants of her mother's perfume. The olive-green Thermos, a throwback from his Boy Scout days, sat wedged between her father's legs and was refreshed at every gas station. His elbow dozed on the edge of the open window, the Thermos lid, now a cup, an extension of his left hand. When he saw a car he liked or a funny billboard, he would point with his whole arm, lifting his glass to whatever caught his eye, toasting the scenery again and again. The only time he ever spilled a drop was in 1959 when he saw his first Lotus. Eleanor wasn't sure if the "Damn!" he uttered was for the car or the coffee burning his forearm.

Even with his pre-GPS sage-ness for direction, El's dad asked her to get out the AAA map and look to see if there were any newly opened service roads or routes they hadn't taken before. Although

Eleanor loved the origami creases and accordion bellows of maps, she lamented the towns that lived on the fault lines of those folds, dots and stars marking places that would be erased after a history of opening and re-pleating. She wondered if the actual cities felt the wear and tear of their enchiridion-like existence, if being a town "on the edge" had an impact on the place in real life. She knew one thing for certain—she would never move to Albany, NY or Marietta, GA, just in case.

Once this two-day traveling circus reached their destination, Eleanor's family settled back into their passive and aggressive roles, the record of their time on the road preserved only in numbers on the odometer. By ten years of age, Eleanor was certain that if she could just keep her family driving, they would continue to get along. In an attempt to sustain the magical road trip bubble, Eleanor suggested that they try Disneyland instead of Disney World. The idea was shot down immediately by her mother, who asked, with no need for an answer, why anyone would want to drive across the country to get to a "land" when they had an entire "world?" Not to mention a free place to stay in Florida. Her mother's immediate and inflammatory response not only burst El's desire for an extended road trip but also silenced her secret dream of healing her family's dysfunction by becoming a traveling circus. She would have loved to see her father as a lion tamer, her mother bejeweled upon a white horse. Alas, it seemed thirty-eight hours a year of familial bliss was all she was entitled to. She tried to be happy and enjoy the view.

The last hour of the drive into their annual rest stop in Atlanta was spent brushing up on their "Varsity Lingo." The Varsity was way off the main highway but well worth the exit. "Get your orders in mind and your money in hand," the catchphrase called out by Varsity employees, echoed through the Page's car as they all recounted the menu from memory. Colleen was the only one who always ordered the same thing—a Mary Brown Steak (a burger with no bun) and a Joe-ree (a coffee with cream), while the rest of the family experimented with the myriad of possibilities that no place up North offered. At the Varsity, a Hot Dog meant a dog with chili and mustard, a Heavy Dog meant extra chili, a Naked Dog meant a plain hot dog on a bun and a Red Dog meant a naked dog with ketchup. The possibilities of combos were endless, as were the joys of the bragging rights for the family member who ate the most without getting heartburn.

When she became the ringmaster of her own errant family, El fantasized about following the same route and spending Thanksgiving in Florida. She saw herself playing co-pilot to Walter, snacking on Red Vines, Corn Nuts, and real Cokes in the back with Jillian, and the three of them sharing a room at the same Holiday Inn outside Atlanta where her family had bunked year after year. She was desperate for some time with her husband and eager to see Jill relax and act like the teenager she was becoming.

The day they were scheduled to head south, Walt pulled up in their driveway captaining a behemoth. He had rented an RV. The intimacy El had been craving was instantly dissolved by the vastness of the mobile home that Walt now proudly helmed. Jillian, looking excited for once, ran to the Leisure-Craft and started exploring. Ok, maybe this won't be so bad if they're happy, El said to herself, trying to assuage the disappointment. Within fifteen minutes of their departure, El's fears were confirmed. Each retreated to their own corner of the RV as if they were back at home—Walter, the king of his own universe, manned the dash and controlled the air, the music, and the map, while Jill migrated to the rear bedroom with her Walkman and agreed only to leave the back curtain open as a courtesy to her mother. El, to be close to both of them, got stranded in the Siberia of the main cabin and ended up reading old magazines on the tan corduroy built-in sofa until she fell asleep. She woke up somewhere outside of Richmond, Kentucky, Walter cursing the Leisure-Craft as he tried to pull into an RV pump to fill-up. Jillian, with her special knack for throwing lighter fluid on every fire, was laughing from the back of the bus. As the yelling became more directed at Jillian, Eleanor closed her eyes tightly and tried to pretend she was still asleep. She knew she should intervene, but she was suddenly too tired to move.

Eleanor spent her days as the middleman, working to keep the peace in her home and peace in the public eye. Walter could be … controversial, to say the least. His stance as an up-and-coming conservative leader in Ohio played well to the far right but pushed the buttons of even the mainstays of his "choir." As his speechwriter, it was up to her to find the words he would wield and bring the press and the people back around to his agendas. Jillian, though she would never admit it, was more like her father, sparking her own inflammatory style with teachers, peers, and, mostly, Walter. The two of them disagreed about everything, especially the election that year.

Eleanor felt sorry for her daughter that, in her first year of political interest, all the Democrats could give young Jillian was Walter Mondale. Walter Murphy was horrified that he shared a name with the former Vice President from Minnesota and campaigned as hard against Mondale as he had for his own commissioner's seat. When the Republican landslide victory was in, Walter paraded around the dining room table playing "Hail to the Chief" through an imaginary trumpet and set the table with paper plates and napkins printed with

Reagan's portrait. Jillian spit her steak into her napkin and yelled, "Where's the beef?!" at Reagan's meat-smeared face, the day's most popular commercial slogan serving as perfect commentary on what the pre-teen believed were flimsy, "Hollywood-style" platforms that got Reagan elected.

Sometimes El thought Jillian was just trying to be combative and start a fight, but after listening to several rounds, she began to agree with her twelve-year-old's assessments of the world. Though annoyed with the constant bickering, El felt proud of her daughter's confidence and obvious political research. She wondered who Jillian would become and what her daughter thought of a mother who had only ever opened her mouth to sing.

Eleanor was hoping for a little more bipartisanship on this adventure, however, and with Walter and Jillian burning bridges faster than she could build them, El was more tired than she had been before they left. She had believed this vacation would serve as a respite from the constant firestorms on the home front. Sadly, they were just barely out of Ohio and already Eleanor could see she had been desperately wrong.

Walter insisted that they sleep in the motorhome. "Why should we pay for a motel when I am driving one?" Eleanor didn't try to argue or share with him her desire to recreate her family's road trip magic. When the signs for Atlanta began to pop up roadside, she did hazard to ask if they could stop at the Varsity Drive-In. Walter refused El's request, saying that any place you couldn't see off I-75 was too far off their route.

Instead, the trio ate at a fast-food restaurant that El wouldn't remember the next day and pulled into an RV campground just off the highway to sleep for the night. With Jill on the narrow sofa bed in the main cabin, husband and wife slept on the pullout couch in the back of the bus behind the accordion-pleated door. Determined to make this trip a good one, El curled up under Walt's arm and breathed in.

"I hear you!" Jillian blared from the other side of the faux wood door. Eleanor froze, just as things were about to get interesting.

"Ignore her," Walter begged. "I'll be silent." The moment gone and the spell broken, Eleanor emerged from under the covers and whispered, "I can't babe, I just can't. Not with Jilly so close."

"Fine," Walt pouted and turned away, taking matters into his own hands.

Eleanor balled up onto her left side, her spine grazing his, disgusted and fuming. After about sixty seconds, Walt's body shuddered and relaxed as he fell immediately into a deep and snoring sleep. Eleanor rolled onto her back, tears pooling in the intertragic notch of her ear, and she wondered how she had come to be so removed from the things she wanted.

To quiet her mind and fall asleep, El listened hard to the sounds that surrounded her. Between the crickets and the soft rush of the freeway, she could make out the music of Jillian's Walkman coming from the main cabin. How could her child sleep through that racket but not the sound of her parents whispering in bed? Eleanor intensified her focus, and soon the driving guitar filtered through the space. She strained to decipher the high-pitched, raspy lyrics, "Why can't I get just one screw? Why can't I get just one screw?" Was that really what the singer said? Was this the soundtrack of her twelve-year-old's days?

Since they bought Jillian a Walkman for her birthday, El realized she had no idea what kind of music her daughter was into and couldn't remember the last time she had bothered to ask. The pair used to sing together in the car, flipping through the stations until they agreed on something, which never took long. Nowadays, locked in her pre-teen isolation chamber of sound, Jill wasn't sharing what she heard or how she felt and seemed to only come up from her sonic depths to argue.

As she listened there in the night, El had to admit that there was something about the music. Even at this muted distance, she heard a rawness and honesty that fit inside the fury of her thoughts. "Don't shoot shoot shoot that thing at me," seemed like the perfect chorus to scream into the mirror at her once-teenage self or her now-husband's face.

Eleanor felt an unnamed emotion boiling inside of her. Whenever anyone bothered to ask how she was feeling, she simply said, "Tired," and left it at that. But she wasn't just tired. She was angry. And she had been angry for a good long while. Where was her someone to take care of her? Was she the only person in her life that felt an obligation to anyone else?

Eleanor whispered the truth of her feelings to her reflection in the skylight overhead, sending it out like a prayer beyond the moths and mosquitoes trapped within the small Plexiglas dome, all the way to the stars. "I am angry," she repeated three times, a smile breaking across her face at the last incantation. All of the guilt she felt for not being a good enough wife and a good enough mother seemed to wipe clean with the admission of her own resentment. She found the muffled intensity of the music calming her, an unlikely lullaby rocking her to sleep. "Day after day, I get angry, and I will say that the day is in my sight when I'll take a bow and say goodnight." Eleanor drifted off at the growl of the last line, the surf guitars carrying her out into a sleepy sea.

One Motel Town

Before she knew it, Eleanor had reached the land of tall thin pines, fern carpets, and cicada choruses. The tick tick tick of the trees as she passed them gave the illusion of life moving by like a film strip, both picture and edge of frame in view. This place still held her as it once had, and she was grateful for the immediate transport to her less complicated self. She arrived at, that Interlochen, Michigan locals called "Corners," expecting to see only Ric's Grocery, the laundromat, and the old bookstore. Not for a moment had she considered that change would have come this far north. Ric's still stood, but the landscape was now blemished with fast food restaurants and the behemoth gas station and convenience store across the street.

As she turned right towards camp, her heart began to pound. Why hadn't she called to make a reservation? Incredibly, there on the left was the Interlochen Motel, and miraculously, the green neon light showed "vacancy." Eleanor remembered her camp days of walking for pizza at Cicero's, the "NO" sign ever flashing red in the summer heat. It amazed El that this was still the only motel in town.

She and Isabel had stayed there once before and had one of the best nights of their sisterhood. It was the first summer El had returned from college in Seattle to be a camp counselor. Her charge: Cabin 19, High School Girls Division. Seventeen light-blue-sock-wearing-sixteen-year-old burgeoning geniuses, divas, and art freaks in one bunk-filled room. Managing this brood was, far and away, the hardest thing she had ever done. El called her sister after breakfast from one of the payphone booths at the Stone Student Center.

"Bust me out of here," El whispered.

"I'm on my way," replied Isabel without hesitation.

By the time Eleanor's night off officially began, Bel had arrived. Always one to make an entrance, Isabel honked loudly at the knotted pine gates where the two had parted four weeks before. Eleanor secretly loved seeing her sister at the wheel of her old blue truck, but loved more the deference Bel paid her by jumping out and relinquishing the keys. Whenever it was the two of them, El always drove and Bel co-piloted. Sometimes Eleanor wondered how her sister got anywhere without her.

"I have everything we need," Bel said slyly, and the two turned left toward the main road into town.

As they pulled up to the Interlochen Motel, El panicked.

"How in the hell are we going to rent a room? We don't have a credit card and neither of us is twenty-five. Not to mention the No Vacancy sign," El worried aloud.

"I'll be right back," Bel smiled, and within moments she was, key in hand.

Eleanor should have been used to her sister's skills of procurement. Their father always said that Isabel was the only person he knew who could ask a waiter for a free refill on dessert and actually get it.

"As soon as you got your schedule, I called ahead and booked the room, stole mom's credit card, and then promised the manager a blow job." Isabel smiled fiendishly at Eleanor's horror-stricken face. "Come on! It's cocktail hour!"

Isabel had raided their mother's travel stash. Inside her overnight bag, stuffed between the bags of potato chips and red vines, were ten tiny bottles of vodka, five miniature Kahlúas, and a half-gallon of milk. Bel had forgotten only one thing, cups.

"White Russians!" Bel proclaimed giddily. "Gargled, not stirred!"

Before long, the two were laughing on the floor of the hotel room, pouring milk, vodka, and coffee liquor straight into their mouths, swishing, and swallowing. It was their first night alone together outside their parents' home, and although neither of them spoke of it, the freedom to laugh with no rules or parameters was more intoxicating than the alcohol.

No bartender had managed to recreate that perfect nostalgic balance of her first "adult" night with her sister. Even still, white Russians remained Eleanor's drink of choice.

Dust billowed around the truck in the empty motel parking lot. Sticky from the heat, the dirt clouds immediately settled on Eleanor's skin as she opened the door and stepped out of the cab. Inside the artificial cool of the manager's office, El was greeted by an elderly fellow, likely the very same who helmed the desk on her last visit. In a sudden flash, she imagined this lucky old geezer with his pants down around his ankles behind the counter and half expected Bel to pop up smiling as he handed her the keys.

Room 5.

The same room she and Isabel had booked thirty years before. Perhaps Bel was there after all. The room was at the far end, away from the road. El dropped her duffel on top of the dresser, set her

Olivetti on the small corner desk, and scanned the room for ghosts. Miniature bottles and chip crumbs littered the floor. Laughter still hung in the air, mingled with the soft purr of her sister's drunken snores. In the bathroom, her reflection warped from girl to woman, woman to girl. These impossible spaces when memory and the moment collided were Eleanor's favorite reminders that our hearts do not beat in chronological time. Love, with its own hourglass, seamlessly merged the past with the present and left her reeling with emotional jet lag.

El splashed water on her face and checked her reflection once more. As she smiled at the memory of herself, the lines and the spots she had earned over sixty-one years reemerged, constellations of her experience resuming their fixed points, telling, in secret code, the mythic journey of her reasonably average life.

"I blame you for these," Eleanor said aloud to her invisible sister as she examined the deep parentheses at the corners of her mouth. "I blame you, and I thank you."

Get Big or Play Dead

Sundays were hers and the woods of the state park felt infinite under the fresh white blanket of November. There was nothing like that first snowfall—the world so very quiet that far north that you could hear the sounds of animals finishing their burrows, tucking away acorns, placing pine needles just so. Sixteen and less than sensible, Eleanor would trudge out across the big road and onto the boy's side, not telling a soul where she was headed. Not that she had any idea herself.

On her pilgrimage towards the unknown, snowmobile tracks forged the weaving paths that she chased through the clean, white slate of winter. Eleanor hiked for hours most Sundays, her yellow rain boots keeping the moisture out, her wool socks, the warmth in. The deeper into the winter wood she went, the more El relished the possibility that there was danger out in the quiet. She savored, as only teenage girls can, the notion that she was not entirely safe and felt the electric whir of adrenaline when a dark patch of scat tarnished the perfect white. She conjured animals of all sizes and power that could match the mound. Her heart beat in her chest as she saw footprints grow in size and shape from those of rabbits to what might be bears or men. Tuned to the muffle of winter, every whisper held possibility.

As the hours trudged on with no one in sight, Eleanor questioned even the crunch of her boots, every few steps turning quickly to see if there was someone behind that tree or over there. The action of suddenly turning her head jolted her at her core, setting into motion a fear response that secretly thrilled her. What if she were to come upon a black bear or a mountain lion? Did they even have animals like those up here? And what was the rule again? Get big or play dead? She wondered this about most things in her life, especially men. What would she do if she came upon one of them? Get big or play dead? When thinking back on it now, Eleanor realized that she had spent most of her quiet hours considering how not to be eaten alive.

One icy Sunday when Eleanor was a senior and had wandered deeper than ever, she came across a town marker that read "Karlin" just as the sky began to turn a yellowy grey. Eleanor knew that her chances of making it back to campus for dinner were slim and that she would be dormed if she were caught this far off campus, so she crossed the big road again over to the bar known as the Karlin Inn.

The bar, originally named Frank's Beer Garden, started as a watering hole for hunters and loggers in 1934, with lodging attached to the adjacent store. With no kitchen in the bar, Frank's served beer and whiskey, peanuts, and cold meat sandwiches. When the bar was sold off from the sleeping quarters and market in the '60s, the phantom limb of the inn somehow remained in the bar's new name, the "Karlin Inn" even though there wasn't a bed in sight. A kitchen was built, complete with a deep fryer and a pizza oven, and the bar quickly became a favorite home to a magical medley of locals and international artists from the music camp. The strange and wonderful cross-section of clientele was one of the best things about the Karlin—violinists from Germany drinking Old Milwaukee next to townies, opera singers doing shots with country music karaoke stars.

The best night of the week was polka night. Every Monday during the summer, tables were pushed back and a polka band made of world-class musicians turned the entire place into a whirling wonderland. Frank, the ghost of the old outpost, played accordion in the corner, smiling down over his "biergarten" as the place ooom-pa-pa-ed just as he had once dreamed.

That evening that Eleanor first found the Karlin, the condensation in the window glowed red, green, and blue, the neon signs illuminating the wooden outpost from within. Lured by the feel of a holiday toy store, Eleanor fearlessly pulled open the blue door, the warmth of the deep fryer and the laughter of the dozen or so patrons welcoming her in from the cold. Behind the bar, a white-haired man pulled mugs of frothy beer.

Looking up and talking with customers as he worked, beer flowed carelessly over the glass and his hands before running down the drain. El was struck by the man's sense of ease and internal rhythm as he moved down the line from one mug to the next without concern for the excess and the mess. Eleanor wondered how long it took to get that comfortable with anything.

"Hey there little lady," the bartender hollered from behind the bar. "What brings you in here?"

"I'm lost," Eleanor answered honestly, her voice sounding strange to her after hours of not speaking. For a moment, she wondered if she had even answered out loud.

"Aren't we all!" whooped a man at the bar. Mugs and cheers lifted around the room in a spontaneous toast to the gods.

"Well, if you don't know where you are, do you know where you're from?" asked the bartender.

"Interlochen Arts Academy," El said quietly.

"Y'are?! Well, hell, you are one of those fancy arts kids. What do you play?"

"I sing. I'm a singer."

"What do you sing, honey?" a woman who could only be kindly described as a "regular" asked from a table in the corner.

"I'm training in jazz, but I want to be a songwriter," El said more confidently. "I write music and play guitar."

"Hippy songs? Are your parents paying for you to go to that fancy school to write hippy songs?" the woman accused, laughing.

It was true. Her parents were paying for her to go to school and write hippy songs. Hearing it called out so plainly made Eleanor smile. "Yeah, I guess they are," Eleanor replied in earnest.

"Well, cheers to that, you lucky son of a bitch!" the woman said and up went the glasses for another round of toasting.

From nowhere a guitar was procured and Eleanor found herself on a barstool in front of one of the big bay windows, the "OPEN" sign glowing behind her. Eleanor blew into her hands to warm them and to make herself breathe; she strummed an F and began to sing.

The bar was instantly silent. As she picked delicately up and down the frets, folks had to lean in towards the sound. A mix of rust and sunlight, charcoal and silk, Eleanor's voice fell inside the bar like the snow piling up outside.

"*Friend, I shall return to you, just as birds return, in the right season. A bright cry beneath the morning, just as you've abandoned all hope of finding me this far north. This far north, this far north, I will return,*" El closed her eyes as she sang, bending over towards the black hole of her guitar. She imagined singing into it as if it were a portal to another world, a direct conduit to someone listening somewhere on the other side. Coiling in towards herself, the "O" of the *Open* sign blinked on and off over her head, a blue halo appearing and disappearing in rhythmic time.

As her last note disappeared into the bar, the room stayed quiet for a good ten seconds before, Ron, the barkeep started the applause. A plate loaded with a burger and fries was brought out and presented to Eleanor like a bouquet of roses. El ate hungrily and gratefully, starving after her day's hike and the evening's performance. It was after 9 p.m. when Ron offered to drive her back to campus, just enough time to make it to sign-in without getting caught. It was only after she got back to her dorm room and took off her wet things that El wondered about the safety of her decision to get in a car, at night, in a snowstorm, with a man she didn't know who reeked of beer. In the moment when perhaps she should have been the most scared, her danger radar was completely down. Maybe all men weren't bears or mountain lions after all? Or maybe this time, she just got lucky.

Patchwork

The park was smaller than she remembered. With graduation just finished and the music camp not yet in-session, it was quiet and the large tent suburb that would soon spring up was in its nascence. A few families who would spend weeks there had already staked the best spots, just far enough from the restrooms to keep away from the flies and the smell but not so far that you couldn't find a toilet at night if you weren't the sort to squat in the brush.

A radio, tuned to a baseball game in Detroit, crackled through the woods, interrupted only by the first chorus of cicadas and the distant hollers of children down at the waterfront. The air was rich with the scent of Michigan summer, and Eleanor drank in every drop, teasing out the humid compounds of moss, cattail, and pine. The nostalgic musk brought tears to her eyes, and though it was only just after three o'clock, the sudden summer storm of emotions made her want a cocktail.

What was it called when you drank before happy hour, she wondered? Unhappy hour? No bar advertised those specials, but they poured them all the same.

Eleanor thought she might try to walk to the Karlin Inn, as she had done that one winter Sunday years before. She had no idea how far it was to hike there. She just remembered it taking about six hours as a lost girl in the snow.

She stuck to the main road and walked along the berm, stepping off the three-foot shoulder into the ferns and mulch when the occasional motorhome or pick-up raced by. The lake glistened off to her right, glimpses of water coming into view between the pines and the cottages tucked in the undergrowth.

She and Walter had visited a few times early in their marriage but stopped coming entirely after Jillian was born. Interlochen was known by its alums as a haven where anyone could fit in. Outsiders did exist however—as "Audience Members" and as "Guests."

Audience Members loved Interlochen. They viewed it from the outside with wonder and appreciation. They traveled from far and wide, taking in the talent of the young artists and the visiting performers, and then they went home in awe.

Guests were different. Guests typically belonged to someone but not to the place itself. Parents, girlfriends and boyfriends, best friends, husbands and wives—Guests were people who came for two or more days and tried to navigate the snow globe of Interlochen, often getting shut out. Not dressed in the customary blues, Guests stuck out like colorful tourists in a foreign land. They slowed down the deli line at Stone Cafeteria and complained about the coffee everyone else had acclimated to. They looked lost in the musical woods and bored in dorm lobbies. Their watches, set to real time and not three-quarter, ticked loudly and made them antsy in the evenings after meals served without wine or beer or television. Guests stood in the last parking lot smoking cigarettes, nodding to one another in acknowledgment of their disassociation, but found no comfort there either. Walter was most certainly a Guest.

Feeling like an outsider was new to Walter, and he didn't know how to behave. He poked at Eleanor for breaking out her old blue knickers and knee socks when they visited.

Both an academy student and a summer camper, Eleanor relished the traditions and held them closer than any religion she had ever known. One knock on her knickers felt like a betrayal of her deep-seeded beliefs. "Dedicated To The Promotion Of World Friendship Through The Universal Language Of The Arts." This mantra, emblazoned upon the lakeside wall of the Kresge Amphitheatre, was tattooed on her soul. To see Walter yawn during a WYSO concert was disturbing evidence that perhaps the "Language of the Arts" was not so universal after all.

The worst offense came after the first time he heard the Interlochen theme. As the conductor's arms floated down, Walt clapped and whistled loudly, breaking the prayerful and customary silence that was meant to fall at its end. Shushed by the entire amphitheater of four thousand people, Eleanor bent her head in humiliation while Walt turned and looked at the audience, laughed, and yelled, "What? What'd I do?" That was the last time Eleanor brought him to her sacred terrain.

She would have loved to see Jillian here as a little girl, navy knee socks pulled up as high as the humidity. Her daughter would have thrived in this wild wood—would have fit in here while she was so violently pressed out in the suburbs.

Jillian's bedroom in their cul-de-sac ranch house was a collage of incomprehensible, unfathomable beauty. Though she was never confident enough to call herself an artist, Jill lived artfully, even as a messy teenager. While most girls her age neatly arranged posters of pop stars and boy bands on their walls, Jillian was busy crafting collages, pastiching the faces of Barbara Thatcher, Debbie Harry, Virginia Wolf, and Joan Jett over the heads of The Back Street Boys.

She stapled her old Easter dresses to the walls and Sharpied them with off-kilter how-to lists:

> How-to survive high school without looking up.
> How-to dress a sheep in a wolf's clothing.
> How-to photograph a vampire.
> How-to feel the wind through your armor.
> How-to stop wanting.

Eleanor couldn't remember why she didn't insist upon boarding school for Jillian. All of those details were lost to her now. She would never, however, forget Walter's famous tirade of 1988.

"If you think I am going spend my money for her to go to a school full of reject art wannabees, just so she can have sleepovers with other little misfit sexual deviants, you are out of your damn mind!"

There were so many chances to save her, to have had her back, to have not been quiet. Eleanor's regret raged inside her as she picked along Highway M-137.

"Mothers fuck up," Isabel used to say to her on the phone. "Hell, look at ours. And here we are. The more you fuck up, the better the material for Jillian to use later on."

Jillian, now a successful fabric artist, had found her way just the same, perhaps in-part due to her mother's mistakes. Eleanor smiled at the thought of her parenting mishaps being woven in, remnant by remnant, with the other found objects of Jillian's world.

Jillian Murphy's wall-size pieces had hung in most major galleries across the United States and were starting to find their way overseas. From the loom that she and her partner built by-hand in her great grandmother's old house, Jill constructed what she dubbed "neo-Americana tapestries," impossibly large, multi-layered works that revealed disquieting, shifting images depending on where one stood. "Queer quilting," *The New Yorker* had dubbed her first show, also calling it a major success. The headline angered Walter during his election and secretly thrilled Eleanor. Her baby girl was patching together her own broken life. And she was making it beautiful.

Eleanor looked up from her daydreaming to see the Karlin before her, just as she remembered it, only now with a blue door and more decorative touches. Wine bottles hung in the window like lanterns next to the neon beer signs, a little class cleaning up the old hunting lodge feel. It was clear that a woman worked this bar now, and Eleanor couldn't wait to meet her.

Since U Been Gone

As she pushed open the door, Eleanor heard the unmistakable laughter of a woman who laughs freely and often. Unlike the frivolous giggle of a child, it was round and full. This was a laugh that knew there was plenty to cry about.

Scanning the room, El saw the "inn" was empty, save the two men who sat hunched over the bar wearing flannel shirts and ball caps. From the back, there was no way to tell if they were in their thirties or nineties, the weight of the hard northern winters pulling their shoulders down so low that they hardly had to lift their mugs to drink.

In the warm and comfortable darkness of the brick-walled bar,

Eleanor couldn't find the source of the laughter until she heard a coin drop in the jukebox. The build of a simple strum, followed by Kelly Clarkson's voice explaining calmly, "Here's the thing, we started out friends," elicited groans from the two patrons.

"Jesus, Sandy, not again!" one teased playfully, his foot tapping surreptitiously under the bar.

As the drums and lyrics kicked in, a tiny and vivacious red head strutted up from the jukebox, swinging a dish rag over her head as she twirled through the tables in the front room. This woman was alive. This woman loved her job, this place, and, clearly, this song. This woman, who could have been mistaken for a teenage girl from far away, was an old soul. And she was exactly the kind of girl Eleanor could use as a friend right now.

"Hi darlin'! Come on in," Sandy yelled to Eleanor as she danced over behind the bar.

"I like the red," the man on the far end said to Sandy as she poured him another beer.

Sandy smiled brightly, touching her new do. "Thanks, Stan. With so much staying the same around here, I needed a little something different."

"What are you having, sweetheart?" Sandy asked kindly as Eleanor slid onto a stool in front of the etched glass cooler. El looked up to see her own reflection behind the bar. Hair frazzled from humidity, dust streaks on her forehead, mosquito bites on her arms. Though it had only been a day, Eleanor already looked like a woman on the run. She wondered if Sandy could see the leaving on her. Her thoughts were confirmed when, without responding, a white Russian was set down in front of her. Sandy grinned.

"How did …?" El began.

"An old parlor trick."

"Some folks read fortunes," Stan explained without looking over, "Sandy here reads spirits."

"Just born with the gift, I guess," Sandy replied, her smile reaching into her eyes.

As Eleanor sipped at Sandy's gesture, regulars poured in as the sun got heavier in the sky. Dale, Sandy's husband, magically appeared behind the grill, and the glorious, summer carnival smell of burgers and fried fish filled the bar. Eleanor drank slowly—the cocktail, the air, the nostalgia of it all—and she let the Karlin's warmth flood her chest and stretch to her fingertips.

"You've been here before," Sandy stated as a fact, not a question, in Eleanor's direction.

"Mm-hmmm," El replied, looking around both the bar and her memory, cataloging the changes and the sameness. El's eyes fixed on a bench made of license plates and bottle caps.

"I love making stuff from something most folks throw away," Sandy nodded in the direction of the bench. "I suppose I will just keep collecting more and more, as long as I have room."

As Sandy bounced away with a pizza, Eleanor looked again into the etched mirror behind the bar. Through the glass, the vodka, the Kahlua, and the cream, Eleanor began to imagine that each patron was a part of this magical woman's creation, that everyone around her was there because they had been thrown away by someone else.

"Since U Been Gone" started up for the fifth time that night. Now, instead of fighting it, most patrons were off their stools and thrown into in a wild, two-stepping mosh pit with Sandy laughing at the center of it all. Eleanor took the distraction as a chance to sneak out unnoticed, leaving a $20 bill on the bar. She wanted to thank Sandy personally, but she knew that she didn't need to.

Outside the bar El could still make out the sounds of the Karlin thumping like a club in the middle of the woods, and she giggled at its absurdity. She was glad she left her truck at the park because there was no way she should be driving now. Walking all the way back in the dark was probably not the smartest idea she had ever had, but with the chorus, "I can breathe for the first time" echoing through her mind, she hung close to the pines and walked on.

The Piano Room

Eleanor was tucked into her first-floor room on the inside "L" of the high school girls' dorm when she heard the small rock fly at the window. She was given this choice room because she could be trusted. With the most direct access to the exit, an exit that led right to the woods and down to the lake, her room was equipped with the perfect route for sneaking out—which everyone knew Eleanor would never do. Everyone including her boyfriend, Lee. Still, every Saturday night, Lee risked expulsion and slipped out of his own dorm on the other side of campus to tempt her from her tower. He threw rock after rock, and night after night Eleanor never appeared. After a while she put a small piece of paper in her window that read,

"I love you. Go home."

But this night, with the quiet of snow falling like heavy down feathers over the pines, with the moon so full it might give way to its gravity and splash into the lake, this night, Eleanor rose to the window to see.

There in the shadows, wearing a leather fringe jacket instead of a winter coat, was her first love. Known on campus as trouble, Lee had already been suspended twice, once for smoking into his vent and once for getting a hallway of underclassman drunk on cough syrup. Lee was the wildest thing Eleanor had ever met, and she had fallen in love with him instantly. She wasn't sure if it has been his eyes, so brown and warm that they melted the world around and within her, or if it was his hands, so full of callous and craft from metalworking that they seemed wiser than their years.

It took almost eight months, however, for Lee to notice her. During that time, Eleanor had written two albums of songs about him. It was one of those songs, strummed at a coffee house performance at the end of junior year that finally turned his head. He kissed her that night in main camp by the wishing well, and they had been together, much to her parent's and the hall counselors' chagrin, ever since.

Standing there now outside in the cold, the seventeen-year-old boy seemed both mythical and small. His long black hair, glistening with snow like stars, hung damply on his shoulders. He looked up at her, aglow in her white Victorian nightgown, as if she, herself, were the moon above. There was something in the awe of that look that shifted her.

Before she could come to her senses, Eleanor threw her long winter coat over her nightgown, shoved her feet in her rain boots, and slipped out the door, through the exit, and down the half flight of stairs into the night. Once outside, Eleanor pressed her back up against the grey cinderblock wall of the building, her heart pounding so loudly she was certain it would give her away. After a moment with no alarms sounding, no lights switching on, Eleanor exhaled and peered around the edge of the dorm to where Lee was standing just moments before. The grove was empty. He was gone.

Of course, he had left, she thought angrily to herself, why wouldn't he? She hadn't given any indication that she was coming, hadn't signaled that she would meet him there.

Disappointed, she turned back around the corner only to be pressed to the wall again, this time by a kiss that caught her scream before she could release it.

"I knew you would come," Lee said, grabbing her hand and leading her down the long wooden staircase to the water.

They ran along the beach, the frozen lake moaning off to the left as the ice cracked and shifted. Eleanor had no idea where they were headed, but she held tightly to Lee's hand as the snow whipped in circles around them. She was too far from her dorm to turn back now and too caught up in the wonder of where they were going to even consider it.

She had heard of couples sneaking into the downstairs windows of the dance building and wondered if that was where Lee was taking her. She imagined the burgundy velvet couch in the women's dressing room, a set piece from an old production of Pygmalion, absorbing the lust of generations of teenage fugitives. She secretly hoped he would be more original.

Turning a sharp right up the slope of the small beach-front, they pushed on until they were behind the smaller of the two outdoor amphitheaters known as The Bowl. Used in the summer for orchestra concerts and the closing ceremonies at camp, The Bowl sat empty throughout most of the academy year.

Why this spot, Eleanor wondered? Full of nothing but snow-filled wooden benches, The Bowl was wide open and unprotected. It seemed like the least likely place they would go.

As if reading her mind, Lee lead her around to the left side of the theatre to what appeared to be a small storage room that Eleanor had never noticed before. He tried the door. It was locked. Eleanor wondered if it was locked to keep something in or just to keep students like them out?

Conjuring an amulet of magical possibility, Lee drew a chain up from the neck of his long underwear shirt. On it hung a small brass key. He slipped the chain over his head and handed it to Eleanor. Dizzy with the curiosity of it all, Eleanor suddenly and desperately believed that this key, the one that had only moments ago been so close to his skin, was the key to her heart.

She slipped it into the lock, opening the door with a click.

It took a moment for Eleanor's eyes to adjust to the blackness inside. Moonlight filtered through the snow-filled window, making it glow like a Japanese screen. Inside that glow, El could see that the room was larger than she had imagined. Puzzled together before her were three grand pianos, deep in hibernation under heavy quilted blankets.

The room smelled wonderfully of cold metal and must, reminding El of her grandfather's workshop. All that was missing was an undertone of apples.

She felt him first on her neck, his lips just under her ear, then his hands firm and warm around her waist. He turned her for a kiss, lifting her onto the piano in the same gesture. Melting against her, El imagined chords ringing out from the just dormant keys, awakened from their deep winter sleep, and sent into sudden song. Lee climbed up onto the piano, and El faced him. As they kissed, crossed-legged, knees touching, Eleanor slipped the key into Lee's hand and pressed it firmly into his palm.

The piano room. I will lose my virginity in the piano room, El thought to herself.

Lee slowly lifted her nightgown over her head. She had imagined the moment a million times, but here, in the piano room, there was no candlelight, no champagne, and no Simon and Garfunkel. Still, in her mind and forever in her memory, the music of Beethoven played from underneath their tangled bodies, filling the background with a perfect three-part rendition of Moonlight Sonata.

Lee assured her that the time most people got caught was sneaking back into their dorms. So, they stayed all night in the piano room, spooned in the crooks of each other's curves, like the instruments they slept upon, until the dawn.

Burial at Sea

It was pitch black by the time Eleanor reached her truck. She opened the passenger side door and grabbed the box she had rescued from her mother's house only twelve hours earlier. It seemed a strange and foreign thing, holding it now. This morning? A lifetime ago. El knew what she had to do, and she knew she had to do it fast before she lost her nerve.

Five minutes of trail hiking got Eleanor out of the state park and back to 31. She crossed the sleeping highway and headed into main camp. After so many years away, it was nice to see the campus first by lamplight; she could take the waves of nostalgia better in the dark. Walking around Interlochen after-hours always thrilled her and made her feel deliciously like she was breaking the rules. Retracing her past, El sneaked behind her old dorm and followed the same route that she and Lee had taken down to the beach over forty years before.

Eleanor wandered up to the edge of the softly lapping lake. With the box tucked under one arm, she kicked off her tennis shoes and stepped bravely into the icy water. Fortunately, the night was warm for early June, and before she knew it, she was drawn thigh-deep into Lake Wahbekanetta. There was no moon and soon Eleanor lost track of up and down, the distinction between the blackness of water and air. With the stars bouncing off the surface, El imagined that she was wading through the night sky.

Body numb and buzz gone, El floated the wooden box out in front of her to examine its contents for the last time. The letters, the teeth, the ribbon, the Polaroid, the stone, the petals, the key. Only one thing was missing.

Fingers shrunken from the cold, her engagement ring slid off easily. She placed it inside its own velvet compartment and whispered the same vow to herself that she had uttered to Walter thirty-five years ago.

"I will."

Of all the things in the box she had recovered from her mother's house, it was that small brass key that Eleanor was having the hardest time parting with. Hoping that this talisman could unlock something new in her once again, El snatched it from its spot and thrust it deep into her pocket.

Lid closed and latched, El dove into the dark and kicked as fast as she could. It was hard swimming without her arms to help her, but after two long sprints, she had to believe she had gone far enough. Down she plunged, one last time, toward the bottom of the murky lake. The box, heavier and heavier as it flooded, soon surrendered to the inevitability of its own gravity. El could feel the pull and released it, rushing back up to the surface for air.

Weightless, Eleanor floated for a moment on her back. She remembered the night she first went skinny-dipping. It was in another Michigan lake, the one by her grandparents' cabin, but it smelled and tasted exactly like this one. She recalled the moment of liberty as she peeled off the bottoms of her bikini, slipped out of the halter of her top. How thick the water felt against her skin, how it swirled around her "privates" and how dangerous it all seemed at the time. To be caught—the thrill of the possibility of it.

That's how El felt now. She was both freed and caught by the universe. Both caught and held. This night was a burial and a baptism, a wake and a wedding. Smiling up at the heavens, Eleanor backstroked effortlessly to the shore.

Within minutes she was shivering onto the land, cursing her welling teenage romanticism and her lack of foresight—why hadn't she grabbed a towel? Sloshing up the concrete staircase by the sundecker, El felt the relief of the small key in her pocket. At its touch, her body warmed from the inside out. "I will," she said again to herself, and this time, she knew she would.

Relief

It was the strangest sensation, falling. Falling and falling and falling. I have been removed from her finger before—I have tumbled end-over-end, but never like this and never, ever, not to be caught. As the lid of the box opened, I was the first to fly out. After a moment's rise, the weight of my one-carat head pulled me down, deeper and deeper into the blackness. With no light to catch my facets, I was lost.

I landed in slow motion, my new earth rising in a poof around me as I settled, like a mollusk would do, into the sand.

In the slow rock of the lake bottom, a heavy blanket of silt sifted over me, burying me completely. After a time, I came to remember my life before sunlight. The pressure of this new underwater world was nothing compared to my fiery beginnings. I could see the blackness I once knew at 180 kilometers below the surface; I could feel the comfort of compression from my cratonic lithosphere; I could remember feeling safe.

I was not part of a meteoric strike; I did not come from a collision sent from outer space. I am of this Earth, of the Long History, and to be cozied back into its depths, even those of a small northern lake, was a relief.

I always felt so precarious on her hand, slipped off and on so casually for lotions, soaps, and gloves. I was not made to be easily removed. In the early days of 2,000-degree heat and sixty kilobars of pressure, I was tucked in, just so, and it felt fine.

When I was birthed from my mantle and drawn forth into the bright world, I was, well, shocked. The openness, the vastness, the wind. It was all too much. Nerves raw and exposed, I longed for the crater comforts of my wedged-in home.

Shuffled along at what felt like warp-speed, changes in me happened before my very eyes. After a billion or so years underground, you tend to get set in your ways. And here I was, transformed.

It wasn't that I didn't like my new-found shine, it was just that it was all happening so . . . fast.

I started hearing words—measurements, describing my hardness, my color, my toughness. I could have told them how tough I was. There was no scale on this green Earth that could adequately measure billions of years of volcanic collision. But I let them label me, polish me, and set me. Oh, how good it felt to be set into gold—the closest I had come in a long while to feeling something almost familiar.

And then I was re-wombed into a small black box with white synthetic satin lining and carried around in a pocket. I spent what felt like a fortnight in that pocket before I was finally drawn out into the sun. I did my best that day, somehow knowing that this was the moment I was meant for. I sparkled, I shown, I asked. She answered and there I was, placed in my new home of her hand, and for a time I felt special.

There is a lot of pressure being a promise of forever. But as I mentioned before, I was used to pressure. I knew how to stand the tests of time. I just wondered, would they?

And here, now, is my answer. As I nestle in deeper to this watery grave, I feel more alive than I have in years. I hope she is as happy without me as I am without her. I don't mean any harm in that, it's just … it's just better this way. I feel her light to my heavy, her bright to my dark, her hand flying skyward without my weight. And as I sink further down, down, down, I feel us both free.

Cocoon

Back at the hotel, El put on clean pajamas and rummaged under the sink, hopeful for a hairdryer. She smiled at the purple 1970s Conair she found there and wondered if it still worked. The blast of heat hit her with surprise. Along with the comfort of warmth after the long walk back from the lake was the smell of burning hair, a nostalgic scent from her teenage years.

It was usually Eleanor in the chair as Isabel played stylist, and therefore Eleanor's hair was caught up in the hairdryer's fan. The high-pitched whir of the hairdryer as it sucked in strands of Eleanor's long brown locks was one of the worst sounds ever created, and the smell that followed worse still. Somehow Isabel always managed to get Eleanor back to her "salon," despite the electric hair-pulling that often ensued.

Eleanor was so tired she could hardly bear to hold up her arm and dry her hair all the way through. It seemed impossible that today was the same day she pulled out of her driveway and sped away from her life and out of town. All she wanted was to be under the covers asleep. But first she had to make the bed. The Interlochen Motel had a policy of leaving the fresh sheets and blankets folded at the foot, proof that everything was clean. Not a bad practice but making the bed alone was Eleanor's least favorite household chore.

After years of running from one side to the other, tugging at fitted sheets, and tucking in "nurse's corners," Eleanor finally got Walt to agree to help her. It quickly became one of their favorite team activities—fluffing the sheets high, letting them parachute down only to be pulled flat and tight. They made a game of it, played with the timing of the billow, challenging each other to not let one wrinkle get by. They raced to stuff pillowcases and measured the height of their stacks with competitive accuracy. And then, after the top sheet and blanket were pulled back taut and even on both sides, they would smile at each other coyly across the serene lake that had settled between them.

Something about the clean of the sheets and all the tidiness stirred a recklessness in them, and within moments the sheets were tossed, the pillows and their clothes were scattered about the room. Nothing was better than those Sunday night bed/love-making sessions; for years just the scent of fabric softener put Eleanor in the mood.

Staring at the neat stack of linens in front of her now, El searched her mind trying desperately to remember when and why they had stopped. Her heart, so liberated in her chest all day, felt instantly heavy and tight. After so many years of crying over Walter, she didn't want to waste another tear on him now.

She stood at the foot of the faux-wood double-bed, the Serta mattress naked and worn in front of her. With her last bit of energy remaining from the day, she tucked in, corner by corner, the flowered sheet; she billowed the flat sheet high, letting its waft remind her to breathe; and she draped the light summer blanket across the top of it all. Shimmying the pillows into their cases, she fluffed them as full as their polyester filling would go and climbed inside the cool of her new cocoon.

I have made my bed, she thought. I have made my bed and now I will lie in it.

Eleanor fell asleep instantly and slept heavy until the buzz of morning. The hammer of a Pileated Woodpecker woke her at 10 a.m. Eleanor couldn't remember when she had slept so long. The night before, she felt certain that she would want to walk around the campground one last time in daylight before hitting the road. But this morning, released from night's endeavors, El was eager to press on. By 10:30 a.m. the truck was packed and the hula dancer, ever ready for an adventure, bounced excitedly on the dash as the engine revved to life.

Pinky Swear

Walter had a theory that he loved to profess every time he and Eleanor went for ice cream. "There are two kinds of people in the world, Nor, hand-dipped and soft-served." Walter would go on to talk about those who believed in homemade and hand-scooped, those who dug in there and got what they needed ("Republican AmeriCANs," he would say proudly) versus the soft-serves of the world who were there for easy handouts and government-produced good times ("the Liberal AmeriCAN'Ts," he would say with a snarl). These talking points took over every summertime treat and eventually stole their way into every political speech that El had written for him, though Eleanor refused to take credit for this narrow logic. To El, it just wasn't that simple—she saw the endless combinations that came when you added the cone conundrum. You had sugar cones and cake cones. The binaries were then further thrown off when a third-party candidate entered the race: the waffle cone, soon followed by the chocolate dipped waffle cone, then the chocolate and rainbow sprinkle dipped waffle cone, truly and beautifully complicating everything. And what about those folks who wanted a dish and a spoon? Walter's habit of over-simplifying had made him an easy ticket for "The People" but had revealed some serious character flaws to his wife.

Eleanor hadn't been to the Dairy King in Honor, Michigan for years, and she couldn't jump back on 70 without a stop. Her father used to pick her up from camp and drive the thirty minutes just to get their Moose Tracks ice cream. The temptation of ice cream for breakfast, and the thought of it without a political diatribe from Walt, brought her back to those secret trips with her dad. She ordered a malt and paused before almost ordering a scoop for her father's ghost who seemed to be hanging around a lot on the ride.

Sitting on the curb outside the small walk-up ice cream stand was a young girl about nine years old, holding nothing but a cone, her ice cream scoop gathering ants at her feet. She wasn't crying or sad, simply contemplative. She seemed liked the perfect company for El.

"You mind?" Eleanor asked as way of introduction to sit down next to her. The young girl moved over a foot, placing them each equidistant from the seam of the curb. It was not in El's nature lately to start conversation, but something about this girl made her want to talk, and so she did.

"Looks like you got trouble," El nodded towards the ice cream on the ground. With the candor that only children possess, the girl responded, "I hate my best friend."

El almost laughed at the perfect honesty of it. But then felt lucky that this girl was opening up to her. When had adults ever listened and taken her seriously at this age?

She supposed her father had, especially when it was just the two of them in the car looking forward and talking into the world as it came at them, their eyes meeting from time to time in the rear-view mirror. They were never often alone, but when it happened, it seemed that their talks carried more weight than anything that was ever said at the dinner table eye to eye.

Her dad was a driving man. He was most himself on the road, most comfortable and playful, even, when he took a wrong turn and got lost. He trusted his inner compass and loved the puzzle of finding his way out from the unknown. He would take new routes almost every time going anywhere, even to the store for milk, making every errand and ordinary outing seem like an adventure. Her mother ruined the fun by worrying and map checking and dramatically begging him to pull over—even when they were just on a new back road coming home from church. When they were alone and her mother's voice wasn't filling up the car, El sensed his exhale, saw his shoulders lower. From the backseat El could feel the solid comfort of him. She loved his silhouette against the windshield. Wind shield. That's what he was, what he had always been to her. A wind shield, protecting her from the gusts of her mother that blew in when you were least expecting them. She didn't blame him for not fighting more for the marriage. He had taken her mother head-on for decades; he had stayed because of the three of them as long as he could. She could see it now—the crack slowly creeping its way across the glass, finally irreparable, until it shattered under the weight of all her mother's dramatic bullshit and debris. She missed her wind shield. She hoped to be that for her own daughter. She needed to get to Jillian and repair the bullet holes in their relationship before they spider-webbed and fractured completely.

El's mind returned to the curb and her present company. She sipped her malt and pressed the girl earnestly, "Why are you friends with her?"

The girl waited a beat, considering the question.

"Because we've always been friends. I can't break up with her now. But man, I hate her."

"Hate's a strong word." As soon as the words escaped her lips, she wished she hadn't said them. Just like my mother, El thought, and pursed her lips tightly in self-reprimand.

"I know," the girl seemed utterly unflappable. "Stronger than love, my mom says."

El felt the permission to stay in the conversation and so she probed deeper, "Why don't you like her?"

"Well, to be honest, I don't like myself around her. I let her boss me all the time. I let her make fun of my brother—he's disabled. I let her have my dessert snacks. And I can't tell anyone about it because she's the only person I have to talk to. And everyone thinks she's sooooo great, so *evolved*."

El had to physically wipe the smile off her face at that one. Who was this little golden child? Who was her mother?

"Don't you have other friends?"

"Who would want to be friends with me? I'm weak."

El had never had to worry about "other friends." She had her acquaintances and she had Bel. She was surrounded by folks she loved and who loved her, but the only opinion that really ever mattered was her sister's. Thus, El was immuned from the drama that ensnared other women—gossip and cliques never seemed to affect her, which made women like her all the more. This notion had never been clearer to her than in this moment and it made her want to call Isabel immediately. She imagined what Isabel would say if it were her in this situation.

"If you told her you didn't want to be friends anymore, wouldn't that make you strong?" El asked, channeling her sister.

"Yeah, strong and mean. That's a sure way to make new friends."

El laughed, "Seems to work for her."

The girl nodded and smiled, "Yeah, but she's been strong and mean FOREVER, so she gets away with it."

Forever. Funny how mercurial the temporality of that word. Forever used to seem like, well, forever. Now even it was finite. Getting older made everything, even the past, seem shorter. When she was young, El luxuriated in time, bathed in it, coming out of a day all prune-y and pink-soaked. Time felt expansive and vast. When did the shift towards the primacy of the second hand happen exactly? It seemed childhood was a clockless nation, the race of middle-age measured by a stopwatch. Now this—this cliff dive into old age, was governed by an alarm with a buzzer set to go off at any minute. Life just moved so quickly, even with long, often arduous workdays, a bad marriage, and daylight savings.

El tried to bolster her own waning confidence, "Not too late to change, right?"

"I guess. I am in the prime of playground years. Pretty soon they take away recess and you're only left with online channels for play-dates. Thanks for listening. Baby steps, I guess. I think I'll start with not letting her grab my HoHos."

"Good place to start," El nodded sincerely.

"You won't tell anyone, right?" The girl looked her age for the first time in the conversation. Her armor off, El could see her little girl heart, could sense her fear of rejection, and wanted to scoop her up and take her away from this bitch of a BFF. That, however, would be kidnapping, so she leaned in and continued to listen.

"I swear," El said, and she meant it.

Holding up her pinky with the sacred austerity of a vow, the girl looked deep into El's eyes. "Pinky swear?" she asked and El knew that this kid understood the gravity of the promise. She and Bel had sealed many a secret under that same oath, and, so far, her track record was perfect. Until now, she had never gone back on a pinky swear promise. It pained her to know that she would.

But this one, she could handle. She could hold this allegiance for her new friend whose name she had never asked and whom she would never see again. And so, Eleanor lifted her right pinky finger and locked it around one seemingly half its size.

"Pinky swear," she said.

The Pretty Way

The trip from Honor to just outside Kansas City was over eleven hours. With her late start out of town Eleanor knew she wouldn't make it in one day, so she opted to hold close to the lake and take the pretty way. The small towns lining Lake Michigan were almost perfectly preserved, pinks and greens updated but not erased. Miniature hardware stores, IGA's and putt-putt courses nestled in among the clapboard cottages and log cabins. The A-frames had always been her favorite. "Triangle house!" she would race to shout before her siblings from the back of the Buick years ago. Winding slowly through all the nostalgia and charm, El began to notice the small cracks and shifts from the world that was towards the one that is. In

Grand Haven, she passed cellphone stores and a Starbucks, even a tattoo parlor named Stain, tucked between the fudge shop and the bait and tackle store.

Eleanor didn't have tattoos. No room, she used to say, with so much already written on the body. Perhaps she would get one now—if ever there were a moment. Something simple or a slogan. One for her this time, not Walter.

The possibility of a rebrand excited her. She had felt her world shifting for a while and knew she was overdue for a new mantra. Perhaps just "be brave" in plain type across her wrist. She could certainly use that reminder now. Everything felt new, was new, and she couldn't tell if that bird in her chest was thrilled or terrified.

> I am a compass with West as my true North.
> I am a hand-pressed book, wishing for the whetted knife.
> I want to know how the story goes.

When Eleanor was first a mother, a teacher, and a politician's wife, she had an unlikely slogan to get her out of bed in the mornings.

"Bring the Fury."

She would say it as she rose at 5 a.m., wakened by her newborn's cries, Walter snoring next to the small warm crater, now cooling, on her side of the bed. She would say it as she poured her second mug full of coffee, packed her family's lunches, and headed into the frozen morning to scrape the ice off her car. She would say it as she applied her lipstick, forced a smile, and walked through the curtains to take her place, just behind her husband, on stage after stage of the campaign trail. She was full of unseen fury and for years, as a rallying cry, it felt fiercely good.

Eleanor was tired. She no longer had enough energy for such vehemence. She needed a new marble to roll to around in her mouth, her hand, her heart. Here, on this slow ride through Michigan, the lake sparkling off to her right, the pines, moved by the most delicious breeze, swaying just so, Eleanor felt the possibility of an alternative path. And there it was, plain as the day before her, her new mantra, "Take the Pretty Way.'"

She could feel the possibilities of The Pretty Way, sense them metabolizing into her being and see how this new slogan would help her face these unfamiliar days and all their changes. She hadn't spent time looking around on the scenic route for years—with so much to accomplish, to tick off the list, with so much to win and so much to lose, El had lost focus of the world around and within her.

On The Pretty Way, the compass needle pointed towards her breast and her hand-pressed pages were blown open.

Patience

It has been a long race, eternal even. Indeed, I am certain that I will overtake both Circus Pig and Gilded Swan if I can just hang in for one more lap. One more lap, that's what I tell myself every day. Just one more lap. Though this epic chase feels like it's been on for decades, I will not tarry, will not tire. Moments have passed when the race slowed to an almost still pace. Strategy then, I think to myself, strategy. And times have come where we stopped completely. It is in those moments of repose where I envision myself running my fastest, getting the jump on the others, catching them unaware as they lean into the rest. I feel the stillness as perfect speed, picture myself running so swiftly that everything else around my lean horse body has stopped, and there is nothing left but my hooves fly-

ing just above the earth, never touching the ground. True, I have suffered disturbingly long passages of déjà vu, but then I notice refinements in the landscape and see that nothing is ever the same. I barely pay attention to the shifts of jockeys as they come and go; I know what is certain, I know who is driving this race. I was born to run and, most certainly, born to win. I know what is at stake and what it will take—patience—and someday, someday soon, I will get that jump that will spring me into the lead and to the finish line before the rest of the field. I have spent my days imagining the finish line—it is a beautiful place, one I have only heard about from others in this strange menagerie of a marathon. Exotic Camel swears he's been there a thousand times over the years and can only mutter, "Just wait, just wait," and then spit. There is one Arabian on my inside flank who seems to have just given up; she's lost pleasure in the running. I can't imagine quitting like that. I will persist—for this is what I am made for. Patience, I remind myself, patience. Patience.

Landlocked

As she jumped from US-31 over to I-94 out of Michigan and around Chicago, Eleanor was sad to lose sight of water. The next long stretch of the drive would be dry until she reached the coast. She hadn't seen the Pacific since college, and though she doubted she would make it as far north as Seattle, she longed for the jagged edges of the Pacific's embrace. When she first arrived as a freshman in 1964, she had loved Seattle every bit as much as she had imagined. That it was home to both the San Juan Islands and Theodore Roethke sealed her fascination with the far and distant land and led her to apply to UW in 1963—sadly the same year her favorite poet and UW professor would die.

A greenhouse gardener like Roethke, Eleanor's father recited his poems of root, rot, and bulb as he pittered away among his orchids in the small greenhouse, built out back as a refuge from the untamable world of their home. During those last years before her parent's separation, Eleanor loved to sit on the stone doorstep and watch him work. Happy for any moment that she had her father to herself, she was undeterred by the acrid smell of fertilizer and the light mist from the sprinklers that filled the air around them. He was a different man there—peaceful, absorbed. The greenhouse was a relief from the everyday of her mother's disappointment. Here in this quiet glass house, there was no blame, no stones thrown. He might have stayed longer in the marriage, if not for his kids, but to keep this sanctuary. Their mother had it dismantled immediately after the divorce.

Some days, the only words that passed between father and daughter there in the greenhouse were those of the Roethke's, and Eleanor found herself rocked by the singsong of the verse.

> Let seed be grass, and grass turn into hay:
> I'm martyr to a motion not my own;
> What's freedom for? To know eternity.
> I swear she cast a shadow white as stone.

With her father's focused attention tuned into the microcosmic rainforest before him, El's presence was almost invisible. Only once did he invite her to reach her fingers into the dirt of the trough.

She remembered how she jumped at the first small zap of the electro-current running through the long planter box. "My experiment," he laughed. "I'm sorry I forgot to warn you, Bird." She looked at him with tear-filled eyes.

"The sting is there to help the yield," her father had said kindly before his attention floated back to the delicate flowers before him.

Though Roethke's death had occurred by the time of her admission, Eleanor took her acceptance into the Creative Writing Department at the University of Washington as a fated invitation to her future. She had applied to both music schools and poetry programs, unsure of how her songwriting career would blossom in college. It soon became clear that her sound was more guided by the melodies of language than the tedium of ear training, and so off to the Emerald City she went, a worn copy of *The Lost Son* tucked into her duffel bag.

El's four years in Seattle were a haze of late '60s drum circles and poetry slams, ferry boat rides and coffee on "The Ave." She knew she was lucky. Her parents sent money for school and for books and she bused tables to cover her rent, a room in a shared house with six other girls in Wallingford. Next door to Dick's Drive-In, the place reeked of grease, an impenetrable smell they battled with patchouli-scented sticks of incense that burned day and night. On the weekends, El busked down by the Market, serenading the tourists of Pike Place and the piers with folk songs she claimed to have learned from the sea. She took on her dad's old nickname for her, Bird, and recorded her first album *Bird and the Mermaid* with the money she made from her guitar case. She reveled in the distance she was from home, from everything, and the freedom she had compared to the curfewed years at Interlochen. She slept with any number of jazz musicians and one of her professors. She smoked pot and tried mushrooms, became a vegetarian and then gave it up after only a few months, the smell of Dick's burgers calling to her and her carnivorous, mid-western ways. Pulled by the Sound, she swam in Lake Union at night, sneaking through the gates of the abandoned Seattle Gas Light Company gasification plant to dive into deep black waters below.

At school, she did well, but was often criticized for the overriding "catchiness" of her prose. She felt if Roethke had been there, he would have understood and mentored her in the ways of rhythm and rhyme. She thought of him often, walked by his old office and grazed her fingers along the glass where his name was only recently scratched off the surface.

That Roethke had died while swimming was an even greater source of obsession and curiosity for Eleanor. With her love of the water, she was always perplexed by its tendencies towards cruelty. She found, however, strange comfort in the notion of drowning. As scary as medical texts made it sound, it was a return—from water to water. A loss of the landlocked ways of the flesh. She imagined the first moment of panic as horrific but that in those final seconds, in the giving over, a blissful pre-evolutionary pilgrimage subsumed.

> In the long journey out of the self,
> There are many detours, washed-out interrupted raw places
> Where the shale slides dangerously
> And the back wheels hang almost over the edge
> At the sudden veering, the moment of turning.

The opening to Roethke's "Journey into the Interior" flashed back to her as El battled through the construction around the outskirts of Chicago. Blessedly, she reached the exit for I-57, the quieter highway that would take her down through the less than tropical Illinois town of Kankakee and all the way to Effingham, where she would finally hop onto to I-70 and begin her real trek out west.

What the Effingham

By 8 p.m. Eleanor was starving. It had been a good nine hours since her chocolate malt that morning and she was desperate for any place that would still serve breakfast. Off exit 160, she found an upscale diner that looked local, clean, and had "all night breakfast" lit up on the sign. Stiff from the road, El dragged her body out of the car and through the door.

Barely on her stool and before she had a chance to order, a cup of hot coffee was set in front of her.

"Hi, Hon. I'm Crystal, and you're skin and bones," smiled the waitress. "I hope you are having more than coffee tonight."

El smiled and ordered eggs over easy.

"Toast?"

"No thank you," El smiled back at the waitress's kind face.

"I'll get you the sourdough. It's great for sopping up the yolks."

Within minutes, Crystal was back with a plate of eggs and two stacks of buttered toast.

The eggs were so glassy she could see herself in them. This was definitely breakfast for dinner after a long day of driving. Evenings were El's least favorite time of day. Where mornings meant the magic of the moment before the world wants something, evenings meant an inventory of failures and to-do lists to come.

When Jillian was little, she woke angry, and El had to be ready for whatever storm was coming. Walter woke slow and preferred to smell his coffee, and ideally bacon, before he hit the snooze a third time. So El woke early, early enough to enjoy a moment in her black t-shirt and soft chair looking out the window and in towards the forever of herself. She could see the way disappointment and guilt sat with pointed clarity right next to generosity and paying attention. Behind the bluing of morning, she knew all the stars still hung above and that the light was just a veil. There, Eleanor could sit in the liminal La-Z-y Boy of knowing and not knowing all at once. The light that needed darkness to be seen was the paradox always in play, just as the ability to hold both side-by-side was the key to letting go. Every cell of her understood that each star was simply light late to her eyes, the darkness of the universe pushing that light forward to her earthly possibility. The safety of being human was not in the concrete but in the slippery, the spaces where belief could mingle with imagination, and El could see that all she needed was right there in the constellations of herself and in the ancestors of the invisible stars. Melancholy and all its unexpected moves was dance partner to joy, and together they tripped the light fantastic. For decades of dawns, El sat with these wanderings until her coffee got cold and the house came alive, and it was there she was her happiest.

Mornings before the house was awake were the times for El to be the woman she was to herself, not for anyone else. Who was that woman now? How, El wondered after sixty-one years around the earth's favorite star, had she lost the pleasure of morning? Her daughter was gone and, before she could leave him, so was her husband. His heavy feet still nailed down the floorboards of the house, his drawn in breath held the air to stillness. But gone was his sweetness. El never knew when his internal intensity would erupt to sarcasm and chiding, or both. Out in the world he was beloved, smart, and funny. In their home, his house, he held the temperature of each room somewhere between static and strain. For years, El had longed to open a window and blow the bound world out, but as her mother-in-law loved to say, "Marriage is hard, dear. You have to stick it out and someday it will all be worth it." It was the when of *someday* that finally had El on the road.

Eleanor pushed her eggs around her plate and sipped her coffee. She tried to imagine the evening sky as the mirror to morning and see the magic in it like she did the dawn.

"You haven't touched your toast," Crystal tsked, playfully taking a piece off of El's plate and taking a bite as she swayed towards the table of truckers all calling her by name.

The few sips of coffee were enough to wire her. Recharged, El was ready to get back on the road for a couple more hours before calling it a night. She tipped Crystal well and headed back to her truck. Her cell rang, startling her as she backed out of the parking lot. It was Walter. She had ignored his other calls but knew she would have to answer at some point.

"Hi," she said in a clipped voice and put him on speaker so she could drive.

"I didn't think you'd pick up," was all Walter could manage.

"Well, here I am," El replied curtly.

"Where is that, exactly?" Walt asked. She could hear the ice against the glass. Checking her phone for the time, she figured he'd be to his third or fourth cocktail by now.

"On the road," El said, smiling to herself at the mystery of the phrase.

"On the road? Goddammit, Nor. Tell what the hell is going on!" Definitely his fourth cocktail, perhaps even his fifth. "Am I on speaker? Are you alone?"

"Don't worry, no one else can hear you," Eleanor said sharply, then muttered "Asshole" under her breath.

"Excuse me? Did you just call me an asshole?" Walter's speech slurring just slightly as his voice raised. "Ok. Ok. I'll give you that one. I am an asshole. A total frickin' asshole. We both agree. Hell, everyone agrees. Great. Now that that's settled, will you get your skinny ass back home—Jimmy is starting to wonder if you are a liability. I told him you were just pissed off and would come around. I told him not to worry. But then I started to. So, are you?"

"Am I what?"

"A liability."

"A liability, Walter?"

"Yes, Eleanor. To the campaign. To our campaign."

"Go to hell, Walter." Eleanor hit the red button and threw the phone down.

Suddenly there, just in the distance, appeared the "World's Largest Cross." Lit from underneath, the almost 200-foot steel behemoth loomed over the left side of the highway. It seemed an impossible thing out here in the plains. Glowing an unearthly white, the cross was undeniable in its presence. El imagined that the number of converts collected on this early westbound stretch of I-70 must range into the thousands. She had an urge to pull off and see it up close, to knock on it and hear its echo. It had to be hollow, she mused, most things trying that hard to be impressive typically are. Walter certainly fell into that category. "Larger than life," people called him. "A giant among men." But the further she got from him, the clearer he came into view. He was a manipulative, empty man. A Trojan horse she had filled up with words he had used to win. And campaign after campaign, speech after speech, win he had. In the process, he had won the Moral Majority, but they had lost their daughter. Her baby. She pressed harder on the gas. The cross she would have to bear to earn Jillian's forgiveness was far larger than the one flashing past her.

Poison control

It was the eve of Walter's swearing-in to the Senate. Eleanor, dressed for the party afterwards not the solemnity of the swearing, was draped in a floor-length, cream-colored gown littered with poppies. "Elegant but bold," Isabel had said when she picked it out in Chicago the month before. Eleanor felt beautiful, truly, and hoped that Walter would like it.

Allyson the sitter arrived at four o'clock so that the pair could get ready and head out for a "pre-game" cocktail, as Walter liked to call them.

As Eleanor floated into the foyer, three-year-old Jillian scrambled around between her legs, hiding in the drapes of the cream-poured fabric.

"Mommy looks vavoom," Allyson had coaxed Jill to say. Eleanor laughed and kissed her, leaving a blossom of red on her forehead.

"We're late," Walter said impatiently, opening the door to usher El out.

"We'll be back by midnight," El assured the sitter and rubbed noses with Jillian a final time.

"We'll see," Walt responded, mussing Jillian's hair as he hurried to the Buick in the driveway.

I will be there for my husband, I will be there for my husband, El repeated inside herself.

The event was both oddly casual and full of self-congratulatory pomp. It was an Old Boys' Club to be sure, "Women's Lib" still a slang phrase spoken with derision inside these halls.

As Eleanor stood beside her husband reciting his vows, she found it strange not to be on the receiving end of them.

She flashed to their wedding day, hosted at the Miami Valley Golf Club, the "only place in town" to be married, according to her mother. El had wanted to have the reception at the new jazz club that had just opened that year, but her mother had dreamed of an event at the French Country-styled club since her own wedding day ("a meager cake reception in the church basement") and wouldn't have it any other way. It would break El's father financially, and now that her parents were divorced, Eleanor was certain this was part of the plan. Walter's family agreed to pay for the champagne, so happy were they that it would be an elegant affair and not some '70s jam session.

Eleanor spent her wedding day floating through someone else's memory. The flowers held no scent, as if they had all been inhaled before; the guests looked like strangers she had never met. The decorations, the music, even the sunset, felt slightly hazy and just off by a shade. The cream lace and satin medieval-styled gown that her sister had picked for her was the only thing that fit. As she walked down the aisle, arm-in-arm with her father, she wondered if the man she was walking towards was actually her own or a concoction of some other woman's imagining.

They exchanged vows, but as was customary in their relationship, Eleanor had written both sides. All of the things that El had wanted to hear, Walter delivered perfectly. There was not a dry eye in the house. And then, at the end of the words El had penned for him, Walter did something out of character. He improvised. Leaning in so that she could smell him, he whispered, "I am yours," and kissed her behind the ear where he had left his truest vow, sealing her heart to his. This kissing spot had become their secret over the years, the reset button that once pressed, could get Walter out of any number of marital mishaps.

Someone from the audience, their old neighbor Mr. Connor, she thought it was, snapped a blurry photo of that kiss—El's clearest memory of the day. She carried that picture, now well weathered, in her wallet as a reminder.

Walter's swearing-in ceremony passed, hands were shaken, photos were posed.

As drinks were ushered around on trays and the congratulatory back slaps and toasts began, El once again had the feeling that she was the star of someone else's scrapbook.

"You look lovely," the other Wives said to her. Lovely. That was a word reserved for "afternoons" and "meals on the lawn." "What a lovely day it's been. What a lovely picnic." Eleanor quickly began to unpack the ethnography of her environment. She realized that if you were here as a Wife, there was no greater a crime than to be "The Most Beautiful Woman in the Room." If she had been homely or under-dressed, the other women could have welcomed her, rallied around her, made her their mission. And then later, when they gossiped about her in the bathroom to one other, they would feel better about themselves. As "The Most Beautiful Woman in the Room," there was nothing that could be said to her or about her, and so all of the words were stored up and the Wives hurled them against themselves. Deeper red lipstick was clicked open from clutches and surreptitiously applied. Hand-passed appetizers were denied while more champagne was consumed. Eclipsed by Eleanor, all of the Wives shivered into their shadow selves, none of the men noticing this phenomenon of disappearance until the car ride home. Then there, in the dark of the front seat but no longer obscured, all of the Wives would pick fights, ruining the night, and go to bed angry before wiping off their make-up, leaving little masks of themselves on their pillows by morning.

At midnight, just as Eleanor and Walter were leaving the party, El received a phone call at the front desk. A hot wave of panic rolled through her.

"Allyson," Eleanor answered. "What's wrong?"

Allyson quickly told the story from the phone inside the emergency vehicle. Shortly after the Murphys had left for their event, the two were playing dress-up at Eleanor's bathroom vanity. In the flash of a moment, Jillian opened the bottom cabinet and got hold of a clear plastic bottle of liquid from under her mother's sink and took a small sip. Allyson, not sure of what it was, tried to make Jilly gag it up. Allyson called poison control after Jill started coughing—it was just a small cough but it seemed strange. It was the attempt at regurgitation that had made it worse, Poison Control said. Jill had aspirated the fluid into her lungs and needed to come in for observation. There was a small ER five minutes from the Murphy house, so Allyson drove her there with the clear plastic bottle—it was determined that the contents were lamp oil.

The goddamn scented-oil lamp that her mother-in-law had given her for Christmas years ago. Eleanor would throw it away like she always wished she had the moment they got home.

After a few hours of observation, Jill fell asleep, and that's when her oxygen started to get low. Chemical pneumonia had set into her lungs, and she needed to be transported to Children's in case her breathing got harder. They were in the ambulance on their way there now.

"Why didn't you call sooner, Allyson?" Eleanor tried not to seethe.

"I didn't want to call and bother you—the nurse said everything would be fine and we would be home by midnight after it had all cleared. I thought we would beat you home," Allyson cried into the phone. "I'm so sorry."

Of all the times Eleanor had imagined something happening to her perfect little girl, nothing ever had. Now something terrible had happened and she had not been THERE. Suddenly, she and her husband were racing an ambulance to Children's Hospital. For the first time in his life, Walter kept his mouth shut. El didn't know if he was more worried for their daughter or worried what Eleanor might say if he spoke.

As they pulled into the circular drive of the emergency wing, Walter briskly offered, "You go, I'll park." Eleanor was already out the door.

As the double doors pulled apart, the sanitized air of the hospital interior collided with the night outside, blowing the folds of Eleanor's dress into a fashion magazine swirl of haute couture. Clearly, the other place not to be "The Most Beautiful Woman in the Room" is in the lobby of the pediatric emergency hospital. El was immediately aware and felt instantly ashamed. She longed to take her place next to the other mothers in sweats and flip flops—superior shoes that said, "I didn't even take time to put on socks so that I could get you here faster."

"Room 533," she announced to the guard behind the Plexiglas.

He smiled at her appreciatively, looked her up and down, and slowly gave her directions. El thought she might scream.

Out of the elevator doors, El made a sharp right towards the nurse's station, her heels clicking across the tile floor like the frantic keys of a typewriter.

"Room 533," El said breathlessly, as if she had run all the way up the stairs instead of taken the elevator.

Behind the counter, three women, wearing brightly colored cartooned fatigues that could easily pass for pajamas, looked up at her from their monitors, clipboards, and bright pink cans of TaB. They stared at her as if she were from a different planet.

"My child, Jillian Murphy, is being brought here in an ambulance," Eleanor annunciated to make certain they knew this was an emergency. "She drank lamp oil. I was told Room 533." Her voice cracked. She stopped herself from going on and on, from asking these women who would heal her daughter, to forgive her dress and her lipstick and her ridiculous shoes and anything her husband might say, to forgive her for not being there when she should have been, and that yes, she'd been meaning to fix that security lock on that cabinet—there was one there, it was just broken and it was her fault, that their sitter was a wonderful girl, really, and that and that and that. ... She felt the guilt rise up in her like poison.

Within a blink of an eye, the nurses snapped into focus—Eleanor was just like all of them; she was a panicked mother with a child in the ER. Meghan, her nametag read, led Eleanor to 533 and asked if she would like coffee.

"No, thank you," Eleanor replied, as she sat in the middle of the small twin bed, waiting for her daughter to be delivered.

"I like your dress," Meghan offered sincerely as she left. "Thank you," El said, blushing to match the field of flowers petaling all around her.

Walt had still not arrived when the EMTs rolled the gurney in. There was Jillian, plugged into an IV and oxygen, smiling at the sight of her mother.

"Mama! I got to ride in an ambulance!" Jillian exclaimed and then barked a small cough like a baby seal.

"I heard," Eleanor feigned a smile.

As she leaned into her kiss her, the sight of what appeared to be blood on her daughter's forehead pushed her back.

"It's just lipstick, ma'am," one of the EMTs replied. "She wouldn't let us wipe it off."

Jillian would be fine; she was strong and already doing better, the nurses said. But where the hell was Walter? Eleanor leaned her forehead against the glass and looked straight down through window. There in the parking lot was the shadowy figure of her husband smoking a cigarette, too afraid to come up.

Eleanor crawled carefully into bed with Jillian, wrapping herself around and through the cords and tubes connected to her little girl. The whoosh of the oxygen and the pump of the drip made Eleanor feel like she was in a subterranean world. As she held her daughter tight, El imagined poison leeching out from both their bodies.

She would get better at this—being a mother, being a wife, caring so much and not caring so much. The list of things she thought she could control scrolled on and on as she watched the oxygen monitor throughout the night. After a while, Walter crept into the room, kissed Eleanor there behind the ear, and quietly crawled into the bed next to them. He was snoring before El could whisper good night.

Regret

Litany. A beautiful word. Except when it is describing a list of things you wish you had done in this lifetime. I know, I know. I flew. I was part of a two-winged team, airborne over the world (well, at least New Jersey—that's where my pigeon was from). Ahhh, my pigeon. How I miss her. What a beautiful beast. I still remember my fall from that grace, from that height. We were regal, royal, relentless. What great creatures we endowed with flight. Oh, my pigeon. It was an honor to be a part of her expanse. The wing is a beautiful piece of architecture, but without us, its plumes, its remiges, its down, there is no up. That's a good one. I would love to write that into memory. To write anything, but I missed my next and greatest callings—and that's what gets me to my list, my litany of failings. The things I could've been. Next. Or now. Or ever. I have lived a life like Icarus—flying too close to the sun only to fall. Oh, that day. That day I plummeted to Earth. Now here I lie, a feather who was meant for so much more. And so, I innumerate:

1. *A quill pen, one who wrote of love, dipped in ink and intimacy. I would have poured sonnets from my tip and left an indelible mark upon literary history—or at least upon the heart of a great love.*

2. *Pillow stuffing, for a queen or some monarch, I am certain. I would have caught the head of one so precious, so worthy, and brought dreams of flights of fancy. I would have held the secrets of pillow talk and whispered them back on lonely nights. I was made for the weary and would have, could have, taken their weight and turned it to the stuff of easy sleep and restful days.*

3. *Fletching for an arrow, one noble and true that shot straight at the heart of food or foe. I would have struck valiantly, solidly, without reserve, as if launched by Diana herself. Oh, the nobility, oh the chance to climb once more, oh the dream to strike and upon striking, to be placed back into the quiver, the favorite to be plucked again for future ventures. The quiver, the thought of its casing thrills me to the hallow of my pigeon's hollow bones. Oh, my pigeon.*

I could go on and on and on, but I shan't. You can see the chances missed, the opportunities unopened, and how they hang heavy on my vane. I can only hope to be collected from this trash heap of an Earth by the fingers of a child, one who sees me as beautiful, one who has an imagination for such things, and find my usefulness again, banishing my regrets.

The Silver Stallion

The last thing Eleanor wanted to deal with was rush hour around the city in the morning, so she pushed on. She fell into a motel close to midnight, somewhere just past St. Louis. She was dreaming before her head hit the pillow.

Since before she could remember, Eleanor had dreamed the same dream. She sits on the back of a wooden horse, whirling in endless circles. The carousel she rides is similar to the majestic, three-tiered merry-go round she remembers from her family's visit to Youngstown's Idora Park in July of 1958. The heat was making them all cranky that summer, so Freddy Page loaded the tribe into the Buick and headed north for a weekend getaway on Lake Erie.

He had heard of the carousel and took a last-minute detour, much to Colleen's frustration. When they arrived, however, it was Colleen who was first to run out of the car and, guided by an unseen hand, circle the ride, searching for her perfect horse. As the three children scrambled upon their chosen mounts, Colleen, trance-like, approached a beautiful silver stallion with a breastplate of wings. She presented her hand to the wooden beast, cupping her palm under its muzzle in offering.

She stroked its wild mane, asking for permission, and then climbed elegantly aboard. Eleanor had chosen a caramel-colored horse just behind her mother's and, instead of looking at the world as it blurred around her, her eyes fixed on her mother. She had never seen her more beautiful. Hair blowing, eyes closed, her mother appeared to be flying.

It was this horse, her mother' silver stallion, that Eleanor was always astride in her dreams. The disturbing part to her young girl's mind was that she knew she was the woman in the dream, even though that woman was far older than young Eleanor. No matter what age the dreaming Eleanor was, the riding Eleanor was always the same—the exact age Eleanor was now.

She awoke in a panic.

She had finally caught up to her carousel self. Not only did Eleanor clearly see the face, the hands, the breasts of the woman she recognized seeing, now, daily in the mirror, but for the first time after decades of constant, relentless spinning, the merry-go round in the dream had slowed. She wondered what it could mean. Now even more restless to be moving, El splashed water on her face, flew out of the motel room and back onto the road.

The Ballerina Swan Lake Mobile Home Country Club

It had been years since El had been to Mass. Growing up as a Catholic, Eleanor relished ritual, still felt nauseous when she smelled incense, and could recite the Apostle's Creed from memory. The feel of any bead reminded her of the tactile comfort of her first communion rosary, given to her by her grandmother on her mother's side. Sometimes while fixing soup, just the touch of dried beans would send her into a mantra of Hail Mary's. Eleanor didn't remember exactly why she had stopped going to Mass to begin with, but she knew that it had something to do with the Vatican's stance on birth control and her new nuclear family's need to be "seen" on Sundays. She, Walter, and Jillian had been to many worship services over the years, especially during election season, but it had been a while since she had gone to church to pray and not campaign.

Eleanor was not thinking about God—about anything really—when the black and white sign for the Ballerina Swan Lake Mobile Home Country Club in Bates City, Missouri caught her eye and pulled her off the highway. She bumped excitedly along on the road that paralleled the freeway, frantic for the magical place the sign described. Finally, Eleanor pulled up to a tired looking gate with a rusted placard that read "No Trespassers. Residents Only."

The pallor of the trailer park was exaggerated by the promise of its name.

Eleanor felt betrayed. She parked the truck, got out, and sat down on the side of I-70. Prepared for the onslaught of a crying fit, El was surprised as she began to laugh uncontrollably. What had she expected—an actual lake full of swans, a country club that played Tchaikovsky on repeat and catered to old ballerinas? Eleanor's disappointment went out of focus. In her manic blur she could see all of the places and things in her life that appeared to have incredible billboards full of possibility but had not lived up to her expectations—her career, her marriage, her relationship with her daughter, and, if she was really honest with herself, her relationship with God. She had expected more from Him. He had great branding, excellent signage, perfect location, and yet somehow in her heart He had always come up short. Maybe, if she were to be even more honest, it was because of her less-than-perfect career, marriage, and relationship with her daughter that she was disillusioned. And what if this Ballerina Swan Lake Mobile Home Trailer Park was what heaven was like? All advertisement and no return? She needed to get back together with God and talk to Him about it. She wasn't saying they would go steady, maybe just a date or two to see if they still had anything in common. Speed dating with God—it would have to be at His place, not hers. She needed a church, and fast.

Aerobics for Jesus

The First Church of Glory was, in fact, the first church that Eleanor came upon. The parking lot was packed for a Wednesday morning, which seemed odd but promising. The sign out front read "Exercise Your Demons;" El took a picture with her phone and sent it to her dad's old cell number that she hadn't yet managed to delete from her contacts. She still texted him from time to time, O-H-ing during Ohio State/Michigan games, sending only the punch lines of jokes and photos of misspellings on menus. And though no "I-O" ever came back, she couldn't help but ask the Unknown, "Can you hear me now?" Perhaps church property might have better service and get her enough bars to reach the afterlife.

For some reason she felt nervous. Eleanor stopped, hand on the door, and was about to turn away when she heard the music. It wasn't a choir of angels to be sure, but something faster, with a heavier, thumping down-beat. Over the base, Eleanor heard women's voices "Whooping" and "Woo-Hoo-ing." It sounded more like a high school pep rally than a religious service. She cracked the door and couldn't believe what she saw inside.

The colors were blinding. Fluorescent yellows, greens and pinks illuminated the room. The pews, presumably mobile ones on rollers, were pushed out to the sides of the great hall, making space for forty to fifty middle-aged women, all of whom were encased in Lycra. Leotards in various leopard prints stretched to the max of their thread-count. Leg warmers slouched around cankles, headbands held hair sprayed bangs aloft.

It was 1987 all over again.

They had a leader, these Jane Awfully Fond-a Jesus Followers; she was the one with the highest hair and the microphone pressed against her bright pink lip-sticked mouth. From her stage, raised slightly above the other Jesus-cizers, she preached the Word of the Workout.

"C'MON GIRLS! DON'T YOU WANT TO BE FISHERS OF MEN?!"

The women WHOOPED back at her, copying her every move.

Working their triceps, they moved forward for four counts, pressing a large, imaginary weight, then back for four, pumping their open palms up to the sky.

Jane chanted. "AND PUSH THE STONE AWAY, AND NOW WE SAY THANK YOU JESUS! PUSH THE STONE AWAY, AND NOW WE SAY THANK YOU JESUS!"

Then pelvic tucks, to work the gluteal muscles.

Jane yelled. "GO MARY! GO MARY!"

It was the strangest workout/worship session Eleanor had ever seen. Were they serious? Was this blasphemous? Or was sweating out your sins a sure-fire way to the Lord?

Eleanor didn't know if she wanted to join or run. Her decision was made for her when Jane, over the microphone hollered out, "WE HAVE A NEW RECRUIT! COME ON IN AND GET DOWN FOR GOD!"

The women circled around her, pumping their arms, and side-touching their feet.

It was both welcoming and terrifying. "GO MARY! GO MARY!" they all began to chant, their knees lifting, their fervor rising. As they got to the higher and higher impact portion of the workout, Eleanor found herself carried away by a kick ball change, kick ball change, pivot turn combination. Soon she was sweating through her clothes like the rest of them.

After thirty minutes of booty and Bible-thumping, the class bowed their heads as Jane talked them through the cool down.

"We are here as vehicles of the Lord," Jane's voice dropped to an almost seductive whisper. "We are here to celebrate His strength. When our bodies feel weak, we lean on Him; when our voices are thin, we sing His song. God works his karaoke through us. We just have to open our mouths and let the words of our sweet Jesus move through. This is the workout of the Lord."

The congregation responded, "Praise be to you, oh Jesus Christ."

"Today's Ladies Lunch will be buffet at the Pizza Hut, hope to see you all there!"

A few "Amens!" whooped through the room. Before anyone could get to her for an invite, El slipped out the door. Freshly baptized in sweat, Eleanor jumped into her truck and sped down the highway, "Go Mary, Go Mary," chanting through her head.

She wasn't sure she was any closer to God, but she had found both her hamstrings and her sense of humor. The latter would get her at least as far as the hour down the road to her brother's house where she would be telling the first person in her life whom she loved that she was dying.

A Four-Letter word for Terrified

Intubate. Eight-down.

Pillow. Thirty-one-across.

In the hospital examining room, El was refining her list of "Things to Ask About My Death" inside the squares of a magazine crossword puzzle, ironically making her questions look like answers. In thirty-four-down she inked in *sedated* instead of the correct answer for the clue "A seven-letter word for brave." Twelve-across' hint of "the five-letter name for gal pal of Roxie Hart" helped El deduce that thirty-four's correct answer was v*aliant*—something quite the opposite of what she was feeling at the moment.

It was the fifth appointment since Eleanor's diagnosis had been made official. Walt was "on the trail," as he liked to say in a cowboy voice, campaigning for another Republican candidate who wanted the Murphy brand behind him on the podium. Walt loved those kinds of pep rallies, much preferred them to hospitals, even if hospitals had good pub shots ("publicity shots, darlin"—also in cowboy voice). Eleanor wouldn't have wanted him there anyway—she still hadn't told him of the diagnosis and didn't want any pity or problems with the divorce (a divorce that he also didn't know about) because he suddenly felt obligated to her. She wanted her marriage over, and as he had managed to disobey the first six of their vows, she had no intention of keeping their final one, "'til death do us part."

El had a list of questions for the doctor today, not questions about procedure and her odds, but uncomfortable, hard questions, the ones she knew she needed to ask before she couldn't—either because she'd lost her voice or her courage. El needed details. Gory details.

She was the kind of girl who imagined the plane going down at every take off. El believed that it was her mini morbid ritual that held the plane in the air. If she could witness every macabre moment, the potential tragedies of her life would feel honored on festive parade with her skeletons and thus leave her alone. Not that she believed thinking about her death would keep her alive exactly, but she did hope that it would at least keep the Reaper at-bay.

Dr. Bannon knocked softly before entering the room where El appeared to be thoughtfully working on a crossword puzzle. The doctor was the most sought after in the area—not just because of his diagnostic expertise but because of his bedside manner. From North Ayrshire, Dr. Bannon's Scottish accent made even the harshest, least hopeful condemnation sound like a compliment to those under his care. El knew Bannon liked her, which would make telling her about her disease all the worse. ALS was incurable and unstoppable. There was little research done on it, and Eleanor knew that all he could really do for her was chart the disease's progression and her digression, suggest feeding tubes and physical therapy, and keep her comfortable until the inevitable. He did make her comfortable, comfortable enough to ask the impossible.

"I have some questions," El said as directly as she could, looking down at the crossword in front of her where she had carefully placed *morgue* in twenty-two-across.

"Let's see how I can help you with them," Dr. Bannon replied, steadying himself for the usual barrage of treatment options and/or homeopathic tinctures and cures that patients read online.

El looked up at him from her magazine and saw the slight panic in his eyes. She couldn't imagine doing such a brutal job, one where every patient looked to you for hope and you had none. Maybe she and her dark sense of humor could make it easier for him.

"How will I die?"

"Excuse me?"

"How will I die?"

"Eleanor, there is no need to go there now."

"Please. I need to know. How will I die?"

Dr. Bannon took a deep breath and tried to redirect, "Like everyone does. Your heart will stop, and so will your breathing."

"No, doctor. *How* will I die?"

By his pause, it seemed like no one had asked him this before. In this moment, Eleanor was not hungry for hope, but for truth.

"You will stop breathing," Dr. Bannon said, thoughtfully.

El considered the word *breathing* as if she had never heard it before and wrote it into seventeen-down.

"Like by pillow? Or drowning?"

"We will have you sedated by that point; you won't feel anything."

"Pillow or drowning?"

An infinity passed.

"Drowning," Dr. Bannon said, in almost a whisper.

Drown. Funny to think of it—she, the swimmer, would drown.

Eleanor picked up her pen and slowly fit the letters into tidy squares. *Drown*, the new answer for five-across where the clue had asked for a "five-letter word (ending in "n") for the mile that prisoners walk."

"If it's the last thing I'm going to feel, don't I want to feel it?"

"Trust me on this one, you don't. It's not like childbirth where you get a hippy prize for going natural. Take the morphine. Please."

She could see he meant it.

"Ok. Put me down for morphine. Next question." El scanned her puzzle. Suddenly the word after seemed too big for its boxes, pushed itself off the page and out of El's mouth. "What happens after?"

"After?" Dr. Bannon repeated innocently.

"Yes, After. What happens after I'm dead?" Eleanor repeated, louder this time, regaining control of her words.

"That's the million-dollar question, isn't it? You'll have to send a postcard so I can do better with that one for my next patient," Dr. Bannon mused.

"No. What happens to me? I mean my body." Thanks to curiosity, Eleanor's courage was building, verging on valiant, as she got the words out. She noticed that her handsome Scottish doctor was wavering and that this, surprisingly, might be harder on him. She hadn't thought of that, or about how handsome he was, and the knowledge that she was thinking only about herself shocked and thrilled her. She pressed on. "Step by step, tell me everything."

Dr. Bannon went on to talk about visitors, how they were welcome to stay an hour, but that after an hour, there would be "a late fee." El laughed, thinking of her body like a library book, gaining value the longer it was off the shelf. She asked what the fee would be and if she could pre-pay it; she knew that Bel would need more than an hour and would be horrified and overly dramatic about any late charges that came her way for a dead body. Bel would stay too long. She always did. Ever the last to arrive at a party and the last to leave, Bel would definitely need more than an hour. She would stay as long as there was warmth in her sister's hands. She would stay until every tube, every piece of tape, was removed from her older sister's body. She would stay to fix Eleanor's hair, parting it on the proper side, the side that hid her cowlick best. Bel would stay to put lipstick on her sister's slowly firming mouth. From her "bag of miracles," Bel would find just the right shade to go with Eleanor's bluing pallor, somehow making her look more beautiful and more alive in death than she ever had in life. It would be their last make-over, and it would definitely take more than an hour for Bel to feel like she had done her best work, over an hour to notice that Eleanor had gone cold and that it was only Bel's own hand emanating warmth, and far more than an hour to finally let her sister go.

"Next," El said more like a demand than a question.

"Well, that depends. Burial or cremation?"

"Ashes to ashes," El answered lightly.

"Ok, first, orderlies will take you to the morgue where your chart will be assessed for an autopsy."

Autopsy. Six-down.

"Barring any signs of foul play, which we don't expect, you will be released to the funeral home."

Funeral. Eleven-down.

"From there, you, your body, will go to the crematorium. Have you picked out a box?"

Box. Twenty-three-across.

"I'm thinking something cheap and ugly so my sister isn't tempted to keep me in there. Have you seen the brass golf urns? They're hideous. We both hate golf. She would know I was fucking with her. "

Dr. Bannon's eyebrows went up, and he looked amused for the first time all morning.

"Oh god, that's right, you're Scottish. Your clan probably invented golf—sorry!" El was mortified.

Dr. Bannon laughed. "No, my clan was more of the sea than of the sand trap."

"Good. Sorry, I mean. Maybe in Scotland it makes sense, but

people who golf in this country, especially in the desert, are insane. What a waste. Maybe I'll get the bonus plaque that says, *One in the Hole*, instead of *Hole in One*. That will kill her. I am totally doing that."

"You're sick, you know that?"

"Yep. And they tell me it's terminal." Eleanor realized that maybe she had taken the joking too far. She didn't want to seem glib, but she couldn't cry anymore, at least not today. She didn't want to get her snot on the nice Scot of a doctor, and she certainly didn't want to get his pity all over her.

"Where do you want to be sprinkled, if you don't mind my asking?"

She didn't mind at all. She could talk all day about the lake by the camp where she sang as a teenager. The musical grove of birch trees by her grandmother's house in Colorado. The rock off the 101 in Northern California that was a pillow and sundeck to a large family of sea lions. Under the painting of St. Joan at the Met in New York. On the carousel she and Bel rode as children. In her guitar that she hoped her daughter would still someday learn to play. The Grand Colbert in Paris where she'd had the best champagne of her life.

"I'm thinking of having a scavenger hunt of all the places I would like to be, leaving something along the path instead of finding something to take." Eleanor imagined her sister, Great Escape style, smuggling her ashes into museums and restaurants, and she knew she would get her wish. Bel loved breaking rules. "I'm leaving my sister my truck. After I'm gone, she's gonna need a road trip."

El looked down at her magazine to see if she had anything left to ask. It was only then that she noticed the puzzle's theme, "Death Row, Hollywood Style" and as she wondered what and when her last supper would be, she laughed so hard she began to cry.

Blood Bath

El had not planned her arrival time quite right. It was just after 1 p.m. and Danny wouldn't be home from the office in Kansas City for at least another five hours. Even the kids, who were in their last week of school, wouldn't be home until three. She was not eager to have one-on-one time with her sister-in-law. Caroline exhausted her. She had no idea how Danny had gotten in and out of the same bed with the woman year after year. There was something relentless about her—her faux niceness peppered with constant judgment. Caroline had a habit of sucking in as a response to something someone had just said, as if she were gulping down her words. With the sound, she managed to inhale all the atmosphere around her, leaving barely any air for anyone else to breathe. Then, after a steadied moment, she spit instead of swallowed, and her opinions got all over you.

It had always been Bel leading the charge against their sister-in-law, the two of them holed up in the bathroom together after a meal, acting more like college girls in the ladies' room of a dive bar than grown-ups in a half-bath of a three-story colonial. Behind closed doors, Bel would be snarky and El would giggle, but they would never confront. Danny would be perched outside the bathroom door upon their exit, waiting, like the five-year-old they still treated him as, to be let into their inside joke.

She loved her younger brother, though they were never close. Their connection did not fulfill her idea of siblingdom, an idea personified by the rhyming couplet that she and Bel had always been. Eleanor remembered a time when Danny was seven, and he said he was changing his name to Mel. He signed "Mel" to everything for one week, changing the loops and lines of the "m" and the "l," shifting between cursive and print, trying to imagine himself transformed by this new organization of letters and font. The family laughed it off and refused to call him by the new name. By Saturday, he realized that it would never catch on. By Sunday, he had changed back to Daniel, by Wednesday he was Dan, and by the following Sunday he was Danny. Out of respect for his efforts, the family got on board, and he'd been Danny ever since. It was only just now hitting El why he wanted the original change to begin with—he wanted to fit in. He wanted to rhyme. El, Bel, and Daniel—it was close but just off, and that's how she had always felt about the intimacy between them.

She knew she was telling him first as a dress rehearsal for telling her sister. She couldn't start with Isabel, even though it was Bel that she most needed to talk to and whom she most dreaded to tell.

Reluctant but sore from her morning's workout and desperately in need of a shower, Eleanor pulled into the driveway of her brother's split-level home. There was, as always, a seasonal wreath on the door. This one was difficult to decipher. With no Hallmark holidays in sight, Caroline appeared to have gone with an end of school/start of summer theme—popsicle sticks, sunscreen tubes, and old report cards. Eleanor knocked and stepped back from the door, anticipating the overly zealous hug that was about to overtake her.

"Coming!" sang through the house as Caroline neared the door. Eleanor imagined toys and dishes scurrying in fright to clean up after themselves as she passed. Caroline would have been perfect for Walter. If she could convince Danny to leave his wife, she might try to make the match.

When Caroline opened the door, her face fell as if she were looking at a ghost. It's true, El had lost weight and was well aware that no amount of concealer could cover up the circles under her eyes that had purpled fiendishly in the past six months, but she didn't think she looked that bad. Caroline sucked in and smiled. "Well, come in, come in!" Caroline's falsetto building. "Did we know you were coming?"

El had been avoiding the phone for the past few months, only answering Bel so she wouldn't get suspicious. Every time her sister called, she pretended she was eating, brushing her teeth, or just back from the dentist with a reoccurring filling problem.

"Dentist—again? What a pain in the ass. You should sue that guy. He's probably putting you under so he can grab your boobs. Do you want me to call back?" Bel would ask.

"No, you talk," El insisted. And so she did.

It dawned on Eleanor that, no, they didn't know she was coming and that she should have called or at least texted. She apologized to Caroline and explained that she was just passing through. She wouldn't be in their hair long.

"You look tired. Would you like a shower?" Caroline cooed.

Usually this sort of back-handed remark would offend Eleanor, but since a shower was exactly what she wanted, she simply nodded and let Caroline show her upstairs to the kids' bathroom that they used for guests.

On the sink were two different sets of toothbrush holders. On the right side, a smiley face sticker bore the words, "For Teeth!" And on the left side, closest to the shower, was a frowny face that warned "For Tile!" Did Caroline make the kids scrub out the shower with toothbrushes, military style? She pulled back the curtain to find the cleanest, sparkliest shower/tub combo she had ever seen. She wanted to lick the grout to see if it tasted of mint. This shower was not a place for dirty people. Presently filthy, she wondered if she should rinse off in the backyard with the hose.

Eleanor turned on the tap, peeled off the clothes she had been wearing for the past few days, and climbed into the steam. It was glorious. She wondered if she could stay right there until her brother came home. She arched back into the spray and, out of habit, let the water run into her mouth. Suddenly she was choking. She could feel her throat constricting, panic flooded her. Goddammit, I am going to drown in my sister-in-law's guest bath, was Eleanor's last thought before passing out.

Nine Lives

When Caroline heard the crash, she raced up to the bathroom to see what had happened. She called Eleanor's name outside the door for fifteen seconds before finally announcing, "I'm coming in!" As she threw the door open, she heard a thud and realized something was blocking the door. She pushed again, harder this time. Another thud and a moan.

Caroline tried to crack the door open just enough to see the obstruction—it was her sister-in-law's head. Caroline screamed. There was blood everywhere. In her collapse, Eleanor had managed to fall through the shower curtain, out of the tub, and across the bathroom floor, but only after hitting her head on the sink corner on the way down.

Suddenly Eleanor's eyes flew open and with the look of a person possessed, her focus jumped around the room, attempting to make sense of her situation. Clearly disoriented, she tried to rise but couldn't. Her legs were like lead, her mouth tasted of acid, and her head buzzed with electricity. When her eyes finally focused, she saw her sister-in-law there with her on the floor, both covered in blood. Eleanor couldn't figure out how she got there, not just to the bathroom floor but to her sister-in-law's house, to Missouri, to age sixty-one, to the Earth. Her mind flipped through the Rolodex of her life, trying to recall how it had all started. She remembered something about angels before she passed out again, this time from shock.

"Eleanor, Eleanor!" Caroline called from the tunnel. "Eleanor, can you hear me? Can you move?" Eleanor knew she could, but she didn't want to. She felt a perfect cool all over, her body temperature matching the atmosphere around her. She couldn't tell where she ended and where the air began. It was lovely. Weightless and floating, Eleanor had the feeling she could, if she really wanted to, stay in this place unbound to her density forever. The annoying voice at the other end of the tunnel kept calling her back to her own mass—"E-leanor, Eleanor!"—until, reluctantly, she returned.

"We need to get you to a hospital, or at least a doctor's," Caroline demanded. "Do you think you can sit up?"

After a Herculean effort and an extreme desire to lie back down, Eleanor did finally manage to sit up. Caroline chattered away with hypothesis after hypothesis of what might have happened, unpacking the crime scene and its clues. As she chatted on, she gently wiped the blood off of Eleanor's head and arms. Caroline handed Eleanor a fresh warm washcloth, one with her own initials on it, CML, to wipe the blood off her chest and thighs. It was the kindest gesture her sister-in-law had ever shown her.

Once dressed in cotton floral pajamas—Laura Ashley, to be sure—the pair made their way slowly down the six steps to the landing and then took a break before conquering the final five to the door. After the fifteen steps to the car, Eleanor collapsed in the back seat, Caroline still rambling away, trying to keep them both out of shock.

In under five minutes, they arrived at a building with a wood-carved sign in front that read, "9 Lives." Even in her bleary state, it seemed to Eleanor to be an odd name for a doctor's office. Once inside, the smell of cat was unmistakable. They were everywhere. Two long-haired Persians draped themselves languorously over the Victorian sofa in the waiting room, while a suspicious looking Siamese guarded the door beside the front desk. A Russian blue scampered under an over-stuffed and well-clawed armchair, his two glassy eyes peered back from the darkness. Five marmalade-stripped kittens bit and mewed at each other in a box in the back corner of the room and a large tabby, with teats full to the brim, greeted the two women with a hiss.

"Why am I at an animal doctor and not a people doctor?" Eleanor said under her breath. Caroline sucked in. "Dr. Mittens is not an animal doctor; she is a cat doctor—she's a specialist."

"Mittens? Are you serious?" Eleanor wondered if she had hit her head harder than she thought.

"She's the only hands in town I trust—you know how important my cats are to me. And besides, I called the pediatrician, and he couldn't get you in for hours, and our doctor is all the way in Kansas City—which would take forever at this time of day," Caroline explained. "Dr. Mittens has been with us for twelve years and three cats. You'll love her."

It was settled; Eleanor would be stitched together by a veterinarian. She wondered how great this Mittens truly was—could she help her other condition? Was there even such a thing as feline ALS and had she treated it before? Perhaps with the lack of research on the disease's front for humans, it would take some crazy cat lady to conquer it. Eleanor sure as hell thought it would take someone or something with nine lives to beat ALS, as vicious and fast moving as it was. Her measly allotment of one life would surely not prove sufficient. She wondered if she might come back as a cat, as The Cat, that solved the puzzle. With her diagnosis hanging over her, the only cat she felt like was Schrodinger's, both alive and dead at once. Her head began to throb. She had definitely hit it harder than she thought.

Dr. Mittens, carrying an angora with two different colored eyes, came out from the back room to greet them.

"Welcome, welcome. Won't this be a treat—no shaving," Dr. Mittens smiled, as she stroked Eleanor's forehead just beside the newly fissured skin. Her touch was soothing, Eleanor almost purred. "Come back and let's clean you up and have a look."

The bleeding had almost stopped completely, so there wasn't much to clean except for some removal of white cotton fuzz from the washcloth Eleanor had been holding to her head en-route.

"I think we can wrap this baby up with ten-to-twelve stitches and have you on your way," Mittens said with authority. "It'll be a good scar. Add character."

El glanced at Caroline, who looked away.

"We'll use a local—you could try some home-brewed catnip tea to take the edge off, if you'd like. We do have a great crop this season." Mittens gestured towards the herb boxes inside the window.

The angora that Mittens had been holding was lolling about in the beautiful grey-green plants. The stalks were dotted with purple buds and flourished almost sixteen inches high, a light camphor smell filled the room.

"When in Rome," Eleanor replied, and the doctor scurried off to fetch the pot.

Mittens returned with a small hand thrown mug, a needle, pliers, and stitching thread. With bifocals down low on her nose, she looked more like a cat than her kittenish company, and Eleanor had to smile. Mittens handed El the tea and gloved her hands.

After a few hummingbird-size sips, Eleanor relaxed onto her back.

It was odd seeing a needle come so close to her eye and impossible, at first, not to flinch. As the anesthetic and the tea took effect, Eleanor softened into the rhythm of the looping in and out and closed her eyes.

"Are you taking any other medications? I suppose I should have asked you that first," Mittens apologized. Eleanor was too relaxed to care.

"Rilutek," Eleanor responded absently.

The doctor's eyes widen, "That's for ALS, isn't it? That's serious stuff. My uncle took that."

"ALS?" Caroline shot up from her seat in the corner. Eleanor had forgotten she was even in the room.

"I was going to tell you tonight, Caroline, you and Danny together, at dinner," Eleanor said sleepily.

"You were coming to dinner to tell us you were dying?" Caroline blurted.

Eleanor felt a sudden need to apologize for already ruining the meal. "It wasn't supposed to happen like this," she said in an almost whisper.

A tear ran out of the corner of Eleanor's eye, pooling into the final opening in the cut. The doctor took her final tug, stitching the tear into the wound. "Saltwater helps it heal," she said, gently petting her patient's head. Eleanor could think of nothing but getting out of the Midwest as fast as possible and heading to the sea.

Happy Family Special

El knew it had been a hard day for Caroline. As she laid back to rest on their Pottery Barn sectional, El listened as Caroline fussed over dinner plans. She had already scrubbed the bathroom, made the bed in the guest room, picked the kids up from school, and regularly checked on El. Caroline lived with a simmering intensity that catalyzed small explosions. Just the ordering of dinner sounded to El like a bomb shelter siren.

"I need you to go to the Chinese place on the way home and pick up the Happy Family Special." El heard Caroline wring out the back of her oak dining room chair. "No, dear. Not pizza. Get the Happy Family," Caroline seethed. El knew Danny was arguing. "Just DO

IT!" and with that, Caroline's phone slammed in its cradle.

She poked her head in the living room. "Sorry to wake you, Eleanor. We're having Chinese food from this adorable spot in Kansas City!" El felt Caroline's songbird intonation echo back from their cathedral ceilings.

At 6:20, Danny, hands full of take-out, rang his own doorbell with his elbow. Eleanor opened the door to greet him. For a moment in his surprise, he looked and felt like exactly like his five-year-old self. Danny threw his arms around his older sister and encircled her, as best he could, with the Happy Family Special.

"Holy shit, Sis! What an amazing surprise!" Danny said earnestly as El took bags out of his hand. "How long have you been here?"

"Since today," Eleanor said smiling, noticing the sounds of marbles mixing in with her words.

"How long are you staying?" Danny took the bags to the counter in the kitchen and kissed his wife hello. "Hi Babe. Isn't this great? Did you know?"

"No. I knew nothing," Caroline replied, holding her face together sternly by pursing her lips. Eleanor smiled. She was feeling sorry for her sister-in-law. The news of her dying seemed to add infinite addendums to Caroline's to-do list: #7: Comfort husband, #8: Dry clean appropriate funeral dress, #9: Purchase waterproof mascara,

#10: Talk to kids about Heaven, and so on and so on. Eleanor could see how taxing it all was for her, how exhausting it would be.

"Aunt Eleanor cracked her head open!" Frankie ran screaming into the front hall.

"You what?" Danny said, jumping to action as if she were still suddenly bleeding.

"It's nothing, I'm fine," El assured.

"I took her to Dr. Mittens to stitch the whole thing up," Caroline said from the kitchen. "She was wonderful, really, to fit us in."

"You took her to the cat doctor? Are you freaking kidding me?"

"You know how good she has been to all of our babies."

"Our babies? They are cats, Caroline." Danny looked at his wife, horrified that she would take his sister to a vet instead of the emergency room.

"Well, they are *my* babies!" Caroline hissed. The tabby and the shorthair wove through Caroline's legs as if on cue. The sister cats could feel Caroline's feline loyalty and were rewarding her for it by brushing up against the bottom third of her calves that stretched out from under her capris. Olivia and Beatrice were of the "cats are to be seen and not petted" variety. Their caress was heavenly to Caroline. She stood shock still until they slipped away and curled back into their own private corners of the house.

“She was great, wasn’t she Eleanor?” Caroline said, snapping out of her cat trance.

Eleanor smiled. As the family set the table and the arguments continued, she could see this conversation was definitely not about her, even though she was the one with the stitches and bandage. True, it was her body they were battling over, yet the war of words clearly had a longer, more vehement history. She watched the drama unfold between her brother and his wife, the weight of looks and tactics of punctuation marks placed between pleasantries of napkins, plates, and water glasses. Ellipses passed for aggression in a not-so-subtle manner. Periods came down heavy, with the finality of a bullet. Question marks raised white flags over conversations, begging for at least a dinnertime truce. As the smoke cleared and the innocents took their seats, Caroline and Danny assumed their chairs at the opposite ends of the table. Eleanor, now mostly a listener, felt like Switzerland and watched it all from a place of neutrality. It was strange to have the heavens hold one’s tongue. She would like to say so much but felt that she had a limited word count left and must choose each syllable carefully. There would be other battles to come.

El sat down at the place setting without chopsticks. Unarmed and marooned with no words, no fork, no knife, the seat with only a spoon clearly marked her territory at the table.

"Eleanor left Walter," Caroline blurted, clearly unable to bare it anymore.

"You what?" Danny asked for the second time that evening.

Eleanor unfolded the napkin that had been origamied by Caroline into a fan in an attempt to make the dinner themed and festive. The linen square seemed to grow in size as El spread it out across her lap like a security blanket.

"Danny, I came to talk to you about something important, something I didn't want to say over the phone," Eleanor started slowly, noticing every chalky word as it stuck in her throat.

"Kids, take your plates to the living room," Caroline ordered, clearly not ready to have this conversation with her children.

Danny looked nervously at Eleanor. That his wife was dismissing their children from the table and sending them off to eat "like savages" in front of the television surely meant that something was desperately wrong.

There was a lot of crying. How Eleanor thought it would be different, she couldn't now say. Of course, there would be crying, and crying was onc of the hardest things for her body to bear. The acronym was a new one for Danny, and so El had to spell ALS out and fill in the blanks, of which there were many. Caroline sobbed silently into her sweet and sour soup. She kept quiet by stuffing her mouth full of chicken chow mein, eating and crying like no one Eleanor had ever seen. Danny couldn't sit still; he was a ball of furious energy. He jumped up from the table angry, ready to kick some unseen force's ass. Then, suddenly exhausted, he slunk into his chair, defeated after only moments on his feet.

"Let's take a walk," Danny finally said, shoving his untouched plate back from him. "I need some fucking air."

Eleanor had been fiddling uncontrollably with the little cellophane wrapped cookie that Caroline had set at each place for decoration, the package becoming a sort of talisman of strength for her as she spoke. Finally tearing away the plastic and breaking the cookie in half, El pulled out the tiny slip of a scroll inside to read, "You are about to embark on the journey of a lifetime." Before leaving the table, Eleanor wadded the oracle into a ball, threw it into the back of her throat like a pill, and choked her fortune down.

The two of them walked for over an hour, Danny cautiously trying to gather details.

"So, you just walked out?" Danny marveled.

"Yep." Amazing how simple it sounded, how effortless.

"That easy?" Danny asked, as if he were getting a recipe or a set of instructions.

"That hard. But yep, that easy."

Now that El was a "Woman Who Had Left Her Husband," she felt all the privilege that the banner came to bear. She could speak up, would speak up, and would speak even louder with her actions than with her words.

"Would you have done it … anyway?" There was clearly no right way to ask this question. Eleanor appreciated her brother's candor and carefulness. She wished they had spent more time together, just the two of them, over the years.

"I mean, would you have left if you weren't … if you weren't …" Danny continued, sensing El's pause.

"Already leaving?" El offered.

"Yeah, already leaving," Danny exhaled.

"I don't know," El answered slowly. "I think so—but there was something about losing my voice in a house where it was already gone that I just couldn't bear. He didn't even notice the quiet. In a way, it was like I had left long ago."

"I hear you."

"I know you do," El said, putting her arm around her brother. "You ever think about it?"

"Dying?" Danny asked.

"No, leaving."

Danny smiled. "I have a bag packed in the garage."

"For how long?"

"Twenty-five years."

"Would the pants still fit?" El teased.

"Bitch," Danny smiled.

It was the longest conversation the two of them had shared without being interrupted by Bel or Caroline. He was stronger than Eleanor thought and, difficult as his wife seemed to everyone else, Danny loved Caroline and he especially loved his kids. He would make the right decisions, with or without his big sister. She memorized his cowlick and his eyelashes, all the details she could take in of his profile as it glowed, illuminated by streetlights. She tried, without over doing it, to imitate his gait so that she could take it on her travels and imagine walking side-by-side with him when she felt alone. She looped her fingers through his for the first time since she had helped him cross at the big intersection by their house decades ago, back when he still needed an older sibling for safe passage. She felt the similarity in the size of their hands and knew that later, in holding her own, she would still feel him.

It was a good visit, but Eleanor couldn't stay. It was the moving forward that was, well, moving her forward. She kissed him and hugged him hard outside the house. To anyone looking on it might have seemed less than innocent, though it was all innocence and more. She changed out of her sister-in-law's pajamas, collected her things from the guest room, kissed Caroline and the kids lovingly but without ceremony, and loaded up the truck. Caroline raced out after her, carrying a doggy bag full of egg-drop soup and one real spoon. She had broken up a set for her, another great kindness in one single day. Eleanor hugged her sister-in-law a second time and whispered, "Thank you" before turning out the door.

The two cats sat on the hood of the old Dodge, waiting to be acknowledged after ignoring their guest all afternoon. Eleanor rubbed them each behind the ear. They leaned into her. The one she thought was Beatrice pawed playfully at the loose end of her butterfly bandage. El pulled it off the rest of the way, exposing the new scar to the night air. She could feel the strain of the stitches as they worked to hold her in place, and she knew that, if she didn't leave now, everything in her that felt so barely held together by a few black threads would unravel. She jumped into her truck and turned the key, sending the cats off into the dark.

Comfort

I am the least dangerous member of my family. I take my place on the outskirts of the war zone, furthest from The Plate. The rest of my tribe have long rap sheets—take The Knife for starters. He's certainly had his share of action. We're related and I still don't trust that guy. He'll stab you in the back right after the entrée, catch you off guard during the cheese course. Just as you're savoring a cave-aged Gouda or a really stinky blue—Bam. One hit. Done.

And then there's The Fork, the ultimate instrument of self-torture. You remember that scene in Dangerous Liaisons when the Marquise de Merteuil takes one to the back of the hand under the table just to test her restraint? Whew. Powerful stuff. Even if you're not into hardcore fork-

ing, you've used her against yourself without thinking. Bite after bite, filling the void, filling the void. Her tines have speared that cake, that pie, that potato, and though you may taste the first bite, savor the chocolate, the berry, the butter, after a while the action becomes rote, and you are numb to it all. In my culture, The Fork is one dangerous step away from the indelicacy of the fingers. As the three- or four-digit extension of your animalness, it is the instrument that makes you feel that you still have control over your appetites and have not yet stooped to scooping food into your mouth with your hands. Even the salad fork has a way about her—bitterly stabbing into lettuce, often used inappropriately by savages for the main dish.

At my worst, I can shovel too much ice cream into a face after a break-up or torture a small child with acerbic grape cough syrup. But at my best and most often, I am built for pleasure and comfort, my slow arch echoing the curves of the sublime. I am the tool you feel while tasting, hot from the soup, cool from the cream. Liberated from the tyranny of teeth, I melt off the tongue, the lips, indulging in the soft palettes of tasting. I am part of the moment of flavor, not distant from it like the other cutlery. I round off the culinary experience. There is nothing flat in my wares.

No wonder that even as a figure of speech, I am comfort. To spoon. To be spooned. Spooning. Cradled. Held. Cuddled. And then there is just the sound of me. The milky "oooo" that feels so good to utter.

Try it.

There's a reason The Dish runs away with me in the end.

Out to Sea

Just barely five minutes on the road from Danny's house, El decided to stop for the night. The audacity of staying in a hotel within running distance from family was deliciously liberating. Dinner had exhausted her. Sometimes she couldn't wait to lose her voice completely so she wouldn't have to tell anyone anymore.

She would get better at this, the telling part. She would have to, or it would kill her instead of the disease. She would lower her voice and her expectations. She would leave out the leaving Walter part. It diffused focus. Really, there weren't that many people for her to tell. There was Danny, Bel, Jillian, any policeman who stopped her, and for some reason, her old high school crush, Lee.

They hadn't spoken in almost forty years, and yet she knew she wanted to tell him, had to tell him, in person. She had googled him last year to find that he was a goldsmith in California. There had been a moment in her younger life when she imagined the two of them living outside of time in a bus or a van, him selling jewelry at Grateful Dead shows, she "opening" for the band in the parking lot for the other gypsies. Truth was, she didn't really make a good hippy and the dream always fizzled at the place where she tried to imagine herself without a shower for more than two days.

It had been difficult to find him online, which didn't surprise her. He wasn't on Facebook or Twitter or LinkedIn. She had no idea if he was married or if he had a girlfriend or had kids. She had simply found an article on the boutique jewelry store he owned outside San Francisco. "Metal Moon" it was called, and since reading that article, she often imagined that it was Lee who had crafted the real moon itself, polished it just so, and pinned it on the night sky as a reminder of the impossible possibility of young love. She had no idea why she wanted to tell him or what she wanted in response, she just knew that he was part of the pilgrimage, a roadside attraction of fierce magnetism, and that it was his gravity that was pulling her west beyond the Rockies.

Not that her story would end in romance—she was too much of

a realist to buy into that dream. At sixty-one, she had come to accept that lack of plot in her life and often felt that she had been meant for a Virginia Woolf novel, not a quick-read paperback.

> She had the perpetual sense, as she watched the taxi cabs, of being out, out, far out to sea and alone; she always had the feeling that it was very, very, dangerous to live even one day.

El, more aware than ever of the dangers of a day, put on her blinker and turned cautiously onto the main drag of town.

Peculiar

El was overcome with exhaustion. She needed a hard drink and a soft pillow. Then there it was on the left, the sign she had been looking for.

Full Moon Bar and Motel.

"It's a sign," she said out loud. The fact that it was literally a sign, and that she had said something so obvious and with such seriousness to no one, made her laugh until her stitches pulled.

The man on duty was the night manager and bartender, both gate keeper and wizard of booze. The lobby entrance was located at the far end of the green-lit bar, room keys hanging next to the top shelf liquors, which in these twenty-three miles outside Kansas City spot meant that Wild Turkey was top shelf. No wonder they put “Bar” first on the neon sign—she wondered if beds folded out of the wall, Murphy style, so you could pass out right off your stool. El, saddled with her overnight bag, strode up to the desk/bar and ordered both a room and a white Russian. The running waterfall clock betrayed her exhaustion—only 8:42 p.m. She was certain it was after midnight.

When the bartender came back with her drink, she thought he might drop her room keys into her glass for effect. He had made it just like she liked it, with the cream streaming through the ice, not yet stirred. She swizzled the short black cocktail straw, mesmerized by the shifting cirrus clouds inside the tumbler. Walter had always called hers “a dessert drink,” one more way he hadn’t taken her seriously.

The bar was pretty full for a Thursday and for a town and a motel of this size. There were about fifteen people, mostly men and mostly older. This wasn’t like any other hotel lobby bar she’d been to with Walter in the last ten years—no piano player, just a jukebox, and no menus, only peanuts on the tables, shells on the floor. There was no worrying about “walking the lobby,” dressing up to make your best showing, as everyone here seemed like permanent fixtures with assigned seats.

As if the bartender had read her mind he answered back. “The

Full Moon is the town's hotspot. You should see this place on karaoke night. Tuesday is trivia night and Saturday we do line dancing."

"What do you do Thursday?" El said, biting down on the straw to mask her failing voice.

"Drink!" said an older man in coveralls three stools down. At that, everyone in the bar raised their glass, toasted one another, and drained their beverages. El laughed and sipped her white Russian through her straw, teasing the ice cubes back and forth across the glass. She was looking to dull the ache around her stitches and her heart. It would take more than a couple white Russians to do that.

"The biggest memorial this town has is the Full Moon's Stall of Fame—the men's bathroom is full of notable quotables that have been here since the early 1940s. Some of the best and brightest from this community have left their John Hancock in that John."

"What about the women's room?" El asked. She suddenly felt like a journalist or an anthropologist doing a piece about Peculiar, Missouri—the town "Where the odds are with you," as the slogan said.

"The women's room went their own direction, it's more about bumper stickers—you'll have to venture a look. I'm Steven. I'll be serving you this evening."

"Steven? When did you become Steven?" The fixture at the end of the bar sloshed his drink. "You grow hair on your balls in the last five minutes? I'm Hank and this is Jimmy. Let us buy the lady her next frufru drink, will ya, Stevie?"

"Nice, Hank. Real nice." Even with the overbearing hue of the green light, El could see Steven blush. She was not used to noticing men, and here she was doing it again. He was probably twenty years her junior, more appropriate for Jillian if Jillian had liked the opposite sex, but certainly not her speed. The mental babbling and the vodka made her smile at herself.

"Inside joke?" Steven asked warmly.

"Way inside," El responded. Feeling a little bold, she slid her straw out of her glass, held it between her first two fingers like a cigarette, ashed it into the air and said, "Thank you boys, I think I will have another," and nodded down the bar at Hank and Jimmy.

Over the next two hours and four cocktails, the three men held El happily captive with stories about the town. When Danny had first moved, Eleanor had asked him, "Why Peculiar?" All he'd had to say about it was that it was close to Kansas City and cost less. "Close" and "less." So very far from "there" and "more." These men didn't seem to think of Peculiar in reference to anything else but the past and the present. This was central. This was home. And home was Peculiar.

Longing

I spent the beginning of my life encased, wrapped in a sheath that kept me as close as "almost" and as far away as "not yet; not yet." From the beginning, I knew my purpose, knew that I was impotent alone. I craved a mouth on my mouth, one to draw life from me and into me, one to fill me with a sudden rush of hot or cold, of frothy or effervescent. The life of a straw appears to be a brief one, usually just the length of one beverage, but we have a fore-life, one that lasts far longer than you can imagine. We live—if you can call it living—cocooned for months, sometimes years, before our unfurling, our quenching, and then our ultimate disposal. Sadly, life is not over after we are tossed into the trash. We are left for almost an eternity with nothingness—nothingness and the recollection of that one sensual moment of our existence. We spend a forever reliving the softness of the lips that knew us ever so briefly, the draw of the suckle, the light brush of the tongue. We ache to be shared, to know the power of another mouth. We remember the death knell of ice cubes clinking against the wall of the glass or the mad, mad hunting at the bottom of the Styrofoam cup for One. Last. Sip.

I was, in the evening of my life, in my happier hour, a Cocktail Straw. We are a damned breed. Some of us never know the pleasure of an embouchement and only ever feel the cold of fingers swizzling and swizzling us farther away from our dreams. I was a lucky one. I felt finger and lip and tongue and tooth, transforming me from pestle to straw to cigarette, extending my time in use well beyond my life expectancy. The mouth of my moment was a great mouth, a gorgeous mouth. She was my own and the memory of her will last me the rest of my landfilled days. The small space between her perfectly imperfect teeth was made for me. Her quiet tongue licked at me as she laughed. I was both instrument of pleasure and of relief. Her bite, flirtatious and coy, sent me into near convulsions—shivers running up me like soda water, firing the sweet headiness of alcohol to my head. I long for that mouth on my mouth, long for the feeling of completeness through my brief expanse. I have known full and that makes empty all the more hollow. Yet it is this empty now that makes the memory of her saturated. I am parched with longing, yet it is longing that brings her to me and sates my thirst with her kiss.

Catholic Phone Booth

El wasn't really drinking anymore, just pushing ice cubes around and chewing on her straw. "Let me get you a fresh one," Steven said about the mangled and contorted piece of black plastic that El had been nibbling all night.

"No thanks. I've gotten kind of attached to this one," El said with the straw gripped between her teeth. It had become a security blanket over the last few hours, a way of inhibiting her full voice and masking its changes. The last thing she wanted, especially this tipsy, was for someone to ask her about it—her voice. There were times when that's all she would have wanted to hear about. During her short stint in Nashville and subsequent "tour," she changed the name of her one-woman band to The Raven and introduced herself as Lenore instead of Eleanor. She was part Stevie Nicks part Janis Ian and not near enough country for down south.

El had played bars like this one throughout the late '60s and, for the most part, loved singing into the sea of anonymous desires. Sometimes their thirsty faces, two too many vodkas, and her proclivity towards a minor key drowned out her words and all she heard were their stories.

A woman she called Heartache sat close to the stage, her eyes closed, and her head tilted into the melodies. She was divorced for the second time, and she often stopped by for "one more drink" before heading home to an empty bed. There was Needy, who clapped too loudly and seemed to always make a big deal about the tip he placed in her jar. Needy always bought her a drink, and she felt she had to listen to him throughout her break. He worked at the local pet store but dreamed of opening his own chain of dog washing establishments. Laundry Mutts, he would call them. It was his pet project, etc., etc. She always knew way too much about Needy by the end of an evening. Desperate wandered from table to table, prowling in her low-cut blouse for someone to see inside her. She usually left after the first set with Wounded or Married, who were always there, sitting in the corner with rocks glasses of bourbon. Eleanor appreciated

Loneliness for his quiet attentiveness, and she usually dedicated one song to him over the course of the night. Then there was Curious, his heart on his sleeve, his intensity honed. His shtick was to seem most interested in the music, but he was only there to get laid. If Curiosity killed the cat, then Satisfaction brought it back. And it was usually Satisfaction she woke up with in the morning.

When it seemed clear that she wasn't going to be discovered, El set out to colonize her own dreams and went to graduate school for teaching. She traded in a barroom for a classroom. There, the smell of peanut butter and jelly mingled with excitement, replacing the stench of beer and regret. At first, she loved this crowd, one more audience for one more show. Though she had never known stage fright in her performing life, the earnest stares of all those young, clear eyes looking up at her started to feel oppressive and daunting. They really believed she could teach them something. She had never felt so listened to and so inadequate in all her life. El switched to one-on-one work with the speech therapy kids. In helping them find their voice, she found hers as well. She spent the next forty years with those kiddos of the speech trailer, and even after Walter's career took off and she began writing for him, it was these students, those with so much to say and not all the sounds for it, whom she remained most loyal to.

Steven set a pint glass of water down in front of El. It reminded her that she had had to pee for the last half hour. She thanked him and excused herself to go use the ladies' room and see what all the bragging had been about.

There were four walls and two stalls completely covered, some overlapping, with bumper stickers. How did they all get here, El wondered in her hazy state. Did folks run outside with hot water and an Exacto knife and peel their favorites off their cars when they found this shrine? Or did they set a pilgrimage for the Full Moon in Peculiar, MO, bearing gifts of over-sized sticky fortune cookie wisdom as a symbol of their devotion?

Where else in the world did anyone appreciate the bumper sticker like in America? And where else in America did people appreciate it more than right here in Peculiar?

Surpassing the flag flying off a front porch, the bumper sticker was the proud purveyor of patriotism, anti-disestablishmentarianism, pacifism, creationism, and other systemic "isms" that could be displayed proudly with an iconic "fish" or "fish eats fish" or "Calvin (of cartoon fame) catches fish." A particular thing about bumper stickers, El mused, was their relationship to their vehicle and their co-passengers—placing a peace sign on a Hummer was either wonderfully ironic or screamed "Hippycrite" as it roared down the highway. "Keep Boulder Weird" was destined to share a seat next to "Visualize Whirled Peas" and "My Other Car is a Broomstick" on VW Beetles. American Flags rode shotgun with red, white, and blue "Support Our Troops" ribbons on Ford Trucks, while yellow "Bring Back our Troops" ribbons most often hitched a ride with a crooked "Snowboard Naked" and a Dave Mathew's dancer on later model Subaru station wagons. The "beater car," the one made of pilfered parts that actually appeared to be held together by its opinions, was one of America's greatest cultural icons. "Thank god I'm an Atheist," worked side-by-side to keep the trunk down and the bumper in place with "Ew! I kissed a Republican," and "I'm rushing to yoga."

Distracted by the sheer volume of confessional wisdom, El hadn't realized that she had company.

"Can you hand me a tissue?" A woman in the stall next to her asked between sniffles.

Loyal to girl code, El tore some toilet paper off the roll and handed it under the stall. This simple gesture sent the woman into a blubbering fit.

"You okay?" El asked, taking more toilet paper off the roll.

"Yes. No. God, do I sound ok? I'm a freakin' train wreck. Fuck." Trainwreck flew even more off-track, a full-blown wail emanating from her throat chased by deep and heaving sobs. She seemed to have refined the art of lamentation. El envied her virtuosity.

"I'm sorry, honey," Trainwreck bawled on. "I'm not mad at you. Hell, I don't even know who you are. Don't tell me. Better if I don't know. You're nice enough to be talking to me, so that probably means I don't know you—seeing as how I pissed off everyone in this damn town. I gotta get something off my chest and it's better if it's un-cog-nito, if you know what I mean? Like those Catholic phone booths, the ones where you put a quarter in, don't know who's on the other end and get to spill it all, tell your sins and then be forgiven. I need me a goddamn Catholic phone booth."

"Ok ..." El responded hesitantly, perversely curious about what this woman had done that warranted this scene. She felt like she had just picked up a tabloid magazine in the check-out aisle and now had to buy it to go past the cover to get to the full story on page twenty-three. She wondered if the priests of her childhood had felt this way, confession as a means of warped and titillating entertainment, the soap opera for the sacred.

"So, how do I start? Forgive me father for I have sinned—or mother—are you a mother?"

"Yep," El almost laughed at the richness of it all, but she didn't want to offend.

"Good. Ok, forgive me mother for I have sinned. I have never done this before—confess my sins, I mean. I've sinned plenty. This latest one is a real doozey."

Trainwreck's words and tears started to puddle into themselves, making El feel like she was underwater. Underwater. The only time El had cried like this was underwater.

It was Valentine's Day, and she and Walter had plans that evening to go out and fake their love life publicly. El was looking more forward to meeting with the Scottish doctor whom she had visited two weeks before when she had finally admitted that something was off. She was eager to get to the bottom of things.

And the bottom it was. El sat stunned on the paper-sheeted bed of Dr. Bannon's office as he handed her the doily-laced death sentence of ALS. After the acronym was decoded for her, Lou Gehrig's spelled out in all its finite ways, she thanked the doctor, shook his hand blankly, and turned towards the door. "Happy Valentine's Day," she had said to him with no sarcasm or bitterness. She had wished him love as she walked out into her despair. As she left, El glimpsed the doctor stepping up to the examining table. As the door closed, she imagined him curled in the fetal position and doing her weeping for her.

El headed straight to the Y, to the locker room, and to her favorite lane. Thank god she had packed her suit that morning, or she would have dived in with her clothes on. It was at the end of the

Silver Flippers water aerobics class and just before the lunch crowd arrived. The lanes were all hers. She jumped into the shallow end, put on her goggles, and pushed off the wall. That first push was her favorite, it was the only one where she noticed the way every part of her body made contact with every part of the water. It felt both exhilarating and grounding. She started to swim free style, as she always did. She made it through her first lap and out of her kick-turn before her mind latched onto the gravity of what she had just learned, and she suddenly forgot how to breathe. She had a terminal disease. She was going to die. Not just sometime in the future like everyone else, she was going to die soon. And horribly.

Her goggles filled and steamed. Once the tears started coming, they wouldn't stop. She felt she could raise the level of the water and flood the gym. In her panic, she imagined the older women in their brightly colored bathing caps bobbing like lost balloons into the tides she was creating. She screamed underwater. She cried so hard she choked. She thrashed. The teenage lifeguards, who could no sooner guard her life than her doctor could, would later tell their friends that it looked like a shark attack in four feet of water. It took three of them to bring her up. She was as heavy as a 400-pound man. Little did they know that she carried the full weight of her diagnosis, like stones in the pockets of an overcoat, into the pool with her that day.

She had hoped she might drown.

"And so, I just ran here, in the deputy sheriff's wife's robe, the one with her initials on it, of course her name is Amy, so I'm branded and locked out of my now ex's apartment just because I danced with the wrong man at my own damn wedding. Whew. That wasn't so bad. Am I supposed to say or do something now to make it all go away?"

El came up from the deep end of her *self* and back to the moment. She wondered how she had missed this woman in a bathrobe emblazoned with an "A" coming into the bar to begin with. She wondered why humans made it so hard. And how long she could carry these secrets with her and still swim. And how much she would miss swimming when that was taken from her like everything else. And how many more laps, how many more Valentines, how many stories, and how many more miles she would live to experience.

El's eyes focused on a bumper sticker that read "Be the change you want to see in the world" and replied like the professional she wasn't, "Say three Hail Marys and be a little nicer to your *self*."

"I don't know that one," Trainwreck sniffled.

"Then just sing your favorite song and really listen to the words."

The most beautiful "Amazing Grace" El had ever heard rose from the stall, bounced off the slogan-filled walls, and saturated the room. Those lungs, trained by crying, were made to sing. El left the stall without flushing; she didn't want to disturb the beauty of it all with something so obscene. She turned on the faucet softly, letting the water wash over her. It felt sacred, holy. As Trainwreck sang from the stall, El caught a glimpse of someone in the mirror. There was something about the woman she saw that reminded her of someone else. Someone she'd known a long, long time ago. El stood for a minute, listened as grace fell all around her, and crossed herself as she walked out the door.

To Oz!

It was only 6 a.m., but with the curtains flung open, the sun was already trumpeting the arrival of the day. Eleanor rose, went to the bathroom, washed her hands and face, and pulled a brush through the wild waves of her coffee brown hair. She noticed a few greys stranded in the bristles. Pulling them out one by one, she watched as they floated, shimmering down into the trash.

Both the lobby and the bar were abandoned at this early hour. El left her keys on the office desk, headed out the door, and out of Peculiar. Head pounding from dehydration, she wondered how she had gotten back to her room from the bar the night before and how she would get enough water into herself without gagging. She longed to chug a Gatorade, but those days were gone.

"You can sip whatever you can handle," Dr. Bannon had told her. "And continue to try small bites of mushy food as you see fit. But just in case, try not to eat alone."

She knew what the good doctor meant, as she had been eating alone for years and the empty scraping of fork and knife to plate was slowly killing her long before her diagnosis. Family dinner used to be such an important time. As soon as Jillian left, Walter saw no need for the ritual gathering and had filled his evenings with "dinner meetings." Stranded alone at the island of the kitchen, Eleanor made up her salads, poured her wine, and ate in silence. Some nights, when she couldn't bear it, she called Isabel, put her on speaker, and propped the phone across from her. On Mountain Time, Isabel was usually still at work, but she would always pick up and put down whatever else she was doing to eat with her sister. El could hear the pluck of a bottle uncorking, one she imagined Isabel pulling from under the register at the store, and the slow gurgle as Isabel poured an afternoon glass of Shiraz. "Cheers!" she would say and the two would clink their glasses across the miles. But she couldn't call Isabel every night at dinner. It would give too much of her loneliness away.

She was a good thirteen to fourteen hours from her sister's place in Crested Butte, and the miles of stretched-out, empty road took their time through Kansas and Eastern Colorado. She opened her glove box and rifled through it, her hand searching for a specific tape. She popped in another old recording, the one she'd made in semi-secret after Jillian was born. This was always a favorite—full of lullabies and love songs to her little girl. She would make the songs up as she nursed her, as she paraded her around the block in her stroller, as she rocked her to sleep at night. When the house was quiet, she would hum them into her cassette recorder to remember the tunes. She sang a couple for Walter, but he seemed more jealous than pleased.

"I like when you save your words for me," he said, cuddling into her.

"I have enough words for you both," El had said, young and sure that her love could divide infinitely between her new baby and her new husband. She never thought she would have to choose, and she certainly never thought she would choose Walter.

It was the campaign of '88. National Coming Out Day had just been established, and Walter had requested a speech from Eleanor that spoke out against the "demoralization of our country" through such a holiday. Though Eleanor had an inkling about her daughter's desires, having read her journal months before, she did as she was asked. She feared that if she stood up too strongly against Walter now, she might give Jillian away. And so, she wrote the potent and inspiring speech that rift against the fabric of her being. It was the second betrayal of her young daughter's heart.

Jillian hadn't intended to come out to her parents that October day, hadn't planned to be one of the thousands, "a gay cliché," as she later cried to her mother, but when her father spoke the words her mother had penned, she couldn't take it any longer.

That night at the table as the family watched snippets of Walter's speech on the news, Jillian asked her father to pass the mashed potatoes and said quietly, "Also, Father, I have a girlfriend." Eleanor's hand flew to her mouth to stifle the sound she was afraid she would make. She wasn't surprised about Jill, but she was more than shocked that she chose this moment to tell all. Walt almost choked on his steak before responding, "Not in my house, you don't," he growled, and then went about his supper. Her move to standing felt glacial, but finally Jillian reached her full height, looked her father dead in the eyes and said, "Then I won't be in your house." She turned to her mother and, in the most hateful voice she could muster, hissed, "How could you?" before running out of the room.

It was Halloween before Jillian came home and, when she did, no questions were asked. The house teetered on a "don't ask, don't tell" basis from there on out, precariously balanced on silence, avoidance, and feigned ignorance. The family still gathered for dinner, but the TV was always on and tuned to the Family Feud, a perfect replacement for the war that raged on silently among them for the next two years before Jillian would move out for good.

“I used to sing my girl to sleep,” Eleanor mused melancholically as she passed signs for The OZ Museum in Wamego, Kansas. El wasn’t so sure that she still agreed with Dorothy and her sentimental assessment of *Home*. She did wonder, however, if somewhere along this yellow brick road trip she might find a wizard who would give her the one thing she needed most. Forgiveness.

Airlock

She held her daughter's journal on her lap and sat down on the end of the unmade bed. I will not read it, she intoned. I will not read it.

Her fingers grazed the cover unconsciously, stroking it with the back of her knuckles as she had once smoothed the pink, pink cream of her daughter's skin.

She used to let me touch her, she thought, used to let me stare at her, unselfconscious, for hours and days and weeks and months. She used to let me in.

Something was different now inside her sixteen-year-old, not just from the other girls her age, but something new, specific to Jillian herself. Eleanor could still read her shadow, if not her face, and her shadow seemed sharper and more distinct at its edge. Jillian's norm was sullen. Her constant cloud hung over the sofa, the bathroom sink, the table. Jill dressed for her life as one would for death. Styled in the funeral garb of a collision of eras, she appeared to be in mourning for the loss of some lone time traveler. Black on black, Jillian mixed torn lace with ripped fishnets with worn velvet and held it all together with a mutiny of safety pins. Her thrift store finds screamed, "I don't belong in the here and now, and I am just barely holding it together, if you really care to know."

But lately, there were splashes, mostly of red. Red on her lips, her laces, her fingernails. But the most arresting to Eleanor, who still, as she was permitted, stole moments to stare, was the red in her cheeks. Her daughter was in love. El was certain of it.

I wish she had hidden it better, Eleanor thought, holding the average looking book in her lap like a sacred text.

The notebook bore no "DO NOT READ's," no "PRIVATE! KEEP OUT's." The obvious was meant to be Jillian's cover. The sacred hidden by the simple; the obscure bared plain. Disguising her most intimate thoughts with normalcy might have worked with friends, or teachers, or even fathers, but not a mother. Eleanor had watched the detail with which Jillian affected every object since the moment she first learned her hands were connected to her body, to her brain, to her imagination. As soon as her daughter could touch and pull the outside into her, she had made it her own. Scraps of paper were not drawn upon but torn and piled into mountains and then blown into avalanches. Legos were assembled into beautiful, incongruous things, temples to upside down gods and right-side up wonders. The unaffected spiral-bound Mead notebook was the surest give-away Eleanor could have imagined for her daughter's most private thoughts.

I will not read it, she said inside herself again, her index finger trembling at the edge of the cardboard barrier. In the smallest and slowest of gestures, her finger rolled over to graze inside the cover. Just the act of touching its underbelly felt deviant, indiscreet, intimate.

Reading her daughter's journal was a last attempt, and a first offense, in a long line of failed tries to connect. She knew there was something, someone, new in Jill's life and she craved inclusion into that new terrain.

How strange it was to bring a human onto this earth and then to watch them float slowly back towards the star from which they came. Never one for sci-fi, El recalled a day she waited, eight months pregnant, at her O.B.'s office engrossed in a *National Geographic* article on spacewalks. "Astronauts trained for them by swimming," she read. That was the language that drew Eleanor in. Always a swimmer, Eleanor felt safest and most alive when freed by the temperaments of water. That caught moment of float, that act of faith, always brought her home. Space seemed too unknowably vast and terrifying, causing TV shows like *Lost in Space* to give her nightmares for weeks. But to think of the night sky and its infiniteness as ocean gave her new keys to understanding the appeal.

And within her was her baby, spacewalking through her inner galaxy. Soon this tiny traveler would be released to transition into the vastness of its life. "There are two doors in an airlock," Eleanor read on, "two doors that must be pulled tight in order to ensure the balance of pressure required to sustain life." The distinction between space travel and motherhood blurred to the point of evaporation, and Eleanor wondered how many women before her in this waiting room had similar epiphanous transports. We mothers are sending our babies into outer space, our outer space. Every day, for the rest of our children's lives, we will labor to let go while still staying connected. We will give them the Universe, but to do so, we must tether them tight. Every over-protective action Eleanor could remember her own mother taking came into crystalline focus. Mothers never truly let go.

When she looked down, again the notebook lay open in her hands. Without further hesitation or thought to consequence, she began to read. It was a terrible, beautiful, gift to see inside her daughter's darkness. She laughed at the descriptions of last month's fight with Walter, how accurately this sixteen-year-old painted the world of their lives. She cried at the bits about "my mother's weakness," not because they were mean, but because they were true. She rejoiced in her daughter's righteous anger and the voice she gave it; she reveled in her daughter's ability to put her discontent down with such acuity. And then there was silence. Page after page of blank. An avalanche of true intimacy. Faster and faster El flipped through the unwritten, hungry for what her daughter felt so strongly about that she could not utter, even here. Until finally, there at the end of the flurry, was one small word, written in red ink. *Her.*

All the air came out of the room. A mother knows things. She has been trained to read between the lines. And with so many blank lined pages, Eleanor could see her daughter even more clearly than had Jillian filled in each detail. *Her.* That one word was enough to confirm what El had believed for some time. But what would she do with this pronoun? What would she do with this new frontier? Her ears popped suddenly with the pressure change.

"The airlock chamber consists of two airtight doors which, in order to provide safe passage between environments of different gases, must not be opened simultaneously." Now that Eleanor had opened this door to her daughter's world, she could not re-lock it. She wondered how long mother and daughter could survive before being sucked into the void of the now Great Known.

Faith

I am just an ordinary, made-in-China, commercial offering to The Mother. One of sixteen of us Virgins, lined up, collecting dust, among the other icons and idols and ornaments at the Our Lady of the Mountains Souvenir Gift Shop and Variety Store outside Estes Park, Colorado. It may seem to some that I am too plain, too plastic, for a miracle, but I do believe I will be chosen one day. I know it with all of my being. Some might call it a calling. If it is, it is a calling from the inside. Someday, something of my blue robe, my pious eyes (my left a bit bigger than my right), and my inclined head will speak to someone, and I will make it to the place beyond this purgatory. I trust it will be beautiful and that there will be riches that I have not known here in this life on my shelf next to the Jesus key chains (which always seem to be chosen first) and the plastic rosaries. There was a bobbly-headed hippy next to me for a while, giving a thumbs up, a real novelty item. His sunny attitude sure worked for him, and he was up and on his way out of this shelf life faster than any curio I had ever seen. I think he barely lasted thirty-six days—a record here in this neck of the woods. We don't get a lot of foot traffic. He was my first true friend, talking me down when I got hard on myself for being just a naïve girl from a small town who would open her arms to anyone. "Our Mary in Perpetual Need of a Hug," he used to call me. My buddy, "pronounced Hey Seus, but spelled J-e-s-u-s," he told me, reminded me daily of my paradoxical depth, my virgin/mother status, my enigmatic attraction—both demure and dour. I would never have made it this long if not for him and his breezy surfer speak.

He was really an all-right guy—it was the people who were oftentimes drawn to him that I couldn't stand. They were, by far, the most loud and obnoxious customers, always pointing back at him "real cool-like," and going on and on about his "awesomeness." Hey Seus was awesome—that bobble-head really had us all green with envy. But enough already. The man who finally helped him make a break for it had two kids and, I remember him telling the cashier, thought his sons would really "love a reminder of their Father." I didn't think Hey Seus looked anything like the dad in the ball cap, but everybody seemed happy, so I felt good about it. Hey Seus gave me one of his classic thumbs up smiles and winked as he went out into the light. I hope someday I will see him again.

"Hang loose, Mare." That's what Hey Seus would tell me, then laugh and make crude jokes about the taxidermy that was placed way too close to the Barbie dolls. Some days I wished I was a Barbie Doll—they definitely seem to have more fun, a totally different sort of figurine—one with a figure—not forced into a potato sack that doesn't even work one curve. I do have curves, you know. But I trust my time here. I believe, with all my heart, that I will leave the fluorescent lights of this knickknack nowhere and move beyond the bric-a-brac to a place where I will be seen as unique and whole and hailed for my simple self. If I can just maintain my graceful composure until my time …

Not Your Mother's Mary

The smokestacks of the oil refinery greeted Eleanor before the Rocky Mountains had their chance. Less "Western Welcome Wagon" and more Terry Gilliam's *Brazil*, these apocalyptic towers served as a not-too-subtle foreshadowing of the world to come.

Desperate for more beauty and more time, El jumped on I-25 north then took exit 243 and Highway 66 toward Estes Park. It was clear to Eleanor that she was driving away from something, not towards, but she didn't care. Once she reached Isabel, she knew everything would change. She would have to start taking better care of herself for her sister's sake, if not her own.

It was incredible how quickly nature took over out here. As Denver dissolved in the background and Long's Peak came into view, El could feel herself breathing more deeply despite the change in altitude. Scents of sage and pine rushed in through the rolled down windows of the truck. The air felt refreshing and cooler than it was, the dryness belying the thermostat's insistence that the temp hit, in fact, 101 degrees. El noticed the waves of her hair straightening and the lines in her hands deepening—sky and earth searching for any water they could draw from. As the old truck clanked along the winding roads towards the national park, Eleanor swore she could see her skin change, chameleoning itself to the parched landscape around her. I will look like a local in no time, El laughed.

After over an hour on this road, Eleanor suddenly made the sharpest left turn of her life, dusting circling around her as she screeched into Our Lady of the Mountains Souvenir Gift Shop and Variety Store just outside of Estes. Eleanor had always had a thing for Mary. Even when she wasn't feeling especially religious, the sight of Her in Her blue and white robes settled Eleanor's nervous system like she imagined meditation would if she had ever really given it a chance. Oprah had once said that if you couldn't give something two minutes then your heart wasn't really in it. In the '90s, El, like every other woman in America, loved an Oprah challenge. And so she tried to sit. After about a minute and a half attempt to quiet her inner voices, El's eyes flew open to check her watch and see if she'd made it to the requisite two-minute mark. The exercise became more of a game than a spiritual awakening, a game against herself and one that she was losing badly. Perhaps meditating was more like sex, set the mood and the "awakening" would follow. El found a low table in the garage and draped a tapestried cloth from her hippy days across it. To complete the makeshift altar, El placed a coiled shell, a photo of her daughter, a lavender candle, a dream catcher she had been given by her sister, and the small porcelain Mary from her mother's nativity set.

Ever since she was a little girl, El had loved this particular miniature trio of Jesus, Mary, and Joseph. Mary was, however, her unabashed favorite. After being given the honor of setting up the scene every Christmas, Eleanor would sneak over and play with Mary until her mother caught her and inevitably told her that this was not a dollhouse but a sacred crèche. After her parents' divorce, Eleanor noticed the mysterious absence of the Holy Family at the holidays and asked her mother about it. Colleen seemed to avoid the question and fluttered on about some box somewhere in the attic, under her breath saying, "I'm sure they'll turn up." And sure enough, one day they did.

It was Eleanor and Walter's first Merry Married Christmas, and they were spending the morning at Colleen's before going to see El's father on the other side of town. The morning, full of the perfectly placed nostalgia of her childhood, went off without a hitch or a battle between her mother and her sister and Eleanor had just begun to exhale when she was summoned into Colleen's "boudoir."

Colleen always looked her most glamorous at the moment she was about to bestow something upon someone. Her beauty towered over events such as these, making the moment and the gift all the more important, the object of her affection becoming as vital as her own heart. To be called in before her, to be handed down something of hers, was to be, in that moment, Chosen.

In her mother's hand was a small gold bag, the kind made for fine jewelry. Eleanor was suddenly overcome with emotion. Her mind raced as to what piece was being bequeathed to her, the new bride at Christmas. There was a small clank as she clasped the bag and when she opened it, she was surprised to find Mary, now a single mother, with her baby, but no Joseph, inside.

"Where's Joseph?" El asked with reservation.

"You don't need him, dear," her mother responded, patting her hand, her engagement diamond now set inside a new band on her middle finger—a gesture El's father hadn't missed when he saw Colleen at El's wedding four months before.

"You know how I love my Mary, Mom, but I would feel funny separating them," El tried to stay light even though she was having a Freudian conversation about the break-up of her own family via the dissolve of the first family of Christianity.

"Men are really quite useless; the sooner you understand that the happier you'll be," Colleen snipped. "But if you'd like him, you can have him." With that, she walked over and snatched the figurine off the side table where she had put him behind a basket of room spray.

"Maybe I'll just put him out at Christmas," El said, trying to appease. Colleen smiled in consent. El sheepishly wondered what would have become of Joseph had she not rescued him from her mother's room that day. Trying to shake the possibilities from her mind, El stuffed Joseph into the bag where, for at least today, he still had a place in the manger. She walked out of her mother's room and greeted her husband, who had been standing impatiently in the foyer holding her coat, with a kiss.

This past week since she had hit the road, El had come to think of the dashboard as her altar, her hula girl, hands clutched to her ukulele, the stand-in for her old Mary, hands clutched to her breast. This brown leather shrine before her now was adorned with road-maps, parking stubs, dried flowers, and of course, Jeremy, who bobbled along playing her soundless song. For the first time in her life,

El understood sitting. And though the road was moving under her, she felt the buzz of inner quiet and a stillness in her mind that she was sure the mystics and the Buddha would refer to as meditation. It would be nice to get a Mary up there on the dash to complete the offerings to the gods, and Our Lady of the Mountains Souvenir Shop seemed just the place to find Her.

The gift shop was about an eighth of a mile away from the actual church and clearly not affiliated with the quaint Catholic parish from which the novelty shop took its name. The store was more secular in nature, as was evinced by the hand drawn signs that advertised "Pope on a Rope! Religious Novelty Items! Boxed Holy Wine!" El could hardly wait.

Inside, Eleanor found the strangest collection of items she had ever seen. Generic Barbies, "Modern-day Mary Magdalenes," hooked on the corner of the cashier's counter in mini-skirts and high heels. Next to them, motion-activated stuffed squirrels wearing mitres carried miniature papal crosses and sang *Don't Stop Believing* when anyone walked by. The place was a treasure trove of iconoclastic icons. Peppered throughout the more offensive items were small plastic statues for every saint, including the really obscure ones that any collector would swoon over. They were all there; St. Gertrude of Nevilles, patron saint of the fear of mice, St. Hubert of Leige, patron saint of mad dogs, and St. Isidore of Seville, patron saint of the internet. Eleanor didn't realize that the World Wide Web had otherworldly intervention and considered buying one to glue onto her laptop now that Walter wasn't around to tell her to log off and start over when something went wrong.

But she was fixed on finding the perfect Mary and hurried along to the big display that housed a hundred different varieties of The Virgin. Most of the Marys held one of two stances, head inclined, hands on heart or head inclined, palms open. If Eleanor were to be honest, she was of the open-palmed persuasion. She saw the gesture as an entrance into the folds of a Divine Mother, one who didn't criticize, turn all conversations back to herself, or introduce her as "the daughter with bad hair." Her mother's Mary, as much as she had loved her, held her hands close to her breast, a gesture that at times felt shut off and riddled with guilt. "Oh, look how you've wounded me, look how you've broken my heart," her mother's Mary sometimes seemed to say. She knew this time she would go for a Madonna whose embrace would hold her, even on her worst hair day.

Then there, out of the sea of Blessed Mothers, shone her very own Stella Maris, her personal Queen of Heaven. It was the statuette's imperfections that tugged at Eleanor, as if this pocket size Mother of God had Her own tidal pull. One slightly wonky eye gave the impression that She was not looking down in judgment upon the "sinners of the earth," but just off, somewhere towards the better parts of human nature. The small dab of blue on the front of Her white gown made Eleanor think of the years of parenthood she spent covered in food and thought to herself, this is a Mary who knows. Without stopping to consider the full ramification of shoplifting a saint, Eleanor snatched the figurine from the display, pocketed Her, and walked out the door into the light.

Siren

Her heart was flooding with blood. El could feel every artery, every ventricle pumping to capacity. The muscle wedged into the cage of her ribs, balled into a tighter fist than ever, worked overtime to quadruple the usual two thousand gallons of blood pumped daily through her body. Eleanor had never felt more alive and more afraid that she might actually die than she did right at the moment she walked out of the store with her stowaway. Her hands shook as she unlocked the truck. She dropped her keys, not once, but twice, into the dry earth of the parking lot. Absently rubbing at the beading sweat on her brow, El replaced its telltale guilt with two streaks of red mud—the ghost of an Ash Wednesday cross shining on the middle of her forehead. She started the car and took a sharp left turn back out onto the highway.

As soon as she heard the siren, she knew it was for her. She was going to jail. Somehow, goddammit, Eleanor always got caught, even if it had been Isabel who had started the trouble. Her conscience was so guilty that it seemed to lead the proper authorities right to her.

Co-conspirator in the Great Bikini Heist of 1961, Eleanor had been in this position before. Ever afraid of breaking the rules, El somehow got herself roped into Isabel's foolproof plan to procure new bathing suits after Colleen had refused them bikinis. It was a simple, five-step scheme that Isabel had drawn up the month after casing the joint.

The department store restocked on the first Monday. Inundated with new merchandise, the clerks were so busy unpacking boxes, steaming, hanging, and rehanging, that they paid little to no attention to teenage clientele. Plus, security was upped on the weekends with the rise in foot traffic. Mondays started the week with just one security guard per floor. It was either a go this weekend or they would have to wait another month, missing the new summer swim wear line, something Isabel just wasn't willing to accept.

Reluctantly, El agreed. At 11:45 a.m., just as the sales staff was starting their lunch rotation and shipments had been brought onto the floor, the pair strolled causally around the store, making their way to the swimsuit section. Isabel talked loudly about how they were to pick out a favorite and then come back with their mother later that day to purchase them. They each grabbed seven swimsuits, tangles of strings and straps, greens and purples, adding to the diversion. Laminated signs threatening "All Shoplifters Would Be Prosecuted to the Furthest Extent of the Law" suddenly appeared to hang on every wall. By 12:02 p.m., sporting a pale pink polka dot bathing suit under her clothes, El followed Bel's lead and strode out of the dressing room and towards the escalator. Then, with the exit in sight, El lost her nerve and ran back inside, drawing the attention of the floor manager. Bel made a break for it, but Eleanor was not so lucky. After ripping off the offending suit and redressing at warp speed, El was met on the other side of the dressing room curtain by a security officer who went through her bags and almost had her strip-searched. Eleanor was finally deemed clean and allowed to leave. Placed "under suspicion," her Polaroid hung in the break room of the ladies' department for the next decade. Eleanor spent the rest of the summer in last season's suit while Bel wore a white fringe halter bikini that netted her three different drive-in dates in June alone.

Eleanor considered throwing Mary out the window, but the consequence of that gesture seemed far worse than whatever the law had to deliver. Palms sweating, she gripped the steering wheel, slowed over to the shoulder, rolled down her window, and stared straight ahead.

"Good morning, ma'am. Are you aware that you made a left turn onto a highway after utilizing your right turn blinker back there?"

El, who had already prepared her "I'm dying and in a terrible hurry to get to my daughter" speech, turned and looked at Officer Maxwell (as his uniform read) and started speaking in tongues.

"And she looked into the cool blue waters of the Man in the Moon's eyes, and he drowned her in a Sea of Tranquility." The first one-line poem El had written for Lee, her high school sweetheart, spilled from her lips with near perfect diction.

"Excuse me, ma'am?" Officer Maxwell said, only then taking off his sunglasses.

His eyes were an otherworldly grey, the color of water on stone. El blinked at the exact moment that Officer Maxwell blinked, and in that quick shutter close, she imagined all their reflexes falling into sync. She could hear her heart slow to match his, his rhythm far more accustomed to the altitude and the race of sirens. She felt their swallow, slow and strong together, the flesh of their throats softening in time. The wind of the world entered their lungs riding the same jet stream. Eleanor smiled—the corners of her mouth magnetized to his. There they were, her sitting, him leaning in, two strangers locked together in time, grinning at one another.

She hoped he would write her a ticket. She wanted to give him all of her information, her name, her address, her date of birth. She only wished her phone number were there on her driver's license. She wanted him to know her height, her weight, her organ donor status. She was, in fact, an organ donor, and for the first time, Eleanor wondered how and if her parts would be divided and who might see the world through her eyes. Which bits of her would be good enough to pass on? She would call the doctor and ask him. She would very much like her organs to get another go around. Especially her heart. It was made to race, made to run. She had a thoroughbred heart, and it loved the chase and the speed. She certainly hoped her heart would race again as it was just beginning to do now.

"I'm Eleanor. What do I owe ya?" El asked, a sauciness to her tone that shocked and pleased her.

"Just your license and registration for now," Officer Maxwell smiled. "I need to run your plates and make sure you are not wanted for anything."

She wanted to be wanted for everything.

Staring into her rear view mirror, Eleanor watched the officer walk back to his car. It was the longest she had ever watched anyone walk, except, of course, Jillian. She had spent hours watching her daughter's gait. Jillian's wobbly steps as she was learning. Jillian's shy shuffle as she wandered alone into kindergarten. Jillian's indignant stride as she stormed out the door after that fateful Sunday brunch. But this watching of this walk—this was measured by a different hourglass. Everything slowed. The dust rose in rarefied clouds from the earth, not because of him, but for him. The swing of his arms felt musical, waltz-like, in harmony with his stride. Eleanor, if she were completely honest, wasn't just watching Officer Maxwell's walk, she was watching his ass. Eleanor's eyes flashed to her own face in the mirror. The mud streaks she had left on her forehead seared with her sinful thoughts. She used the bottom of her t-shirt to wipe them away. For the first time in her life, Eleanor was afraid of what she might do.

No longer worried about getting caught, in fact wanting to get taken in, El had unconsciously pulled Mary out of her pocket and had begun rolling the figurine between her fingers. As the heavy footfalls of boots approached, Eleanor forced herself to look down into her hands at the Virgin. She was pressing her luck. She said a quick prayer for guidance.

"Well, I couldn't find anything on you, so I'm gonna have to let you go," Officer Maxwell smiled. "Let this be a warning to you—we don't take kindly to outsiders giving mixed signals."

Eleanor sucked in hard. The Mother had spoken.

"Be careful, young lady, you don't want to run into me again. Unless maybe you fancy a two-step. I spend my off-nights at the Grizzly Rose." Officer Maxwell smiled his perfect crooked grin, handed her back her license and paperwork, and tipped his hat. "Good day, ma'am."

"Good day, officer," Eleanor said, exhaling, she imagined, for the first time since she had heard the siren.

Eleanor watched him walk back to his patrol car and climb inside. Just as his left foot was slipping inside the door, El noticed that he was wearing black cowboy boots with his uniform instead of regulation lace-ups. Fancy a two-step?!? She was just trying to put one foot in front of the other. She gripped her Mary so hard she thought she might pop Her head off. Officer Maxwell turned his head has he drove past her, tipped his hat again, and was gone.

The Color Red

Eleanor poured out through the truck's door and slid down onto her knees, right there in the dirt on the side of the road. Elbows resting on the cab's step, she folded her hands around her Mary, closed her eyes, and prayed. She prayed that her thighs would stop shaking. She prayed that she might someday hear again over the pounding of her heart. She prayed that her daughter would forgive her the choices of her life and that her sister would forgive her the compressed inevitability of her death. She prayed that she would meet that delicious looking officer again and not waste another moment of her life wondering. But mostly, over and over, Eleanor prayed for the strength to get her ass back up in the cab and keep driving. She knew she was wasting time spinning her wheels on Colorado back-roads, trying to avoid the inevitable. She had turned right off of I-70 towards Estes to stay blind. Blind to the huge and impossible reality that she was one of the 5,600 who would be diagnosed this year with Lou Gehrig's. That, if she was lucky, she was one of the 5,600 who would get at least one or two more years to live.

Eleanor opened her eyes and tears pooled out of them onto the ground, splashing the earth, bringing out its rich red. It was almost as if she were crying blood, the color was so intense. She had never before thought about how Colorado got its name or what it meant, but kneel-ing in the red-speckled dirt, the answer was clear. Something uncorked in her, and Eleanor was unable to stop crying. As the tears fell faster, El could feel the anger washing out of her eye sockets, burning its way to the ground. The cliché "seeing red" had never been more accurate. From this unstoppable expulsion, a question emerged.

"Why me?" Head down, snot draining, Eleanor asked the earth, again and again, "Why me?" And, before the sun could completely suck the moisture out of the dirt and render it back to its less vibrant menstrual brown, the answer came plain as day.

Why not you?

Eleanor sucked in hard at the clarity of the response.

She held the three words quietly in her mind until her legs

started to go numb and she ached from kneeling, ached from wanting to believe that she could hold this nobler question as truth.

She blew her nose into her tank top. She took a deep breath.

The earth was right. Why not me? Eleanor thought. With all that had been good in her world, with all she had seen and felt and done, why not her? Children were dying of cancer and being taken too young. Soldiers had given their lives for her without knowing who she was. She had lived, was still living, a rich and vibrant existence, so why not her?

Eleanor pulled herself up slowly, her legs buzzing from the electricity of falling asleep, and side-saddled back into her truck. It was time. She needed her Thelma. After unwrapping a piece of gum she found in the glove compartment, El chewed it just enough to make it tacky; its juicy fruitedness working her salivary glands harder than her swallow could handle. She rolled the gum into a small wad, stuck it to the underside of her new Mary and pressed Her down hard onto the dash next to Jeremy, her hula girl.

Eleanor started the old Dodge, "flipped a bitch" in the middle of US-36 and headed back toward Denver. The hula dancer smiled at her new company and nodded her head in approval as the two of them, now sisters, watched the mighty mountains become smaller through the back cab window.

Dust to Dust

Burnt meteorite particles. Remnants of shooting stars. Comet crumbs. Eleanor read online that the silt covering so much of her life was made of the memories of old planets. It could also be the fecal remains of mites, but she was too obsessed with the notion that the Universe had come to her to latch onto anything so ungodly as microscopic insect poop. As she imagined little pieces of the cosmos making themselves at home in her living room, she felt more a part of the Big Unknown than ever before.

Eleanor had never understood dusting as a singular act—you brush something off something, and it lands somewhere else. It felt so Sisyphean. So every third Sunday of the month, El would rethink the intimate world she lived in and not just dust but re-arrange: a blue glass bottle moved to the mantle, a chartreuse throw pillow reseated on a wooden rocking chair, enamel-framed pictures of her and her guitar by a lake rehung and given placards with quotes from her mother like, "I hate that shot of you. We fought all the way up North because you wouldn't cut your hair."

Eleanor reveled in the French Country meets Middle Eastern medley of her home. "Shabby Sheik" she joked to friends, and, like a good Moroccan stew, it was better when stirred. In the world before Walter, El's "Dust Sundays" were delicious.

On these Sundays, Isabel would stop by with croissants and coffee from the only real French bakery in town and watch Eleanor work. Isabel would direct from the overstuffed armchair, the sole piece of furniture in the apartment that was never to be moved. It's never moving was "The Rule," crafted one boozy night who-remembers-ago, and The Rule often stranded the old wingback like a lone island separated from its archipelago of footstool and coffee table. There from that chair, sometimes with no side table, Bel would point this way and that, bits of croissant flying from her hands, flaky patisserie particles joining with the silt of the solar system as Eleanor vacuumed the old carpet grooves away.

Dusting for Walter was a different story. Dusting was a chore.

The only pleasure came from the absurdity of the feather duster itself—an impossible array of feathers plucked from an implausible bird. The plumes were huge and dyed to almost fluorescent hues of pink, blue, yellow, and orange, and the act of waving them at the muted blue-grey Precious Moments statuettes tickled El every time she rubbed a feather under their little turned up noses. She half expected them to sneeze.

Per her husband's instructions, she was to dust from the top shelf down to the bottom for obvious reasons that eluded her when left to her own haphazard ways. She was to dust from the heads to the sides, then lift and dust under and around. The next step was critical. Each figurine must be placed back on the shelf exactly as it was—no new view for Little Girl and Kitten, no new relationships between Angel and Hobo Baby that hadn't been set in place years before. There was an order. A hierarchy. A way.

Once El thought it would be a fun game to rearrange the collectibles, mixing them up and giving them a little "Dust Sunday" for dessert after so many years of dutiful service. Walter had barely walked in the door when he turned to his curios and started to sweat. "What have you done?" he said in a yell contained to a whisper. He ran to his Precious and, with the hands of a surgeon, placed them back as they were meant to be. Husband and wife didn't speak for three days.

From then on, dusting was done on the first Wednesday of each month, which meant she would certainly leave Walter on that first Tuesday of June. Even if he didn't miss her, he would at least notice the trail of comet dust in her wake.

Toast

After twenty minutes on the road, El's cell interrupted the silence by singing a terrible synthesized rendition of, "Come Dancing" by the Kinks, announcing that she was back in the land of cell reception and that Isabel was on the other end. It was almost 9 p.m., which meant that Isabel was home from work and would want a long chat. Back in Dayton, at 11 p.m. her time, El relished these late-night calls, using them as an excuse to get out of bed from beside Walter, sit at the counter in the kitchen, and eat toast with her sister over the phone. They had established this practice of "toasting" in junior high and kept it through Eleanor's returns from boarding school. Each of them home from different directions, the sisters would sit at the kitchen table, recounting the events of the night, breaking bread together as if they had baked it solely for this scared ritual. Now, forty years later, the two synchronized their toasting unintentionally, the dings of their machines ringing out in almost perfect unison.

Lately, El had wasted a lot of good bread. She worried her sister would miss the bell if she didn't enact the ritual, and so, letting the light burn of sourdough fill the kitchen, Eleanor toasted slice after slice, night after night. She buttered the bread, more and more butter each time, slathering the nooks and crannies with greasy white film, filling in every crack. It was wishful buttering, she knew it, but the action was as good for her soul as any comfort food she could devour. She broke pieces off close to the phone to sound like chewing—she used the "chewing" to mask her failing voice. After at least forty-five minutes and two or three pieces of toast, the sisters would say goodnight and their usual "I love you mores." Eleanor would dump the remains of her charade into the trash, brush the crumbs off of her robe, lick the butter off her fingertips, and, for the time being, feel full.

Eleanor hit OK on the cell phone, interrupting the steel drum bridge of the ringer to say hello. She missed her sister's voice so badly that it was worth the risk.

"Where are you? You sound like you're in a car," Isabel asked before saying hello.

Without waiting for Eleanor's answer, Bel launched into the recap of her day. Eleanor heard the familiar sound of the seven-grain being unwrapped; she heard the ding of Bel's toaster, the fridge opening, the clank of the butter dish. It was as if, since losing her ability to swallow solid food, her sense of hearing had sharpened, every detail of Bel's actions coming vividly into focus. As she toasted and buttered and chewed, Isabel talked about the debt consolidator she'd been to see that day, how he was helping her streamline her finances and how, if she'd been ten years younger and if he had been only slightly less married, she would have stapled him to his desk and underlined his assets. Lost in her recap fantasy, Isabel didn't notice the absence of tandem toasting on the other end.

El remembered how they used to prank call friends and try to trip them up by pretending to be the other. As her sister rambled on between crunches, she realized how much she missed the sound of her own voice and how lucky she was to have a facsimile. Too bad, she thought, that her sister was never a singer and couldn't match pitch to save her soul. Listening to her sister's voice now, even with its throatier accents and higher laugh, Eleanor imagined it was herself talking. As her voice left her completely, maybe Bel could learn to throw hers, turning them into a two-person ventriloquist team and traveling the country, Isabel eating toast and talking for two.

"Wait, where are you?" Isabel interrupted herself out of the blue to ask again. "Heading home," El smiled. "Heading home."

The sisters "I love you'd," El hanging up quickly before she spoiled the surprise that she would see her sister tomorrow. She considered continuing on, pushing it and arriving in Crested Butte sometime around 1 a.m., but she knew she needed one more good night's rest before the firestorm of tears that was about to ensue. El took US-36 through Boulder and over to I-25, thinking she'd find a motel in Denver and then start fresh in the morning. That's when, at the sight of the neon lights of the Grizzly Rose, her truck yanked her off the highway, led her forward, then left, back across the overpass, through a few backstreets and spinning into the gravel parking lot, seemingly against her will.

The Grizzly Rose

The Grizzly Rose stood off I-25 in defiance of the highway. Built in the 1980s to appeal to both the old and the contemporary cowboys of Denver, the saloon stretched out wide, yawning into the landscape as if she had come long before the traffic and the hot tub stores, the Mattress King and Furniture Row. Trucks and cars rolled by like tumbleweeds, exhaust swirled around her foundation like the dust storms of the past. Still, she shone her bright lights and opened her petals to the passersby—a beacon from modernity, a Venus Fly Trap promising cold beer, live music, and a place where folks still danced in straight lines and two-by-two. Her marquee, never missing a letter, announced performances by the Two-Step Two-Timers and Reagan McGrath. Like an old timey saloon girl, she was painted up on the outside, but her insides bore the weathered, rustic look of a thing that had always been there and had "danced" with every cowboy who came through town.

Eleanor had always wanted to go to "The Rose," as the regulars called Denver's favorite country western nightclub, but Walter hadn't danced with her since their wedding and he wasn't about to sit on the sidelines and share her with a cowboy. The first time she said those two antonyms together out loud, Grizzly and Rose, she wondered what such a flower might look like. She tried to picture a bud with the ferocity of a bear, a flower whose aroma and hue were so powerful that one single stem, laid at the foot of a beloved, could capture a heart for all eternity. As an avid gardener, El had done her fair share of research into the family of thorned beauties, imagining their roles in love affairs across the centuries. The "Old Red Moss" of deepest red and double petal, sent to turn a lover on the road to another; the "Madame Hardy," whose white petals pleaded innocence, delivered by hand and on bended knee, begging forgiveness of one who had been scorned; the "Complicata's" potent blend of pinks that had likely filled the bouquet of a young bride, matching the not-so-chaste blush of her cheeks. Roses were the horticultural equivalent of lie detectors—when read for all their meaning, the scent and colors said more about the honesty of the heart that bore them than words ever could.

As Eleanor looked up at the sign that now read "Saloon and Concert Hall" instead of the old "Saloon and Dance Emporium," the truth about the Grizzly Rose hit her. The bar was not named for its enduring ferocity. It was named for the dictionary definition of grizzly—"greying." This was the "Greying Flower," not "Raging, Growling, Fearsome Flower of the Bear." The realization smacked of personal revelation. She, too, was dying on the vine. As she aged, El hoped she would be more like Jane Seymour or Susan Sarandon, only getting sexier and more herself with age. She had prayed that she would be a late bloomer before it was too late. Well, the time was now and, wilting or no, she wasn't dead yet. She could still rustle up a cowboy or two. After years of driving by and dying to see what was inside, a terminal diagnosis seemed the perfect excuse to go on in and grab the rose by the thorns.

Eleanor dug through her gym bag next to her to see if there were any shirts left in it that smelled better than the one she had on. She would do laundry at Isabel's—that or throw everything away and go shopping. The decadence of the thought made her smile and feel conspicuously like her sister. She found her favorite soft black T-shirt gifted from Lee all those years ago and slipped it on, its form looser on her than she remembered. With no luck finding clean underwear, Eleanor changed out of her shorts and opted to go commando under her jeans, something that felt wonderful and wildly inappropriate for a senator's wife. She hooked the pair of Colorado turquoise earrings that Bel had given her years ago into her lobes, making her look more like a local, and carefully applied the emergency red lipstick that was always zipped into the inside pocket of her purse. Her mother believed that to go out without lipstick was a cardinal sin, and she told her girls again and again that, if you were in an accident, only a few people would see your underwear. But everyone would see your face.

With her hair pulled up in a high ponytail and her reserve tugged up even higher, Eleanor walked through the double doors of "The Rose" and back in time. A cobbler's room, where cowboy boots were softened and shined back to life by a Kenny Rogers look-a-like, was just to her left inside the door. Kenny tipped his hat to her, then went back to banging on the soles of a worn-out pair of Justin's, pounding in time to the rhythms of the country music that filled the air.

Before her, the largest dance floor she had ever seen brimmed with lines of dancers aged twenty-one to ninety-one, sprawled out under rotating hues of blue and red. Cowboy hats of different shape and color trimmed the bar. El looked around for a moment, half expecting to see horses tied up somewhere and drinking from a trough on the other side of the well. The musky aroma of old beer mixed with the fatty grease of the deep fryer and swirled around her, reminding her of trips to the Ohio State Fair with her dad. Full of wonder and excitement, Eleanor pressed on past the entrance into the vastness of the dark wooden room. The Rose was more than she had ever imagined.

It was a Friday and, as the calendar nailed to a hand-hewn post read, it was Singles' Night. El wondered if she could blend in, if anyone would notice the suntan lines trapping the negative space where her wedding band once sat so prominently on her finger. She didn't feel single yet, whatever that meant. However, there was nothing in their last phone call or in any of Walt's messages that would convince her that she was otherwise. At first, he had sounded concerned, worried they had been robbed. "What the hell is going on Eleanor? Where's my collection and where the hell are you?!?"' The first message ended with a click. By the second message he sounded more put out. "Eleanor, I've called the police and will file a missing person's report if you don't call me back this instant." He was threatening to look for her, not promising to find her. Almost immediately after that one, clearly now having seen The Note, he sounded panicked. "El, honey, you can't mean it. You can't do this to us. Not during an election year …" El had erased the message after that utterance and tossed her phone aside.

"During an election year my ass," she had said to the dash. "Sorry to inconvenience you." She was so relieved that she had left him, depriving Walt of sympathy votes for her illness and all his suffering. She would not leave him that glory.

For a singles' night at The Rose, there were but three people left standing alone near the dance floor. This place seemed to couple up like the ark before the storm, men and women pairing two-by-two, swirling and gliding counter-clockwise around the large penned-in dance floor. There was a magic to the rhythm, something that pulled at all of them like the same sea, a current causing the couples to float along at a tempo that moved like summertime. The six-piece band on the stage at the south end of the floor played a classic romantic country waltz that people sang along to as they skimmed round and round and round. The footwork of the couples was mesmerizing and utterly impossible for Eleanor to decode. As her feet shuffled unknowingly underneath her, El looked like a high school wallflower begging for a dance. When the song ended and El came to, there was a line of men as long as a Texas border waiting to ask her onto the floor.

"Howdy, Ma'am, I'm Clyve," an elderly gentleman in a white

cowboy hat announced, "Would you care to dance?"

"Sure, but …" El began to reply, Clyve cutting her off mid-sentence.

"No buts! I'm the best partner here, ask any of the ladies, and it's my job to make you look good." With that, Clyve strode out onto the dance floor with El just as the fiddle player started in, setting a tempo about twice as fast as the last song. The last thing El heard Clyve call out over the music and hollerin' was, "Just try to keep up!"

The next thirty minutes was a whirl of rotating gentlemen suitors, most of whom seemed twice her age. By then, El had at least learned how to not step on the tips of even the pointiest boots. In spite of herself and her blisters, she was having a blast. It was nice to meet people through movement, not words. For the first time in her life, she felt relieved to be dancing instead of talking, and for a moment she was grateful that she was losing her voice first, not her body.

Parched and exhausted, El wanted a drink. That was another thing she had wondered about—drinking. When would that stop? Not just the alcohol, but her ability to get liquid past her throat? She knew she shouldn't drink liquor now and vowed that, after she reached her sister and they had one last good round on the porch, she would cut it out. If her calories were to be limited, they all needed to be of use. Dr. Bannon wasn't thrilled with the idea of her having any alcohol at all, so El, like just about everyone else, lied on her intake survey about her number of glasses per week. Doing the math, she counted two drinks a night, more during a campaign. She wondered if she might have a small issue when she saw the five-to-ten drinks per week listing and turned the page over to see if there were any more options to circle on the other side. If ever there was a time someone deserved a cocktail, El believed that leaving her husband, her home, and this life, warranted such an opportunity. But Eleanor was a woman of will power. She could eat just one potato chip and put the bag back, something Isabel wouldn't dare attempt. El would cut out the booze at the end of this chapter of her adventure, sobering herself to what was ahead. First, she would saunter up to the bar and ask for a whiskey and Budweiser, two straws.

As Eleanor approached the bar, the wall of cowboy hats parted and a round of "Excuse me, ma'ams" allowed her in and up to order. She felt eyes on her from everywhere, and to be honest, they felt good. They were the kind of eyes that she used to dress for back in her twenties, the kind that felt appreciative roaming over her curves, her hair, her face. As a feminist at heart, she felt guilty for absorbing the attention. As a woman in body, she felt great being appreciated and seen. She ordered her drinks, and the bartender waved her off, not letting her pay. She tipped him ten dollars and her best smile, and then she waded down towards the sea of two-steppers.

She heard the boots before she saw them. The earth seemed to move underneath her as they got closer and closer. Beer in one hand, whiskey in the other, Eleanor turned and looked down to see the dusty, worn tips of Colorado's finest. And he was truly, truly the finest thing she had ever laid eyes on. Wearing the same black boots as earlier but dressed now in the unofficial uniform of the Grizzly Rose—perfectly faded, perfectly fitted blue jeans, a soft but ironed black button-down shirt, and a white cowboy hat. There, for the second time that day, was Officer Maxwell. When her eyes landed on his, she felt that unexplainable audacity rise again into her throat.

"You gonna arrest me for drinking and dancing?" El flirted, straw between her teeth.

"Not if you're doin' it with me," Officer Maxwell replied. In a single gesture, Eleanor's straw was slipped from between her teeth, her drinks set on one of the side tables that lined the floor, and she was swept up in the arms of the most beautiful man God had created.

As they danced, El took in every detail. At least six-foot-two, she had to lean back slightly at this close range to look into his face, which she did unabashedly and without turning away. Officer Maxwell returned the stare, causing El to wonder if he was accustomed to women starring at him this way, if this was his "normal." She snapped mental picture after mental picture, taking him in as if he were the last thing on Earth she would experience. The tiny gap between his front teeth, the clefted squareness of his lightly stubbled chin, the flatness between his eyebrows that went up only towards the middle, the broadness of his forehead that rose ever so elegantly into his hairline. His features were so big they appeared drawn on. So textbook in their desirability that they seemed ridiculous. Yet somehow, on him, they worked perfectly.

At the end of the band's last song of their first set, Officer Maxwell leaned in close and whispered the invitation El could not refuse, "Let's get outta here."

She was already gone.

It was as if they found a portal from the Grizzly Rose to the Comfort Inn on East 58th Street, one that plummeted them instantaneously into their motel room and into each other's arms. It had been a long time since El had felt want or wanted. And here she was, with a man whose first name she didn't know, pressed to the edge of her nerve endings with desire. Unlike other men she had been with, this cowboy didn't start by kissing her mouth—he breathed her in and worked his way from hair to neck to breasts to hips, washing her over his face like he would have splashed water from a stream on a hot day. Eyes closed, his hands seemed to read her goose bumps like braille—each touch exactly what El wanted without ever uttering a word.

Desire

I have only really known touch from underneath, the warmth of intimate contact emanating from the contours of my Eleanor's body. I love this body, her body, though it is mostly torso, breasts, ribs, and back, especially back, that I have come to feel. I am the lucky one who knows her skin through the delicious shifting of my fibers, her bones through my easy hang across her broad swimmer's shoulders. And then, then there is that momentary pressure that comes from opening to her as the top of her head presses through me … the briefest of encounters when the smell of her hair, perfumed with soapy greenness or the sweat of summer, consumes me. I, Black T-Shirt, am worn thin with habit, made softer by her, more perfect with time.

Worn mostly at night, my Eleanor sought me after the shedding of suits or garden clothes. I am the refuge that means Home, the article of clothing that means Complete. My short sleeves are stretched from the nightly ritual of my Eleanor pulling her bra through the holes, an instant of release that sends her nipples into reflex and thrills me still to this day.

I have been with Eleanor for over forty-five years, a gift stripped from the back of her previous owner, a muskier human whose youthful and ever-expanding width pulled at me, leaving me threadbare before my time. Eleanor seemed to like me this way, calling me "pink" as a term of endearment—color representing texture instead of hue. I know I make her feel sexy, easy in her skin, more desirable than any lacy lingerie. Pity her Mr. didn't seem to see the two of us together that way. Walter, as my Eleanor calls him, would demand that she "take off that rag" before moving to his side of the bed. Many nights, at that demeaning request, Eleanor would roll the other way, choosing me over him.

But tonight? Tonight was different. I felt something I hadn't known in a long, long while—touch, sensation, coming from everywhere. Hands—large, gloriously demanding hands—feeling me from the outside, as my Eleanor tried to press through me towards those hands from the inside. Breathlessly caught in the middle of desire, I felt the roughness of skin from one direction, the soft aching from the other—these hands, this new powerful torso, wearing both me and my Eleanor down com-

pletely. Callouses scratched over me, threatened and invigorated every fiber of my being. Hands this good wouldn't allow me to come between them and her for long. I ached to be torn in two, to be ripped open, to be laid bare. I prayed this was my end. More, I begged, more—I couldn't feel enough. Minutes felt like hours. Eventually, the kneading subsided and the hands that had almost torn me to pieces softened and slipped lovingly underneath and up the sides of my seams where I had just touched ribs and moved over heart. Elegantly, effortlessly, I was lifted over her head and puddled onto the floor. Spent on the outside from the heavenly chaffing, melted on the inside by my Eleanor's heat, I lay there, grateful to be all cotton and not a blend, for I would surely have burst into flame.

Parts and Pieces

The first thing Eleanor saw when she came to after hours of lovemaking was a human leg propped against the side of the bed. As her eyes shifted into focus in the early morning light, she registered that this was a prosthetic. Her mind raced, culling through images from the night before—her shirt off, his, her bra, her jeans, his, his underwear. In all this taking off, how did she miss stripping a limb? How drunk was she last night and how in the throes had she lost this detail? She looked over at him wrapped in the sheets, even more beautiful asleep than awake, the contours of his body belying the absence of this three-foot extremity.

The only fake leg she had ever seen exposed before belonged to a creepy fisherman in South Florida. When Eleanor was ten years old, the family drove down to visit her father's mother in Sarasota. Nana Elaine, a feisty sixty-seven-year-old with a perfect figure and drawn-on eyebrows, was taking her and Isabel to see the Sailor Circus while her mom stayed home with little Danny and their dad slept on the couch after nine holes and at least as many beers. The girls had gotten new outfits for the event, matching culottes, in alternating colors of pink and green. Before the show, they went to get burgers at a restaurant with cloth napkins and a raised bar that had a pinball machine. Eleanor loved pinball, the pull and release of the spring, the smack of the white buttons, every small action sending the little silver ball into a new orbit, an entire world erupting into bright and whirling chaos that she could alter with the flick of a paddle. Standing on a little step stool generously placed there for kids her size, she hovered over the machine like an angry god stirring the tides. It felt so good to her ten-year-old self to have some modicum of control. Bel was busy playing the bowling game on the opposite end of the bar when a man wearing a Hawaiian shirt and a dirty ball cap with flies hooked into it came over and asked if Eleanor would like more change. Though she knew she shouldn't take money from strangers, Eleanor said yes. The fisherman put a coin down on the glass face of the machine and pulled a barstool up behind her to watch. Without thanking him, El dropped the nickel in, tugged back on the spring, and leaned in as the ball raced toward the bumpers. After ping-ponging back and forth at least six times, the ball zoomed straight down the middle lane, between her paddles, and out of reach of any possible defense. El smacked the sides of the table hard in frustration.

"Wanna 'nother?" the fisherman smiled wolfishly.

"Sure," she said quietly.

"Well, then come 'ere," he said, with a syrupy drawl.

As El walked closer to the chair where he was sitting, the fisherman pulled up the leg of his khaki pants and patted his thigh. "Have a seat, lil' lady," he said, but all Eleanor could do was stare. A skin-colored piece of plastic, poorly molded to resemble a calf, sat atop a metal rod that fed into his dirty brown leather topsiders. "You remind me of my lil' girl," he said encouragingly. If not for the shock of the artificial leg, El might have dutifully obliged and climbed onto his lap, feeling as if she had owed him something for the earlier game. As it was, she was too scared to move and stood there staring until Bel came over, grabbed her by the arm, and in her most ferocious nine-year old voice said, "Creep!" and led her sister over to their table where Nana was on her second "CC" and their cheeseburgers and curly fries had just arrived. Eleanor remembered nothing from that night at the circus but couldn't get the fisherman's daughter's name out of her head for years. Seeing Maxwell's leg propped up there against the pine headboard of the motel bed brought it back to her again in a flash. Betsy. Eleanor closed her eyes and prayed that young Betsy had made it out of South Florida unscathed.

More curious than shocked, Eleanor slipped out of bed, put on Maxwell's button-down shirt, stood in front of the perfectly color-matched synthetic leg, and touched it. Maxwell woke with a shiver. Eleanor turned to him and smiled, leaving her hand there without recoil. As she shaped her hand over the calf, the ankle, Eleanor gently and unknowingly returned his lost leg to him with her touch. As she caressed his prosthetic knee, tears came to Maxwell's eyes, and he told her everything.

How he joined the Army after 9/11 because he wanted to do something—to get out of Colorado and be a part of something greater. How, at first, it felt like playing cops and robbers, good guys versus bad guys, until he lost three guys to mines and friendly fire within two months. The sand flies, the heat. How he struggled to get his bearings in long patrols through that arid landscape—it felt like he was slowly seizing up under the desert's buzz. Then, one night, an airstrike that went sideways.

"There was nothing noble about it, nothing patriotic, just a lot of dead kids in uniform from both sides."

El stood there, tears pooling in her eyes, her hand on his prosthetic thigh.

"The next week I was honorably discharged. The report read that the gun went off in my hand as I was cleaning it. The truth? The truth is that I couldn't stand those damn flies anymore and I didn't want to die with them swarming over my head—so, I shot myself in the leg. I don't know why I didn't go for a finger or something. I didn't want to miss. At the last second, I closed my eyes and shot high—hit a major artery and they had to take my leg to save my life. When I woke up it seemed a fair trade for cowardice."

As the weight of the truth dropped off his body, his shoulders slumped, and he began to bawl like a little boy. El went to him and sat in the hollowed-out absence of his right leg. Wrapping her body around him, she rocked him like she used to rock Jillian. He clung to her arm, nails dug in tight, and it took all her strength to hold him. After a time, his sobbing subsided and he turned to her, little boy gone, and grabbed her face with both hands, drawing her mouth to his. Eleanor didn't resist. She wanted to know how far she could go before going under. The waters of their kiss flooded her both emotionally and physically, and, without being able to stop the natural response of her disease, she sputtered up from the depths coughing unable to breathe. She was literally drowning in his embrace. Maxwell jumped into rescue mode and whacked her on the back. The action didn't actually help her choking, but it did jolt her back to reality, slow her breathing, and help her focus her swallowing until it became more manageable and steadied.

Well, Eleanor thought to herself out of the panic, that's it for kissing. Maxwell stared at her, looking confused and a little hurt. El could read his face and his fear that she'd choked on his shame, so she shared a truth of her own. "I have ALS, the swallowing kind," she said softly. He tilted his head like a puppy trying desperately to understand. "Lou Gehrig's disease?" she added, more like a question to see if he understood. There was just so little known, so little shared about the illness and its prognosis that El realized she would have to explain in more detail. "It's a disease that typically attacks the spinal cord," El swallowed, she hadn't spoken this much in a while and felt her voice slur. "It's terminal. You, my handsome cowboy, were my last kiss."

Telling someone that he was your "last" instead of your "first" was never something Eleanor had considered. It felt bittersweet and wonderful and anticlimactic at the same time, kind of like losing her virginity all over again but in reverse.

"I may not be able to kiss," El said seductively. "But, if you're game, I can still fuck."

"Fuck." It sounded both foreign and familiar coming from her mouth, though it had been decades since she said the word out loud, let alone in bed. And here she was, with so few fucks left to give, she might as well name them. She pulled the covers back and slid on top of him. She straddled him at an angle, wrapping her legs around his pelvis and his left thigh, pressing him deeper inside her the closer she clung. Their broken bodies locked together in a puzzle of misfit pieces, forming a picture that wasn't on the cover of any box, but together, felt beautifully whole.

The next morning was spent quietly. It was not the kind of awkward one night stand silence accompanied by the flurry to get clothes on and out the door. It was more of a prayerful quiet, one where every action had its own ritualistic purpose, the back and forth bristling of a toothbrush mimicking the brush of robes against a monastery's stone floor, the sound of a zipper echoing through the tiled bathroom like a throaty "Om." With an instinct to be closer to his skin, El slipped her black T-shirt on backwards and silently vowed to wear it that way for the rest of its life. She watched as he reattached his leg, not as a voyeur but as one might observe a blacksmith hoof a stallion or an artisan blow a glass vase. With no self-consciousness, he smiled as she looked on. Even in this state of intimacy, neither held tight to any illusion that this moment would be more, for this moment had been more than enough, and enough was something that neither of them had felt for a long time.

"I need you to do something for me," Eleanor asked seriously.

"Anything," Maxwell said.

The Light of Morning

El peered over the edge of the twenty-foot cliff, the pink of the early morning slowly warming into orange. The gun in Maxwell's right hand caught the glint of the sun as it rose over the Mars-like landscape, sending a metallic blast of light out from his hand like a star. El had followed Maxwell to a small town called Idledale, a remote clutch of homes that, so far, were spared Denver's expansion. Eleanor turned, hair ablaze, face in shadow, and reached for him. He walked forward, placed the gun in her hand and then retreated, giving her room to do her worst.

A glove, "they" said proverbially, "It fits like a glove." She'd always had a hard time with that cliché, with gloves in general, ladies' in particular. Eleanor had "man hands," as her mother called them. They were just like her father's—identical, down to the callouses and the raw bitten cuticles. Isabel loved to talk about hand twins when they were growing up. She believed that everyone had one out there in the world—your "dopplehander," as she liked to call him or her. Bel naturally imagined hers as some mystical being with hands saved from industry of the common folk and used towards artistic betterment—hands that played the harp or knit hats for sick babies or salvaged the embroidery of nineteenth century garments for The Smithsonian. El, however, was never disillusioned. She couldn't imagine that her hand twin was anyone besides a cabby or a meat packer or, worse, her own dad. Bel encouraged her to dream bigger, like Peter Pan in the nursery coaching Michael to "think lovelier thoughts," but El still saw the man in the half moon of her nail beds as her father and her imagination stopped there.

The fact that her hand twin was her dad and not some redheaded classical Pan flute player was one thing that had always disappointed Eleanor until her father died and she took his waxen grasp at the funeral. As they held hands for the last time, and possibly the first in forty years, the song he had sung to her as a little girl, "Sur la Pont d'Avignon" flew suddenly to mind. "The real bridge of the French tune was the Pont de Saint Benezet," he had once told her after singing it for a fourth time in a row. Legend had it that the real bridge was built when a twelve-year-old shepherd boy, Benezet, told the town of Avignon that angels commanded him to build the bridge. As the town mocked his prophecy, he miraculously lifted a huge block of stone and threw it effortlessly into the Rhône, starting construction there and then. Now here it was being built again, the mystical bridge of her childhood, commanded by angels, arching across the divide of the living and the dead, connecting her to her father with more realness than she had felt in years.

It was a slow build. She inched her hand into the casket like you would reach into the crib of a sleeping baby, careful not to wake him. She placed her right hand on top of his right hand, ten arching fingers intertwined, little bridges each, connecting the island of the body to the outer world. His delicate system of bridges now touching the unimaginable so long out of reach. And then, feeling a little like a smuggler or a serial killer taking a trophy from the scene of the crime, El snapped a picture of their hands with her cell phone. Later looking at it, she couldn't tell the two hands apart, which thrilled her but also made her question her need for Vitamin D.

These hands were great for playing guitar, pulling up root vegetables, and waving from shore. They just weren't made for gloves. But this, this pistol she held so solidly, fit her like one.

She was definitely not going to pull the trigger she told herself, though it felt deliciously like a lucky stone or a worn bone in her palm. She tickled its underbelly, stroked its metal curve and felt … comfortable. She stood as she imagined a cowboy would stand, a plain's woman: wide-legged, steady, sure. She felt huge against the backdrop of her mind. A tumbleweed blew in front of her thoughts erasing all fear. She was larger than life. Larger, especially and gratefully, than her own life. She was as big as her hands. She was suddenly of the mind for murder.

The first blast erupted into a fine white cloud, chips and fragments, like shards of small bones, flying at her face. As she gained confidence, she fired faster and faster, debris sticking to her lips and her lashes. Through the massacre, Eleanor did not stop, did not tarry, until the very last Precious Moments statuette, a young girl and her cat, gave her pause. But it was too late. The bullets were fired. They all lay now in wreckage at her feet, their bits and pieces bathed by the full light of morning.

Forgiveness

I watched the others go, one-by-one, down the line. A powdery white film filled the air. The kitten at my feet was almost entirely white from porcelain debris. Looking like this, I would have named him Snowball instead of Coal all those years ago. Each who'd gone before me had done so in stoic silence. There was no begging, no pleading, no cheap promises. Most kept placid smiles on their faces, staring blankly forward as the mad woman who used to dust them and place them lovingly "just so" stood before them now, pistol in hand, their executioner, their one-woman firing squad. There was nothing that I could say, no words I could find to end the slaughter. As they fell, one-by-one, it was clear that the Missus was a good shot—all the better, less suffering. To be dropped to the ground, only to lay there with a broken ear or shot off leg with no Superglue for miles ... Eccch, I could hardly think of it. Yes, a slow, painful end seemed a much worse destiny. As the shots rang closer and closer, I tried to imagine how I would go—would it be in a cloud of glaze and smoke, or would I crack down the middle and feel myself halved?

All I could think was, "How could the Missus do this?" What had driven her to turn on me and the entire Collection with such vehemence and hatred? Sure, we were outdated, but this seemed a dramatic way to clean house. But there was something in the look of the Missus' eyes that made me all the more sad for her. I spent a life kept in perfect order, rarely to be touched and certainly never to be played with. The feather duster of the Missus was the only physical pleasure I knew. Even my ceramic cat sat just out of reach. Truth be told, I was lonely. I had always been lonely, now that I thought of it. I had done my best for years to be perfect, quiet, still, and look what good that had done me. Here, in these last precious moments of my life, I saw that there had been no life at all. And then I imagined that the Missus felt this way, too. The look in those big brown eyes as they stared down the barrel of the gun was familiar. As the trigger squeezed, the bullet released from its casing and sped towards me. I felt a flood of something I had never known. I closed my eyes and exhaled, and at the exact moment of my last breath, I heard the Missus scream, "No!" drop the gun, and attempt to outrace the bullet bound for me.

Breaking the Mold

Well, now she had done it. She had finally, thoroughly, cleaned house.

Eleanor imagined each figurine like a voodoo doll of her husband's body. The blasts would reach him for sure—each shot, each fragment, sending Walter to a slow grave, his so distant, so tainted flesh, stuck with exploding needles. In her mind's eye she saw him at the office conference table, the one she had picked out for him, body in spasm in the middle of a meeting, convulsing and shuddering from an unknown, unseen, assailant's fire.

No, he was not somewhere dying. But El could feel his body, pale with the shock of 59 invisible bullets slowly twitching to a calm. She had no regrets, except one. She had really liked the little girl with the kitten. It was a pity to see her go.

From nowhere, a white feather blew onto her flip-flop. She picked it up, remembering how her mother never let her touch feathers as a little girl. "Filthy things," she had said. "Filthy things from filthy creatures." Had she ignored her mother's phobia, what a collection she could have had by now. Certainly enough for wings.

Helium

The pair was silent as they held hands and walked back to their cars. Nothing was said about the events that had just passed between. When all was done, Maxwell had simply taken the hot gun from her hand, placed it back in its holster, and wiped the dust from her face. No questions asked. El looked down now at their interlaced fingers and remembered the last time she and Walter had done the same. After winning his senate election, Walt had grabbed her hand in his and stretched her arm high in the air like an announcer calling a fight. That victory pose graced the front of the *Columbus Dispatch* and the *Dayton Daily News*. Walt had it framed for their anniversary. Looking larger than life while his wife hung weightless from his grasp, Walter never seemed to notice all that was off with the picture, but Eleanor did. Barely captured in the photo were her feet—her heels pulling out of navy Chanel pumps just enough to make it seem as if she were about to float up out of her shoes, out of her marriage, and far, far, away.

Eleanor parked the truck just far enough from Officer Maxwell's car so that, as he left, she could watch him walk away. This time she would not disguise her stare as he turned to go. So much had changed in twenty-four hours. Now, after seeing him naked, she was no longer undressing him with her eyes but was, layer by layer, putting him back together. She knew his stories, the sensitivity of his earlobes, the small moans he made when forgetting himself. As he walked, she noticed the slight limp she hadn't seen that first time, the uneven weight shift adding to the perfect rhythm of his gait. Looking backward, the details that were once obscured came into focus and made better sense of the aggregate. Officer Maxwell caught her eye in the rear view mirror and smiled. El wondered, what did he see now of her that was invisible on first read? How had she changed? Was anything left of her that was the same?

Glancing over at Jeremy, her hula girl, Eleanor wondered what privileged information her little Hawaiian friend held from always looking backward at the past. Before she changed her mind about going forward, El cut back to Morrison, Colorado and south on US-285, saluting the Red Rocks Amphitheatre and tipping her grass-skirted mascot into a gyrating, ukulele playing frenzy. Jeremy's silent solo filled the cab with a lusty and melancholic tune, as Mary, beside her, sang back-up and ached for a tambourine.

Now I Can See the Moon

Eleanor had been driving on US-285 for just shy of an hour, and she was hungry but wasn't sure what sounded good or what she could handle. Tired of milkshakes and smoothies, Eleanor thought about the tuna melts her mother had made the three of them on "Sick Days." Even if she couldn't swallow one, she wanted to taste one. Sick Days were a household tradition in the Page family and perhaps the primary thing that kept the team loyal to their mother. Sick Days were always their mom's idea, and you never knew when one would hit. Usually, the smell of waffles wafting up the stairs was the signal for a day off. Once she had dropped them at school only to return and collect them an hour later, lying to the school nurse that one of her children had complained of a stomachache and fever earlier that morning and that she was certain an epidemic was about to hit the Page household and that none of the other school children should be exposed. El panicked when the nurse arrived at the narrow window of Mrs. Granger's fifth grade door—she was certain that someone close to her must be dead. By the time the three Pages left their classrooms and met suspiciously in the main hall where fifth, fourth, and second intersected, they knew a plan was underfoot and picked up their step, the silver Cadillac shining in the distance like a promise of adventure through the double-glass doors. First, there would be ice cream and coffee for everyone. "Four cones, four coffees," their mother would order from the Dairy Queen. Bel pretended to be sophisticated and like hers, but she secretly poured it out onto the sidewalk, only really tending to her cone. El reveled in the magical adult elixir and sipped it slowly, alternating bites of ice cream and sips of coffee. The cold of the ice cream mingled with the bitter brew in her mouth so perfectly that she believed she had invented a new flavor. Danny always shot his coffee back like whiskey, burning the roof of his mouth. The effects of the caffeine and sugar seemed to impact him immediately and he went from zero to sixty in about two seconds. Next on the day's agenda was the zoo, the arcade at the mall, or a movie, then home for tuna melts.

Their mother's tuna melts were works of art. She slathered the thick white bread with butter and grilled it on both sides (the underside first), then piled it high with rich, mayonnaisey tuna salad (no celery). Extra sharp cheddar oozed from the golden-brown bookends until the overflow hit the skillet and hardened into that wonderful crispy cheese film. Cut into triangles and served with potato chips—the really salty ones that she usually bought and never shared—these sandwiches were the promise of the perfect childhood. They tasted of abundant domesticity and gave comfort to the un-sickest of them all. After the richness of tuna melts and the caffeine crashes, there was nothing to do but nap.

It was her mother's tuna melts that made her turn into the Jefferson Convenience Store. The store, painted bright turquoise and boasting of a deli and homemade fudge, looked a good place for provisions. Chimes hanging from the door announced her entrance as she walked into what seemed like a moment out of the *Twilight Zone*. The bright façade was a mask for the store's insides. Everything, save the fudge and the small blond girl behind the register, seemed old. The shelves were lined with dusty boxes of Rice-a-Roni and dehydrated potatoes. Fluorescent lights blinked like flycatchers and a radio broadcast of a baseball game played to an audience of one. The single fan, an ancient looking man at the deli counter, was so bent over his lunch that he hardly had to raise his sandwich to his lips to take a bite. El imagined he was an old prospector who came to Colorado looking for his fortune, found a wife, had a family, and never made it farther than Jefferson County. She could envision him walking down the streets of this almost-town, back hunched, forever searching the sidewalks for gold. She decided against the deli, since bread was too difficult these days, and tried the cooler. There she found snack packs of vacuum wrapped tuna and mayonnaise with an expiration date that seemed further out than her own.

El piled her packages of tuna onto the counter. The girl working the antique register, framed by fudge and Colorado postcards, seemed impossibly young and decidedly sad.

"You have a cat in your car?" the girl asked out of nowhere.

Caught off guard by the very idea of a conversation with anyone, "Huh?" was all El could get out of her mouth.

"That's a lot of tuna."

Eleanor smiled at the thought of her driving cross-country, packed to the rafters with cats.

"I'm Serena," the girl continued. Eleanor was about to introduce herself when Serena kept going.

"I'm living in my car right now, too. Well, my sister's."

"I'm not ..." El managed to get out before Serena patted her hand. It was a gesture that a much older person would do, a grandmotherly gesture, and it made El smile.

"Us neither," Serena said consoling, "Temporary, just since the fire."

And then Serena started to cry. Big tears splashed on the brown bag that she had been loading with the tuna that El would never be able to eat. El stood there for a moment, imagined patting her hand, when a much larger version of the same girl materialized from behind the deli counter.

"Go take a minute, Serena," the giant Serena ordered. "Ma'am, I'll be right there to ring you."

A slew of *I'm sorrys* hung in the air with the door chimes as Serena sobbed herself out of the store. Reminded of her daughter, El ached as she watched her go.

The woman, who she could only imagine was Serena's mother or much older sister, squeezed behind the register and finished ringing her up. She talked as she punched the old cash register keys, the percussion of the numbers a perfect counterpoint to her words.

"It's been hard on her since the house burned. Cat died in it. Police say arson. Could've been one of my ex's. You like chocolate?" The woman dropped some fudge into the bag. "Of course, you do, who doesn't. I had an ex who didn't, that's part of why I divorced him. That, and he couldn't keep his mouth shut about how much butter I put on my baked potatoes. Wanna know a secret?"

El smiled and nodded.

"Three-quarters of a stick. That's how much. I always fought him on it and said I only used a few pats. Three-quarters of a stick and I am not sorry about it. That baked potato is gonna be my glass slipper someday. Yep. Someday, they'll be a man out there who doesn't say shit when I am loading that baby up. In fact, he may even ask if I need more. Hmmm … now that's a man. I'm Coral. My mother had a thing for the sea. She wasn't made for the mountains. She's gonna die out here of dehydration one day. Come see us again sometime," and she handed El her bag with a well-meaning smile.

Come see us again sometime. It seemed a funny thing to say to a person passing through, but El returned the smile and walked out the door just as the old prospector started swearing at the radio about a call the umpire had made. The force of his vehemence tickled her. Everybody needs something to care about, she thought as she heard muffled sobs over her shoulder.

At the side of the store were three brightly colored theatre chairs. El wondered how they had gotten there and if they had ever seen a film or a play before finding their permanent home here on the side of the highway. Serena was sitting in the last of the three seats, knees tucked up to her nose, crying into the holes in her jeans. El sat down next to her and silently offered her some of the fudge from the bag.

"Thanks," Serena sniffed. "I've never had anyone offer me something I made before."

"You made this?" Eleanor asked disbelievingly.

"Yep, at 5 a.m. this morning. It tastes better when you share it," Serena perked up. Without a moment's hesitation and with the innocence of an even younger child than she appeared to be, Serena asked, "Is something the matter with your voice?"

"I'm losing it," El replied simply.

"Laryngitis?" Serena pressed.

"Something like that."

"I had that once—no one noticed—everyone in my house talks so much. I'm the youngest, fifteen, almost sixteen, so there's a lot of talking over my head. Steams my clams. Old enough to work, not old enough to matter." Serena looked up into the cloudless blue sky and fixed her eyes there as if she were looking at something solid.

"Barn's burned down. Now I can see the moon," Serena paused for a moment afterward, as if she were contemplating the very thing she had just uttered. "It's on a magnet we sell in the store," she said to Eleanor, by way of explaining her meaning.

El "hmmmm-ed" as if Confucius himself had spoken.

"I burnt down my house," Serena suddenly blurted. El looked up from her fudge thoughtfully and smiled at the girl.

"You won't tell, will you?"

"I can't," El mused, tapping her throat. "Laryngitis."

"God, I was going to explode if I didn't tell someone. You should have seen them—running around, throwing things in suitcases, out windows. Mom starts yelling, 'Grab only what matters!' All those bags and nobody grabbed Mr. Marmalade. I walked out of there empty handed and sat across the street and watched it burn. Do you want to know why I torched it? Do you know how I could do such a thing? When I was little, I read how Native Americans used to send smoke signals to neighboring tribes to communicate. I wanted to know if I had a neighboring tribe. There it was, everything that ever mattered, everything that I had ever known or loved since I was kid, everything just burning up into the sky, telling my story. I was trying to see if somebody could read my smoke."

"Did anyone come?" El asked earnestly.

Serena took a breath, licked some chocolate off the side of her hand, sat back in her theatre seat and smiled. "You did."

"I did," El nodded.

The two sat there quiet for a moment. El was imagining Walter coming home to her gone. She pictured him frantically looking for clues of her disappearance—her wedding band left on the ring holder that they had bought on their honeymoon in Costa Rica, her favorite sunhat, gone from its hook in the mudroom. When he missed those signs, she imagined him collecting the more obvious threads—no coffee in the morning, since he had never learned how to work the espresso maker; no paper on the roll, stranding him with his pants down on the toilet, calling out to no one to save him. She imagined little places that would expand immeasurably with the void of her. She wondered how long they would take for him to fill.

"I guess I kinda burnt my house down, too," El said finally, breaking the silence. The admission felt good to Eleanor. She liked the camaraderie of it, the thought of her and this not-yet woman going rogue together.

"You did? I knew it!" Serena beamed. "Is that why you are living in your car with your cat?"

El laughed. "You could say that."

Looking at El, Serena's eyes widened like saucers and pooled to the rims with tears. "So, you don't think I'm crazy?"

"No. I think you are wise beyond your years."

Bird

She wanted to know how much longer she could swim. Eleanor made the appointment for Monday morning, already set in her mind that she would be leaving the next day. She was certain she wouldn't tell Dr. Bannon about the road trip, in case he forbid her or scared her out of leaving town. She needed this—the motion, the drive, the moving forward. Eleanor would call him from the road.

"The exercise is good for you for as long as you can do it, but you might want to start thinking of what else you would like to do besides swim." Dr. Bannon looked at El's chart as he spoke. She had already lost a considerable amount of weight and he was worried about her dropping more as swallowing became difficult.

"Swimming is my religion," El said plainly. "I don't want to be converted."

"Eleanor, there will come a time when you will have to."

"Doc, I can give up eating, I can give up talking, but I'm not sure what will be left of me if I have to give up swimming."

"You'll find other things—Tai Chi, yoga—"

"How long do I have left then? To swim, I mean?" El interrupted.

"Once you get the feeding tube, you'll be landlocked. It could be anywhere from three-to-nine months."

Eleanor could hardly picture it. A feeding tube. El imagined herself in a giant nest made of twigs and I.V.'s, guitar strings and bits of old love letters. In the nest, she saw herself hooked up to a machine that fed her like a mama bird feeds her babies, a machine that chewed and swallowed then reached beak-down inside her throat and regurgitated sustenance deep into her gullet. Would she ever taste again? Would she chew? Once she entered the nest, would she ever leave? Would smell still stir her appetite or, fed like a machine, would she become like one, hit empty, and simply need refueling? Did machines get hungry?

No swimming. There would come a time when there would be no swimming. It seemed no longing could bring that back. The cut of bubbles rushing past her skin. The weightlessness. The everywhere-held. When her world went dry, she wondered how much longer she would want to stay. Maybe that's how you know, Eleanor mused. When there are so few things left to hold you to this earth, perhaps that is when you begin to let go.

"A lady always knows when to leave," Colleen Page was fond of saying.

Eleanor hoped for once in a long while that her mother was right. Soon to be a thing of feather instead of fin, she prayed that when her baby bird wings dried, she would be able to make the leap from the nest into the unknown.

The Atlas of Lost Causes

Serena waved Eleanor out of town. There was no back and forth to the gesture, just a hand held high, an arm reaching upward to be called upon, a hopeful sign that someday she, too, might be chosen to leave. It was a wave of confidence, not drowning, and hours later down the road Eleanor could still see the slight ghost of a girl in her rear-view mirror, hand aloft, pressing her on.

She knew she was about three hours from Crested Butte and Isabel, but the dread of what was to come made the last beautiful bends through the valley seem endless. She pulled the AAA map out of the glove box and unpleated it next to her in the passenger seat. A red line moved across the route like a waveform on an

EKG. She had been marking each leg of the trip with a sharpie and was surprised to see how much the course really did follow the ups and downs of her pulse. The line would peak again as she pointed North, only to come down and then flat line after the Rockies as she headed to the coast. With the graph of her heart laid out so clearly before her, she saw the inevitability of the path ahead, heard its long "beeeeep" as she moved westward.

In an attempt to sync the speedometer to her heart rate, El pressed the gas down hard. She did not want her life to be a road map of mistakes, an atlas of lost causes. There were things to be said while she still had the words to say them.

She had written over a hundred speeches for Walter in her life, but none so important as the one she needed to give to her daughter. After years of finding the perfect tone and length, El knew exactly how to craft the musicality that would gather the masses into chorus, but she had no idea how to reach just one. When it came to Jillian, Eleanor felt like she had already lost her voice.

El squeezed her eyes tight, driving blind for a moment. No crying fit now—phlegm was her worst enemy when it came to this disease. Tears clung to her lashes, distorting the road. She blinked again only to open to a glinting of lights. Ahead in the distance, a whirling and wayward menagerie spun in slow motion. She rubbed her eyes, but the image still remained. There, as real as the mountains, was a carousel. Her carousel, dusty from the red earth and the road, but her carousel all the same. She could just make out a figure on the back of the dulled-silver horse when suddenly the road dipped down and El lost sight of the horizon.

"C'mon!" El yelled at the old Dodge, kicking the gas pedal like a jockey would a steed. As she crested the small hill, Eleanor stretched up high, pulling herself forward out of her seat. At the top, she screeched the truck over to the shoulder. Nothing but rolling green and a few cabins dotted the landscape. Mary had taken a tumble on the abrupt stop. El fished around under the seat for her, hand dipping into the terrifying abyss Isabel used to refer to as "The French Fry Graveyard." Face smashed against the steering wheel, body bent at an impossible angle, Eleanor's hand hit metal and crumb and plastic until it eventually came up with both Mary and a crumpled piece of notebook paper. El stuck Mary back on her post next to the dashboard hula dancer and smoothed flat the blue-lined page. Folded in two, the outside bore the words "To MOM," written in Jillian's second grade scrawl. On the inside, a drawing of a little girl with pigtails carried the message, "You are here!" an arrow pointing to the stick figure's heart. This was the atlas she was looking for, a perfect map—one El could follow with her eyes closed. And this, the route that would take her home.

Alchemic Gifts

The main drag of the old coal-mining town of Crested Butte was Elk Avenue. Turning right onto the five blocks of restaurants and mid-scale boutiques, Eleanor imagined the herds of elk that had once barreled out of the hills, furrowing this path as the digging and the dynamite began, giving the street its name. Now a seasonal resort known more for its wildflowers and snowboarding than its mining industry, Crested Butte had been home to Eleanor's sister for over a decade. After leaving the Midwest for the Old West, Bel had lived in Santa Fe, Denver, and Idaho Springs before finally inching her way out to Crested Butte. With a healthy population of males under fifty to enjoy, Bel said the choice was more for the men than the mountains, but Eleanor knew her sister better than that. While Isabel liked her fair share of gentlemen (and the occasional not-so-gentleman), she was ultimately shy and liked the quiet of the town and the transience of the tourists. Isabel never had to worry about pissing anyone off or owing anyone anything, because the population of people rarely stayed the same long enough to deal with them.

Besides the small base of locals who were as committed to Crested Butte as the mountain itself, this vacation hot spot was the perfect way for Isabel to feel like she was still a gypsy without having to repack. The panorama of people moved around her like a green-screened scene in a 1940's film. Between the seasons and the tourists, Bel's backdrop changed so much that she felt she, herself, might never have to again. The town had a population of just over 1,500, most of whom worked for the slopes or the many resorts sprinkled around the base of the mountain. Isabel leased a small storefront on the corner of 4th and Elk, where she refused to sell the standard sightseer fare like pillows and boxer shorts reading "Butte-i-ful." Uniquely her and poetically odd, Isabel's store, Alchemic Gifts, was one of "darker magic." Featuring strange yet perfect presents, customers always left with something they didn't need but had always wanted, even if they had never seen it before.

Eleanor stood before her sister's newest window display, marveling over the unearthly tree full of tiny copper-wire birds' nests, each full of what appeared to be robins' eggs. On closer inspection, the eggs transformed into miniature Día de Las Muertos inspired skulls carved out of blue stone. Tucked in among the nests like multi-colored leaves, were the single winter gloves that Isabel had been collecting off the streets for years. These misfit mittens added the perfect balance of melancholy and whimsy to the weeping birch and would have made Eleanor want to go inside the shop, even if it hadn't been her destination all along.

The sign on the door read, "No Shoplifting … Video Karmas on Premises." El laughed out loud. Leave it to Isabel to guilt her customers before they had even entered her establishment. Bel would hate to hear it, but she had gotten this gift from their mother.

Through the glass door, standing behind the wood-hewn sales counter, was Isabel. A lump the size of one of the window's eggs sprang instantly into Eleanor's throat at the sight of her. To watch Isabel now, before she knew El was here, was to see her as El wanted to hold Bel in the locket of her heart. Without the weight of this terrible thing—without the burden of this awful illness—this was her sister in the moments before the telling and on.

A silver-streaked lock of Isabel's hair drifted into her eyes as she hand-wrote price tags on creamy parchment. She brushed it away without a thought and tucked it back behind her ear. El remembered the sudden and seldom seen seriousness of her sister's face when engrossed in specific tasks. Between the two of them, Isabel had the much harder time at school. El could still picture her sister suffering at the kitchen table, their mother looming in the background, holding an egg-timer as it ticked off the remaining seconds that Isabel had left to sit in her chair while working on her homework. Just staying in one place was hard enough on Isabel, let alone getting through a chapter on biology or math or anything that didn't immediately appeal. But when she was working on a visual presentation or any sort of hands-on project, Isabel would find her zone and could sit for hours. Had doctors been diagnosing kids with ADHD back in their day, Isabel would have been medicated by the age of seven.

Thanks to the discouragement from her mother and the school systems of the day, Isabel attended one year of junior college before dropping out and making her own way through the world of retail. Isabel could sell anything—clothes, art, jewelry. She could craft a display of the hardest to move items and have them sold by the day's end. After all of those years casing department stores, Isabel had learned the optimal topography of a showroom floor. She knew its hotspots and its traffic patterns, rerouting customers through last month's inventory as if it were next season's previews. Unable to curb her honesty, Bel won customers over by telling the truth. If a pair of over-priced pants didn't give the shopper a $1,000 ass, she wouldn't let her buy them. So, when she told a shopper that something looked good, they believed her and handed over their credit cards and their retail loyalty.

Eleanor had relied on that same fashion frankness her whole life, and she would never make a public appearance without having had her outfit vetted by Isabel. Once a year, the sisters met in Chicago and shopped for Eleanor's season of events. From Saks to small boutiques at the Water Tower, Isabel came to life as Eleanor emerged from dressing rooms transformed from behind-the-scenes mother, teacher, and speechwriter to camera-ready wife. No matter how formal El might have felt in the new silks and tweeds, Isabel always managed to keep her in something of her own skin. Bel had a gift for reading people's colors and knew how to pull the right shade of sapphire, the exact match of moss. She was deft at mixing fabrics, layering textures that added shape and complexity to the whole. And there was no one, no one on this earth, better at understanding the subtleties and communication of accessories than Isabel Helene Page. Eleanor had not known the potency of a purse before her sister coached her on the clutch, nor had she understood the true value of grouping things in threes before her sister instructed her in this higher math. Sure, early on it was she who had shown Isabel how to button a shirt or tie her shoes. But her little sister was the one who taught her how *to dress*.

As time passed, however, the retail world of fashion became too emotionally messy for Bel, and she turned her attention to objects and their ability to transform people without the need for a dressing room and the required therapy. If a piece of art didn't fit the customer, it wasn't the customer's fault or the fault of her trainer. It was the object's or the artist's problem. The blame could be put on the thing, not on the person, thus creating distance and a far less dramatic work environment. Isabel personally believed in the right fit between "Pretties," as she called them, and people, and she delighted in delivering objects that appeared to fall out of the unconscious treasure trove of dreams. The more the Pretty was off and "just weird enough," the better the Pretty sold.

Anything that carried with it some latent content that had not yet been decoded by the waking mind moved the fastest through her store. Folks would come in thinking they were looking for a throw pillow for a neighbor's hostess gift and leave cradling a worn doll made from the pastiched parts of figurines salvaged from different eras.

As El pushed open the front door, the jangling chimes announced her presence before she could say hello. Isabel turned and greeted her sister with the smile she donned for customers. That smile quickly shifted at the recognition of her sibling and best friend.

Isabel flew over the counter screaming and swearing, catching Eleanor up in her arms and "Holy Shits!" before El could cross the threshold of the shop. After about thirty seconds of an embrace, Isabel cast Eleanor out at arm's length.

"What's wrong?" she demanded.

Eleanor walked to the window and reached into one of the copper nests, careful not to disturb the other two eggs that remained. She felt the cool smoothness in her palm. She turned and, without a word, placed the tiny skull into her sister's hand. Isabel reeled back, reading the tarot of the object and her sister's intent. In that moment, the world around them was transformed in a dizzying rush. All the words Eleanor had imagined over and over were useless to her, and worse, with none uttered, there were none to take back. Her sister, who had always known everything about El, once again, knew all.

"No," Isabel said with quiet command. Though it had caused most of their fights in the past, Eleanor found herself instantly and wildly in love with her sister's stubbornness. She knew it would be the biggest force, rivaling both fear and love, that would get her through the next many months and hold her longer to this life. Tears pooling in her hazel eyes, Eleanor nodded the smallest "yes" in the world. The blue orb slipped from Isabel's hand and rolled end over end across the floor. A tiny crack, beginning just under the eye socket, slowly splintered down to the mouth of the carved-out face. Eleanor watched it warble away and smiled softly, wondering what sort of animal lay wait inside.

Truth

An egg is meant to be a symbol of Hope and Possibility, a promise of birth or at least a good breakfast. I was made of a different sort of matter. I am an ovum carrying an omen, a harbinger of Despair—not an augury, but an eggery here to say, "Un oeuf is un oeuf." I am an egg timer announcing the end of a hard boil.

I'm sorry for the puns. Really, I am, but I'm a Deviled Egg, long burdened with a dark secret, incubating for what feels like an eternity. It's interesting living a shelf life full of something rank, something sulfuric in its malodorousnous, knowing your destiny is to deliver bad news, waiting to see whom your news is for.

I must say I feel relieved, honestly. The lonely truth was scrambling my insides. After a while, it's not the news but the waiting that is the hardest. I soon became desperate to know for whom I carried this yolk of devastation. Was it a child, a thief, an artist, a mother? Who would cradle me, make a nest of their palms, think me beautiful, only then to have me hatch my secret and serve up betrayal? You may find me vile, rotten, but I assure you, I am just the messenger. I, myself, am not to blame. There are bigger eggs to fry. If you want to point fingers, ask the guy who knows the answer to this one, "What came first, the chicken or the egg?" I have an idea, but again, I am only the messenger.

Sister

Sister, there is never enough time.

There wouldn't be enough time if we lived forever.

There wouldn't be enough time if we met in the afterlife and had an eternity.

And even there, there in the ever after, there would never be enough coffee, enough wine, enough chocolate to get us to the bottom of it all.

Sister, there is too much to say for us to ever say everything.

Too much to do to do it all, and certainly not enough time to talk about it afterwards.

These truths and more passed silently between the two as they sat huddled on the tiled floor of Isabel's store. Isabel was the first to break the quiet.

"Tell me everything."

Eleanor held her sister's hand as she described the last six months of changes in her speech and swallowing, the slow slippage of sounds that had always come so easily to her. She felt Isabel get steadier as she talked, felt her fixing, like cement, under her grip, waiting to hear what would come next. So, this is how it will be—I will lose strength and she will find it, Eleanor thought to herself.

El explained her drug regimen and the physical therapy that would soon follow. She described Dr. Bannon and blushed a little, giving his handsomeness away. For the first time at the description of an attractive man with a great nose, Isabel didn't flinch. Eleanor talked about her life expectancy—three years if she was lucky—about the order of events, the radiating out of the disease from her center like a starfish until, eventually, she wouldn't be able to swallow or speak or move. She talked about the thing that scared her the most, the glass coffin of her body as her thoughts inside stayed perfectly lucid, as her personality, her memories, her wants, stayed exquisitely intact but frozen within a body that would betray her inner life. She talked about Walter and the liberty in leaving him, the devastation in knowing that at some point, if only for his health insurance and her doctors, she would need to return and then would lose the ability to go. She talked about it all—except one thing—the pain of waiting.

These next few years would be full of it, Eleanor wanted to say, waiting for what will go next, for what will leave, for what will remain. She not only feared her own wait, but her sister's. You will have to wait, she wanted to say to Isabel, to be patient for my death. Some days you will want it to speed up, you will not want to see me suffer. But you will. You will watch my body become a hull and you will wait until I say or write or gesture into your hand, ENOUGH.

All this waiting will make you stronger, Eleanor knew, but didn't say. Wait training. It all starts now.

It was dark by the time Eleanor finished. Isabel's stomach growled loudly.

"I'm … I'm sorry," she said and started to cry.

"One of us has to stay human," Eleanor whispered into the hair of her little sister, who she now held sobbing in her lap. As sad as El was to have Isabel cry, she was happy to have one last moment as the protective big sister. It had been a long while since she had stroked Isabel's hair.

Eleanor could still see the yellow light of the chandelier as clearly as if it were overhead. Their parents had fought across the dining room table under that light as the girls sat hidden, curled into one another, in the dark at the top of the stairs. Listening to the exchanges, they collected clues on how to be grown-ups, tricks like how to polish your armor with your opponent's spit, how to sharpen your words with your tongue, how to win at a game that is not worth playing. Even at ages nine and seven, before the front door had opened and his slumped figure disappeared into the night, they could tell that their father was outmatched. The pair sat frozen until they heard the clink of the crystal decanter cork and the slow pour of amber, their cue to sprint to their bedroom before they were found out.

Huddled together on Eleanor's twin bed, Isabel cried herself to sleep. How far did it go, El wondered, how many times did the night unfold? This mental game of stretching her thoughts out into space usually terrified her, but this night, when she already felt so small, Eleanor was comforted by the knowledge that none of the words thrown angrily about this house really mattered much inside the vastness of things. That night, she fell asleep slumped over the easy-breathing body of her sister, imagining herself a part of everything and nothing all at once.

The sisters assumed that same position now some fifty years later, but sat tucked in together, wide awake.

"Let's get up," El said as nobly as she could and pulled her sister from the floor.

"So, this is what's happening," Isabel exhaled reluctantly, trying to summon her earlier resolve.

"Yep, this is what's happening," El smiled weakly.

"What now?" Isabel asked.

"Food for you, bed for me, and then a couple days to come up with a plan," El replied. "I still haven't told you about my one-legged cowboy ..."

Isabel brightened for the first time since she her sister walked into the shop.

"I'm not going out without a fight," El grinned. "I did learn something from our mother."

After a moment of stretching their nerve-tingled legs, the two sisters stepped out arm-in-arm, walking into the dark of what was to come.

Drop Dead Gorgeous

"What do you want to do today besides talk about dying?" Isabel yelled from the bathroom.

El smiled. Her sister was the only person she knew who could immediately turn something horrific into a punch line. It was self-preservation at its finest and El was grateful for it.

"Shop?" El answered, trying to conjure the one thing the two sisters could do no matter what.

"Yes! I know the perfect place—there's a new boutique that just moved in from NY. They even brought their own guy. He's like a 102 and smells like silkworms … In the best way."

"I don't need anything that fancy," El said.

"Not for now, but you will," Isabel said, mouth full of toothpaste.

"Are we really doing this now?"

"It's the only way I can cope. Seriously. The first way I need to prepare for your 'imminence' is to shop for it."

Isabel spit into the sink unceremoniously and El laughed. This was full denial mode, but there was no room for arguing. El got dressed quickly, wearing the nicest underwear she had packed to prepare for the dressing room.

She would be cremated, Eleanor knew this, but she didn't want to take away the pleasure of this day from her sister, sick as it may be. Since the first campaign, Isabel had dressed her, because "There's no room for an Earth Mama at the podium." Somehow Bel always made her feel beautiful and like herself, even when she was wearing a tailored suit.

"The accessories get you access," Bel would say, and it was true. For Eleanor, a liberal at heart, performing the bride of a Republican politician in Ohio could be a tricky business. But with the right jewelry, El discovered she could more clearly speak her mind and veer conversations, at least among the other wives, in new directions.

"Wear pearls to the country club and then talk dirty." This was Isabel's mantra and Eleanor adopted it, trying her best to use her powers for good and not evil. Eleanor had been instrumental in the "Forget the Cookies, Just Give the Dough" fundraisers for the schools, insisting that money should not be raised one snicker doodle at a time for our future leaders. Her message, spoken through Chanel lipstick at tea instead of a megaphone on the courthouse steps, was heard louder than "Bake Sales for Bombs" in that particular circle. The fundraising goals were hit within a week and El was off on her next quiet crusade. She had to be careful, however, not to conflict directly with any of Walt's platforms, and there was one issue she could not touch—gay marriage. This pained her. Her Jillian had come out to them almost a decade ago and she wanted nothing more than to see her walk down the aisle, any aisle, in a dress or a suit, towards the person of her dreams. But because she was the wife of an Ohio Republican Senator, her hopes were adamantly silenced.

The boutique was gorgeous—one-of-a-kind items in never more than two sizes, everything as rich in texture as it was in price.

"No pant suits," Bel yelled from four racks over.

"Why not?" Eleanor replied, sifting through the gorgeous wools and crepes.

"This is not a campaign. It's a funeral, for god's sake." Bel was in her element. "You need something a little sexy but not too necro-feel-you-up."

Eleanor couldn't help but laugh at her sister's warped sense of humor—something they had shared for all of the past lives lived between them. Out of nowhere appeared an elegant man with a pocket square, a confirmed bachelor since before Elton John was born.

"Ladies, can I help you with something special or some sizing? I'm Percy."

Of course you are, thought Eleanor.

"We need a funeral dress," Bel said plainly, tearing through the evening gowns.

She shopped like a Tasmanian devil, destroying floor displays and hanging racks, mannequins left in varied states of frenzied undress. She was a fashion prospector, able to dig through even the roughest terrain to come up with one shining piece of pret-á-porter perfection.

"Oh, I'm so sorry. … For whom, dears?" Percy asked as if he would know the deceased and send flowers immediately.

Eleanor suddenly wanted to tell him everything.

"For me," Eleanor replied quietly.

"Classic black? Navy is big these days. Subtle. Let's find something more about lines, architectural but not outlandish, nothing that says look at me, look at me, I'm grieving." He loved his job—that was obvious. Years of large department stores had led him to this small mountain boutique, and it was here where he imagined he would spend his golden years as a retail therapist. Percy was obviously accustomed to smoothing out any shopping wrinkle—the mother of the groom dress debacles, the teenagers who wanted hooker costumes not prom dresses.

"I won't be … I mean, I need something a little flashier, a little more stand out," El responded awkwardly.

Bel was there, unabashed as ever, to cause trouble and drive the point home. "She's the star of the show darling, and this is like her last supper of shopping dates, so you better serve the good stuff."

Percy's eyes lit up. El smiled as she witnessed his transformation. Could this be the Holy Grail of shopping adventures for a connoisseur like Percy? Had he been waiting for her? What if this moment of collision was as much about his destiny as her own? Could she, and The Perfect Dress for All Eternity, be his hall pass out of retail hell? What if this was her final dress, and she, his last customer? Maybe he would move to Palm Springs. And maybe, just maybe, he would never shop for anyone but himself again.

Mischief alight in his eyes, Percy put his arm around Eleanor and led her to the back of the store, "In that case …"

Percy opened a door to a room neither sister expected. Here is where he kept the good stuff. It was like walking through the looking glass into an enchanted land. The sequins, the silks, the feathers. This was going to be one hell of a dress to go up in smoke.

It was the oddest of fashion shows. Anyone else looking on would have thought them all insane and, frankly, a little sadistic. Eleanor modeled dress after dress, lying down on the showroom floor's chaise lounge, crossing her arms over her chest in a classic corpse pose. Bel and Percy would line her imaginary casket and give thumbs up or thumbs down from their bird's eye view. It was amazing how different couture looked from this perspective. Some things that looked impossible on the hanger were a different animal altogether when horizontal.

Like holding onto a piece of a jigsaw puzzle, there was one dress Isabel had saved for last. It was a sapphire blue satin gown, identical to one, to be sure, that was worn the night the Titanic took her icy plunge.

"When's the last time you were a four," Bel asked a little grouchily. "Sadie Hawkins, Kent Riley?"

"He died senior year," El said vacantly. She was caught off-guard by the woman she saw before her. She was beautiful.

"I forgot that." Isabel came out from behind the zipper and froze. "Damn, you look good—so frickin' skinny," she said casually, as if this were any other shopping day.

"Benefits of not being able to swallow," El tried to laugh.

"I'm so jealous," Bel played along. "Killer diet plan." Bel stopped and took an unaccustomed step back, "Do you want me to stop?"

"Stop? You? No, I need your irreverence—and this in a size two."

"Bitch," Bel said playfully. "I love you, you know."

"I know."

The dressing room, bigger than any that they had snuck into together as teenagers, shrank around them.

"This is impossible." Bel was on the verge. Eleanor could not see her sister lose it now.

"But we're doing it," El demanded.

"Sickest game of dress-up we've ever played." Bel started to walk out to get some air and ask Percy for the two.

El's voice caught her at the door. "Don't let Walt bring a date."

It was coming. One of those conversations that you never forget. One with requests and song lists. One where odd things come into sharp focus—the pattern in the rug, the angle of the mirrors.

Bel hesitated for a moment then answered, "No date. Got it."

"And no coffee before 'The Viewing.' I hate coffee breath," Eleanor tried to laugh. She needed Bel to hear her and not freak out. She needed someone to take care of things.

“No coffee breath, check,” Bel answered, staring at the rose and vine pattern in the carpet.

“And only Mary-Louise Parker can play me when I’m gone.” Eleanor tried to catch her sister’s eye in the mirror.

“And who will play me?” Bel demanded.

“A young Barbara Hershey,” El replied, as if it were decided.

“Anything else?”

“You’ll know.” The sisters’ eyes met in the mirror. They looked different in so many ways, but their eyes gave away that they were sisters.

“I won’t know,” Bel pleaded in an almost whisper. “I never know anything.”

“You’ll know,” Eleanor insisted. “Now get me the two.”

Nightswinging

The summer of her sixteenth birthday during the last weeks before Eleanor was to leave for boarding school, she and Isabel hatched a plan to sneak out of the house and ride their bikes across town to the O'Henry's house. The O'Henrys were a large Catholic family on the other side of the golf course who, in the middle of a tribe of six girls, had boys the exact same ages as Eleanor and Isabel. Bel, of course, liked the older O'Henry boy Charles, leaving no suitable suitor for Eleanor. Still, El relished the thought of breaking the rules, of breaking anything after the summer they'd had, and leaned into Bel's scheming.

Getting beyond their mother's door would be simple. She would have long since passed out thanks to her evening cocktail of vodka, "tension pills," and resentment.

It was getting past their pre-teen brother Danny's room that would be the true test. If he heard them, he would invariably want to come. And if he came, he would ruin everything. Too old to be cute anymore but not old enough to be an asset, the girls spent their twin-like lives that summer pushing him to the edges.

If their father had still been in the house, they would have never attempted the escape. It's not that he was a light sleeper and they feared getting caught. Their father was known to sleep through anything. One night, after a bad dream, Eleanor approached her father's side of the bed. On the downslope of his bear-like snores, Eleanor whispered, "Daddy, Daddy," over and over to no avail. After a time of trying to stir him, she finally slid under the blankets between him and the edge of the bed, cuddling up to his warmth. Tucked in tight to the mountain of his body, El forgot that her mother was there on the other side of the mattress, forgot about the dream that had terrified her, and forgot that her father was not hers alone.

No, the girls would have never tried to leave if he were still home. It wasn't fear of his anger that had kept them to their beds at night but fear of his concern. Had their father risen in the night to pee or to get a glass of water and discovered their empty beds, his panic would have sounded through the neighborhood like a four-alarm fire. Then, after the girls returned safe and unharmed, his panic would have turned to disappointment. It was the fear of this disappointment that kept them to their curfew. But now, this summer, since it was he who left first and they who were disappointed, the girls felt free to go.

The pair creaked past their mother's door, slipped successfully past Danny's room, and tiptoed down the staircase. As they turned down the long hall toward the back door, they were met by a small shadowy figure.

"Take me with you," the figure begged. "Please?"

As her pupils adjusted, Eleanor could see the longing in her brother's eyes. Before she could move, Isabel grabbed both their hands and pulled them out the back door into the night.

The trio, on bicycles and still in their pajamas, kept off the streets and sidewalks so as not to be seen. Flying over the wet grass between houses, a silent race built up between them, a wildness of horses untethering their timidity. The metal *tick tick ticking* of their spokes seemed to fall in-sync as they bumped over garden hoses and stone walkways. The three had never felt so lucky to live in a neighborhood where fences did not separate this from that and yours from mine. Weaving through the suburb as if their route had been planned, they wordlessly headed toward the elementary school. A huge moon hung over the playground, illuminating their destination in an almost corny Hollywood way. As their tires slid into stopping just at the edge of the baseball diamond, it occurred to each of them that they had not seen a playground at rest, never imagined its solitude, its stillness. The absence of laughter and children's playful screaming was both eerie and mesmerizing, and it froze the Page children in their tracks. It was Eleanor who led the charge for the swings that set them back in motion again.

Side by side the siblings pumped their legs, swinging higher and higher into the darkness.

"Close your eyes just as you reach the top!" Isabel ordered.

At the peak of her upswing, Eleanor's body lay out almost parallel to the sky. At that highest height, Eleanor gulped the night with her eyes, closing her lids just as she began her pendular arch back down. The repetition of this devouring made her feel drunk with moonlight and momentum until she couldn't stop herself from laughing. Soon the three were all in giddy hysterics, laughing together for the first time in ages. In that moment, unbound from the laws of gravity, they understood what their father might now be feeling.

The blood metal smell of the swing set chains stained their hands as they remounted their bicycles and headed for home. As much as they hated to go back, inside all of them bloomed a secret awareness of freedom and a small forgiveness of their father for leaving.

Inheriting the Earth

Meeker, Colorado, the home to the girls' maternal grandmother Grammy Doyle, was a four-and-a-half-hour's drive, fish-hooking north from Crested Butte. Grammy Doyle was a blazing icon of pioneer bad-assery, and about as different from their mother as any woman they could imagine. Typically outfitted in heavy work boots and wartime-styled overalls, Grammy Doyle always appeared dressed for disaster. That she had survived The Great Dayton Flood of 1913, The Great Influenza Epidemic of 1918, The Great War, and The Great Depression, may have informed her fashion sense in her later years.

"Colleen is my delicate side," Grammy used to say. And it was true—the girls' mother could hardly endure her own bouts with depression, let alone a "Great" one. And after the death of Colleen's father, their grandfather Hugh, one would have thought it was Colleen who was widowed, not Grammy Doyle. Shrouded in mourning, Colleen locked herself in her room for a month after the funeral. When she finally emerged, she begged her husband to move back into the old Victorian in Grafton Hill, claiming that her mother needed her there. Freddy knew full well that it was his wife's way of getting closer to her father's memory but was so relieved to have her back among the living that he agreed.

Before the movers could deliver their furniture, however, Grammy had packed up and headed West, never to return. Even though she was from Dayton, had met and married her husband and raised her daughter there, she would say after that she hadn't known home until she moved to the mountains.

Tucked in along a ridge known locally as "China Wall," Meeker was still a cowboy town of a little over 2,000 people. Cattle and sheep drives droned on through Main Street, and big game hunting was the area's main attraction. Grammy fell in love with the town immediately and sent a postcard back to Grafton Hill that read, "We in Meeker have inherited the Earth!"

The summer their parents divorced, the girls spent two months out West with Grammy, while Danny went on a fishing trip with their father. Why the three were separated, no one ever questioned, but the time in Meeker was like none other. Their mother's mania and depression had obscured the joy in their lives for years, leaving only a thin halo of light glowing around the edges of birthdays, holidays, and cartoon-soaked Saturday mornings. If the sun was happiness, Eleanor's mother had been the moon in full eclipse, occulting the vibrancy of every moment with her unpredictability and propensity towards rage—silent or otherwise. That summer without her mother was the first time Eleanor felt unobstructed delight. And there, at 6,200 feet, was the first time Eleanor truly felt the sun.

The summer of '63 was the only time El had spent at the homestead. Over the years, however, Eleanor had relived the memories of the dry heat, cottonwood showers, and sudden thunderstorms enough times to trick herself into believing she'd passed her entire childhood there. Isabel had returned the following summer as El moved to Seattle for school. And though both headed West, one by truck and one by train, it was then that the sisters' lives began moving in opposite directions. "Home" would rarely hold the same zip code for the two after that. Isabel tried returning to Dayton for a six-month spell when El was first engaged, but, like Grammy Doyle, the West had won her over and she found she could no longer breathe at sea level.

There aren't enough long-distance phone calls to make up for lost moments shared without ceremony—the baton passing of toothpaste, the bartered exchange of clothes, the inside joke laughed at before uttered. We lose our sisters twice, El thought as the pair drove silently on. First, from the mirror above the shared sink in the too-small bathroom of our parent's home and again from the mirror of our eyes in this too-small life.

There are silences that sound like loneliness and those that sound like love. The quiet between the sisters now on Colorado State Highway 13 North was definitively of the latter. With so much to say and so much of it hard, the two rode for hours listening to the crackle of earth beneath the truck tires.

"How did she live alone out here so long," El finally asked, breaking the quiet as she looked at the vastness of mountain and prairie.

"She wasn't alone," Isabel smiled.

El's eyes went wide. "What do you know?"

"Do you remember Connie, Grammy's 'housekeeper.'" As Bel slowly winked air-quotes, El's eyes widened, and the story became clear. Bel laughed and launched into how she found out that Connie was more than a woman who helped Gram with the garden and goats—how one night she discovered them beautifully intertwined in a thunderstorm.

"It was the first and only time I ever saw Grammy's hair down. It was so long and beautiful, red woven with silver, wild tendrils reaching to the small of her back. I stayed and watched them kiss, limbs and sheets all entangled, and then I crept away. The strangest thing was how strange it wasn't. They were beautiful."

"That's why she left the house to Jillian," was all El could say. "But you didn't tell me?"

"At first it felt good to have something that was mine—something in this world that was not a hand-me-down—even if it was just a secret. And then later, when I would have told you, you and Walter weren't mincing words in his speeches. And I didn't want to hear you disagree with her life and love you any less."

Quiet fell around them again. Tears welled in Eleanor's eyes. Her throat worked hard as she struggled to swallow back the guilt of her judgment. Their kin had survived a flood, and here she was, overwhelmed by her saliva. It was time to buck up and muster some of that pioneer courage that was there in her genes.

Eleanor knew that she was going to have to summon her strength and that of her ancestors if she was to inherit any bit of this wild earth before leaving it.

Surface Tension

She imagined dropping her on every new surface she encountered. This new baby, this precious thing that she brought into this hard, hard earth, was her charge and all she could imagine, though she never told anyone, was dropping her on her head every time she crossed the threshold onto a new flooring. What would the splatter pattern be on tile, concrete, stone? She couldn't stop. She was grateful that their house consisted mostly of wall-to-wall carpeting, but the kitchen and the bathrooms were treacherous. Most terrifying was the outside world, with its asphalt and brick, new surfaces changing underneath her like the tides, new possibilities for that sweet round head to crack open and spill out little Jillian's memories of heaven into the gutter. She didn't leave the house for the first six weeks. That seemed an acceptable amount of time to stay indoors with a newborn. After that, there were lunch invitations, coffee dates, and a mother from her birth class who thought a playground might be fun. "Not that our nine-week-olds can do anything at a playground, but at least it would get us out of the house," she had said.

Out of the house.

El declined, lying about a cold the baby seemed to be catching. So this is what agoraphobia feels like, El thought, as she imagined Jill's head tumbling toward the sand, the mulch, the sidewalk. When she was a kid, she remembered hearing the word *agoraphobia* for the first time and thought it was someone who was afraid of sweaters. Now, it seemed perfectly reasonable to want to stay inside where there were only three types of surfaces to navigate. She had never imagined herself a worrier, at least not to this extreme. And it wasn't poisons or drowning or choking that scared her. It was the slow-motion tumble as she let her baby fall. The compulsion was building towards paralysis when Bel coaxed her out to go shopping and noticed her pause before entering the store. Wide, off-white tile. A totally new and treacherous surface, one that showed everything—blood, brains, bone—awaited her beyond the revolving doors. As soon as the vision was complete, down to the last details, she was fine and pushed through the entrance. But those first few steps were gruesome.

"I just dropped my baby!" El wanted to scream, but she knew she hadn't, knew she wouldn't, and tried to stop herself from looking down.

Melinda

El gripped the steering wheel until her knuckles blanched. She was terrified of seeing her daughter and wasn't sure which was haunting her more, telling her she was dying or that she was sorry.

So many years had passed since she had been to their grandmother's homestead, and, as they rounded the bend beyond the enormous cottonwood, Eleanor gasped at the sight of it. Exhaling slowly, her hands relaxed a bit at the wheel. Through all of the weathering of this world, the white clapboard farmhouse held its poise. The large front porch opened like a smile, greeting them from a quarter mile away. The old swing still hung off balance, a front tooth loose in its grin. With all the windows opened wide, the white lace curtains blew out like lashes from the eyes of the house. A banner of laundry was being hung on the line, strips of fabric in every imaginable shade sparking the scene with Technicolor prayer flags blowing in the late morning wind. Even from this distance and after so much time, El could easily tell that the figure before them was not her Jill. This woman, a poppy on the horizon, moved with grace and confidence. Braids flew out from under her oversized straw hat. Light seemed to stream through her. Dressed in nothing but a peach silk slip and workman's boots, the curves of her body came into clearer and clearer relief, making El blush the nearer they came. Here was her daughter's lover. She felt a strange pride in this woman's beauty.

The figure turned and waved generously, as if she had been expecting visitors all morning.

"Ready?" Isabel squeezed El's hand.

"No," El smiled back as the two got out of the truck and walked towards their hostess.

"Eleanor!" the young woman called confidently, rushing over to embrace her. "Aunt Isabel! It's so good to see you again! And so soon!"

El shot Isabel a look. Why hadn't her sister told her she'd been here recently? "El, meet Melinda," Isabel said by way of avoiding the other ten thousand questions Eleanor's eyes asked. Without realizing it, Eleanor went into politician's wife mode and stuck out her hand stiffly and smiled.

Melinda swatted it away and hugged her a second time. "Come in! Come in!" she smiled irrepressibly. "The house is a mess but mess is where Jill finds beauty, so we wouldn't have cleaned it even if we'd known you were coming." Melinda's laughter rippled over the landscape like the breeze.

"What a surprise!" she exclaimed, without a sardonic hint or sarcastic note in her tone. Melinda took the sisters in-hand, walking between them as a child would, and led them up to the house. El had the sudden flash of walking that way with Walter and Jillian when she was two or three, swinging her over the cracks in the sidewalk on their way home from church. The physical memory was so strong, she almost lifted Melinda off the ground.

The front door was open and through the screen, Eleanor could see into the belly of the house. The furniture had been removed to make room for the giant loom, and there, working like a magnificent spider at the center of her web, sat Jillian. There was a steady rhythm to her work, a machine-like constancy inside the chaos of fabric, color, and form. The paleness of her neck, the elegance of her fingers—Eleanor could have watched her for hours. As the three entered the house, Jillian looked up with a smile. It was the kind of smile you save for a beloved, and it was clearly intended for Melinda.

The music of the loom was silenced as Jill froze at the sight of her mother in the doorway.

Melinda was the first to break the quiet.

"Hiya, babe," Melinda sung cheerily. "We have company."

She wove herself effortlessly through the threads, as much a part of the art as anything caught in the loom.

As she leaned in to kiss Jillian on the cheek, El heard her daughter whisper, "Mel, did you—" and Melinda quickly respond "No, babe," as she swept an errant piece of dark hair from Jill's eyes just as Eleanor used to do.

El didn't know how to approach Jillian from this side of their divide, let alone from this side of the loom. She wanted to run to her and scoop her up, but she had no idea how to navigate the space, the physical obstacle between them almost comical in its literalness. After a moment, Jill rose and made her way to her mother.

"Are you here to tell me dad's dead?" Jillian said without flinching.

"Sadly, no," Eleanor replied. A small smile passed between the two women and Eleanor exhaled.

"Jilly!" Isabel lauded, throwing her arms around her as Eleanor wished she could.

From the kitchen, Melinda magically appeared with a pitcher and a tray of glasses, "Lemonade! Porch!" yelled more like an order than an offering. The women fell in line and trailed out through the door as they were commanded.

The four took their places around the small, white, metal table as if each seat had been assigned to them. Isabel and Melinda, across from one another, chatted away about the drive and the morning heat and the recent rash of evening storms. Clearly at home with uncomfortable tension, the two moved the conversation from one banal topic to another like great hostesses at a state dinner. Holding tightly to Jillian with her left hand, Melinda's right flew excitedly around her like a butterfly as she talked.

Eleanor was entranced by this woman who so clearly held her daughter's heart. Seeing them together made perfect sense, and El wondered if this whole saga would have played out differently—if Jill would have felt safe enough to bring someone home. If there had there been a face to the love that Walt *and* El, through her silence, forbade. Tears sprung to her eyes. El could feel herself swallowing hard to dam the waterfall building at the back of her throat. Straining against the oncoming flood, she caught Jillian's eye just as the coughing began. Isabel jumped up and whacked her on the back as Jillian looked on in horror. It was a quick but violent spell, and, after Eleanor had gathered her wits, she quickly excused herself and raced to the bathroom.

As she pressed her handkerchief into the sockets of her eyes to stop the tears, there was a knock at the door.

"May I?" Melinda's voice implored.

The downstairs wash closet, as her grandmother had called it, was just that—a closet, but back in the day it had felt like a luxury salon compared to the outhouse. Barely large enough for one, the two women met face-to-face upon Melinda's entry.

"Listen," Melinda hissed. The air about her palpably changed—gone were the butterflies and out was the lioness. The bathroom shrunk in tighter around them. "If you're here to tell Jillian some shit like you're sick or dying, you'd better clean up the mess you made with her before you dump some truckload of guilt or expectation, you understand? She has been hurt enough by you, and now is no time to go *Steel Magnolias* on her ass. Got it?"

Eleanor's face softened into a smile. Her daughter had found a fighter. It was clear that Melinda loved Jillian with a fierceness and a fearlessness that she, herself, had never been able to show. Jill would need that strength in the coming months and years. Perhaps, despite her choices, she had taught her daughter to choose well, and Jill certainly had.

"Bless you, you perfect girl." Eleanor wiped her eyes, and, kissing Melinda on the forehead, sealed a secret truce with her embrace.

Hate Speech

Eleanor had been typing out two letters over the course of the road trip, one to Riordon, her wonderful student back home, and the other to Jillian. She was always better written down than aloud. Soon, she knew from Dr. Bannon, writing would be the only way of getting her insides clearly out.

"You'll want a good wipe board," he'd said like a stock boy at Staples. "Or a notebook and pen. It's really whatever is easiest for you."

Eleanor thought she would be one for erasure—why should her every thought need to stay after she'd gone? And she knew Isabel couldn't be trusted—she would keep every entry. The last thing El wanted was Isabel alone in a room full of words written in manic scrawl. Wipe board it would be.

The letter buzzed in her pocket like she imagined an engagement ring might. Eleanor knew she couldn't make it through a meal without questions or seeming rude. And she knew she didn't want to open with the disease—that wouldn't be fair. Melinda announced that she and Isabel were headed to the kitchen to fix up some lunch, the kick in the ass Eleanor needed.

"You look happy," El said, looking directly at her daughter for the first time. Jillian's eyes followed after Melinda and lingered on the door frame of the porch where she had just disappeared.

Without hesitation she replied, "I am." Before she could stop it, a small smile spread across Jill's face.

"I have something I would like you to read." Eleanor took out the letter, slightly damp from the heat of her pocket.

Jillian crossed her hands over her chest in refusal. She looked all of sixteen, and it took every last ounce of Eleanor's energy not to laugh at her daughter's beautiful obstinance. "Please," she begged, hoping to god Jillian wouldn't be so stubborn that she would have to read the letter aloud.

Jillian snatched the paper from her hand, turned slightly away, and began to read.

My Dear Jillian,

I have long since owed you tomes of words, careful words that worked hard to be worthy of you. And if these words here are not good enough, not true enough, I will remake the alphabet, fashioning it to better say all that I need to say, all that you deserve to hear.

I have failed as a mother. And I don't say that so that you or anyone else will offer me false confidence. I have failed. And I am deeply sorry. I have put myself and my fear before your happiness and trust. It is not that I put your father first, though I can see how, on the surface, it would appear that way. My loyalty to him is better understood as an act of self-abandonment, as a wicked gesture of self-loathing, as an affirmation of my insecurity.

Imagine me for a moment, not as your mother, but as a girl. All I wanted was to be loved. And in a house of such large voices, to be heard was to be loved. And yet I was silent. Silent or ignored. People only listened when I sang—but then my mother never said, "I love those lyrics" or, "what a great song." Just, "doesn't she have a pretty voice?"

It didn't matter what I had to say—just how I sang it. No one was really listening. I had a failed music career. I did. It sounds romantic when your Nana or your aunt talk about it, but it was not much more than a few dive bars and a summer living in my truck with a pile of handmade cassette tapes. Lonely, I slept with lonely people. Needy, I woke up with people even needier. Remember, I was not your mother then. I was a girl trying to figure out how to be a woman. And then I met your dad.

It was your father who gave me voice, both literally and figuratively. He made my thoughts seem grand and palpable. He was, is, a megaphone of a man, and I quickly fell for the sound of my words pressed through his powerful *boom*. I stopped listening to what he said, to what I wrote, a long time ago. But there was something in it for me, just hearing my voice come out of that man. I was not only heard, I was spoken. After so many years of a mother not listening and a father out of earshot, it felt like LOVE. Soon, what had been mine became his. I was relegated to catchphrases and insincerities, bad song hooks made up of conservative, game-winning rhetoric that no longer held power for me. But I was in it by then and too attached to raise my voice and say No.

I/he/we said hateful things. Things that I wish I could take back. Even if our daughter wasn't gay, I should have thought about the fact that someone else's daughter was. I wish I could take back every word. I can't. But I can write new ones.

You are stronger than your mother. In this singular act of parenting, I have succeeded—though I fear you are stronger in spite of me. I can live with that, if you will forgive me.

You are a perfect girl—a perfect woman. Your parents are hypocrites, traitors. But you? You are loyal and true. You are the best of us, and I will try, for the rest of my days, to be better for you, to be worthy.

I love you, Jillian. Please forgive me.

With all my heart,
Mom

Eleanor had imagined this moment for hundreds of miles. The moment when Jillian put down the letter, tears brimming, and she forgave her everything. She had seen the scene so many times that when Jillian looked up, her eyes the color of hate, Eleanor was shocked and a little afraid.

Silence that Eleanor felt she could not endure rent the next minute, as a forever of silence passed. And then, Jillian spoke.

"You fucking poets. One dulcet fucking tone, one broken cup of a metaphor and you feel like you should get off. But I know you, mother. You are a snake charmer, a fucking snake charmer that acts like they're afraid of snakes while living in the nest of them."

Eleanor sucked in her breath, waiting for the punch to land.

"You're a goddamn sorceress! You turn ordinary things into magic and make people believe and love *you*." Eleanor almost felt Jillian's jaw straining at the word. "And it made me love you, while you made me think my love was wrong. You could turn a cardboard box into a goddamn boat that I thought we'd sail together, off through night and day—"

"And in and out of weeks—" El began.

"Do *not* tell my story," Jillian seethed.

Jillian's strong hands wrung the letter like she was squeezing the words off the page. Eleanor could feel Jillian's ferocity building. It was the same as when she was a little girl, El remembered. Jillian would emerge from her corner, suddenly huge, her anger looming over the room. Her rage was its own wild animal, and Eleanor could see it now—all these years, El was the reason for it. El had fed its fury.

"I saw you as the victim and him as the asshole. When you were complicit all along. You weren't magic, you were manipulative. And I fell for it! For you!" Jillian screamed, breaking into sobs. "And for you, I broke my own heart, again and again."

Snot poured out of Jillian's nose, and she spat as she screamed. Eleanor drew the monogrammed handkerchief from her pocket and offered it to Jillian. Jillian batted it away.

"You wanted a voice? Well, you fucking got one. One full of hate that thrived on ego. I told myself for years that dad was the mastermind. But how could you have written those things if somewhere you didn't feel them? If you didn't believe them to be true? You had that hate in your heart. You had that hate for me."

"Jillian, I never hated you! I could never hate you," Eleanor said, reaching out her hand to touch Jillian's thigh. Jillian recoiled and jumped to her feet.

"But that's just it, mom. You did. You do." Jillian punctuated each sentence by pointing at Eleanor. "Hate speech. You wrote hate speech. Hate fucking speeches. PLURAL. I don't know why the actual fuck you are here, but there is more for you to do than write a goddamn letter."

"Jill, I need you to forgive me," El begged. "I will do anything—"

"I forgave you years ago. It's the only way I could forgive myself. But I am mad, mom. I am still really fucking mad."

"What can I do, Jill? Retract my life? I'll do it. Publicly take back every word? I will. Write new speeches? March? Fight? Become the goddamn P-FLAG mother of the year? I will do anything. I was WRONG, Jillian, wrong. On so many levels. I am trying—"

"Mom, I hear you, but I need a minute. You show up here to tell me you're leaving, have left, but what you don't see is that you left *me* years ago. Just when I needed you. I am proud of you for leaving him, I am, but I am still so very sad that it was so much easier for you to leave me that you didn't even notice that you had."

There it was. El had done it. She had dropped her baby after all.

An ocean of regret poured between them as Jillian tossed the letter on the table and walked out into the yard where the cottonwood tree glimmered its leaves in the evening light.

Loyalty

Some had thought me out of fashion. But now, with everything "green," I am making a comeback. Not that I care about fashion. What I care about, besides a gentle cycle and a nice, crisp ironing from time to time, is her. I have been there at the best of times and the worst, and I will always be there, in her pocket waiting for a light afternoon rain to turn into a downpour. My mistress is prone to sudden crying jags—it's not because she's sad, she says, but quoting a favorite poet, it's "because life is so beautiful and so short."

As her Handkerchief, I am chief in charge of carrying her emotions, dabbing away the tears and the rest, and holding fast until she needs me again. This is a noble post. I know, I know, you're probably wondering how snot and saliva are poetic. They aren't. But the act of wiping them away and enfolding them is. I am grateful that she doesn't wear mascara. First, she doesn't need it—she has the most beautiful hazel eyes that need no decorative frame. And second, I would be sure to stain and a stain on a hanky is like a blemish on a bride, very unsavory indeed. Stains give away too much and can wind a girl up in the rag drawer.

No, in my many years of service, I am proud to say that my ivory linen skin has come clean with every wash. No one wants a smudged or yellowed reminder of their past—we all want to start fresh, as if there has never been anything to cry about at all. And yet, we know that there may be something to cry about, must be something to cry about, in the future. That's where I come in—a protective measure slipped into pocket or purse, one so delicate that I go unnoticed and could never seem strong enough to hold forty years of tears. I remember the day I made official rank. My young mistress, no more than ten, embroidered her initials, EPD, into my fine yet unstained face, a permanent badge of loyalty and completeness. Her stitches were deft and quick, unembellished but clear. I was hers and she was mine, for all the torrents and for all of time. And I will be there as she requires until the bittersweet end, to dry her last tear.

I pray that one will stain.

The Game of Impossible Questions

The screen door slammed behind her. Isabel had a knack for letting doors fall hard. She never tried to buffer her wake.

"Do you remember that game, *Impossible Questions*, we used to play?" Bel asked abruptly.

Jillian had long disappeared inside. Eleanor, alone and heartbroken, sat on the same porch swing that had been her favorite spot since the girls' first visit in 1963. The swing hung at an angle so that someone always sat higher than the person next to her, giving the illusion that your swinging partner was much heavier.

As a girl, Isabel used to plop down on the swing next to her sister after dinner and say, "I had waaaay too much dessert," as her side of the swing sunk with her imagined weight. It made El giggle every time.

Why the chain was never adjusted was a family mystery, but the pleasure that came from the over-used joke seemed to be great enough cause to leave well-enough alone.

Eleanor was swinging on the high side of the swing as usual, when Bel sat down and it tipped considerably. Bel patted her belly and they both chuckled. Truth was, Eleanor was looking transparently thin, and Bel didn't have the stomach to say the old punch line aloud. They sat there in silence for a moment before Bel continued.

"Do you remember the question about the phone line and your death?"

Eleanor nodded. This question had haunted her since she was fourteen, though she never brought it up again to her sister after the day they had played *Impossible Questions* for the last time. It paled her to think that Isabel had held onto the very same scenario that troubled her all these years.

"It is the moment of your death, and you have a telephone receiver that can either allow you to talk or to hear. Which would you choose?"

Isabel seemed adamantly convinced that she would want to be the one to talk, would need every last moment to say every last thing.

"I know you love me," she had said, "I won't need to hear it. I'll need to talk, and you'll need to hear me—to know I'm ok or just to know I really love you or to apologize for something I fucked up at the last minute and had never apologized for or whatever. I would DEFINITELY need to be the one talking."

Eleanor was never so sure about her answer, and she was glad that Bel had taken her turn for her.

For the last forty years when she couldn't sleep, the question would come back to her. Eleanor would lie in bed replaying the scenario—she was always in the same room, an all-white box with nothing but a heavy black receiver on the wall. After all these years, she could still feel its oppressive weight in her hand. This phone, the last thing she would touch, was her lifeline to the other side. Over the years, the person on the other end changed—her sister, her mother, Walter, Jill—and with the change of the person on the line, El's answer changed.

With her mother, she would let her do the talking. She knew, or at least hoped, that the woman who was there with her when she was born would know, for once, just the right things to say. With Jill, she would sing to her the song she had sung nightly from her birth, "All of Me." "Take my arms, I want to lose them. Take my lips, I'll never use them. Your good-byes left me with eyes that cry, how can I go on without you" hung in the air around her in this version of her imaginings and brought her to tears in her own bed. With Walter, there was just silence coming from both ends, as if neither one of them had understood the rules of the game. With her sister, she switched from talker to listener, depending on the need and the night.

The hardest part of the impossible question thing for Eleanor was trying to figure out the parameters. When did the speaker get cut off? Was there a time limit, or did they get to finish their thought, say "I love you," tell her not to be scared, and then leave it to Eleanor to actually have to hang up the phone? Or could she die listening, the earpiece falling to the floor, the speaker's voice crying, "Are you still there? Are you still there?" into the hollow of the white room. If she were the one talking, did she die mid-monologue, or did she find completion, finish the song, trust that the silence on the other end was still listening, say good-bye, and have the courage to hang up the heavy black receiver and leave the other side alone with a dial tone? It was this part of the game that had troubled her for years. She was grateful, in a way, for the particulars of this damn disease. The choice was made for her. She would be on the receiving end, and it would be Isabel, talking away non-stop, as if her sister could stretch out the inevitable for eternity, rambling on long after her good-bye.

"I change my answer," Bel said quietly.

"You can't change it now. No gimmes. No take-backs," Eleanor smiled.

"No, I change my answer," Bel demanded. "I want to be the one listening, and I want to be the one dying. When we played all those years ago, I answered your *Impossible Question* for you—as if you were the one dying. How fucking selfish. I wanted to talk, and I wanted to live. Well, now I change my answer. You talk. You live. Game over."

El could see it wasn't worth arguing the point, plus she was too tired to go another round on this ridiculous topic where no answer would ever be good enough.

"Ok," El relented. "You win. You listen. I live."

The swing creaked as they swayed gently off-kilter. Eleanor reached for her sister's hand. She imagined her sister, the constant receiver of all her dreams and wishes, every secret, every fear, sitting there listening quietly to the silence on the other end of the line, waiting for one last word, for as long as the game would allow.

Better Ancestors

El didn't sleep well that night. Lying in the single bed of her youth, she was tossed between dream, memory, and the moment. Everything was disorienting and surreal. As hot as the night was, the full moon shone through the eyelet curtains, creating a gobo of snow across her body. She shivered as she sweat.

Her dreams flashed under her lids, channels changing with rapid fire. She was at the edge of the sea, waves lapping her feet, a winter storm whipping her hair. Was she in California? Scotland? She had never been to Scotland, but as soon as she thought it, she knew it was where she was. The midnight blue dress she and Bel had picked out for her funeral puddled around her feet. "It will be stained with salt!" El whispered, but she kept walking forward, deeper and deeper. Her foot touched something under the water. She bent to collect it. It was her Mary figurine. It changed to her hula dancer as she brought it out of the sea. Touching the talisman propelled her into a new corner of the dream, a cinder block practice room. Almost a prison cell, it was stark and small with no windows and harsh yellow light. Still in the blue gown, El sat at the piano and tried the keys.

Instead of notes, words came out. Each key pressed held the tone of someone she had known. When she hit the pedals and the low C, there was her father. She worked the combinations, creating chords that spoke to her. "Home," her father said over and over. "Home." And then there she was, on the lawn of the Page's old house, three bikes cast off in the driveway, a lemonade stand on the edge of the lawn. El walked up behind the three Page children, eager to see her younger self. Eleanor, age eight, turned and offered her older self a Dixie cup of lemonade, which immediately transformed to a wine glass in her hand. Transported to a table in the small Indian restaurant where she and Walter had eaten on their first trip to New York, Eleanor sipped the wine and smiled across at her husband.

"I like your dress," he said, and, for a moment lost in the magic of the dangling multi- colored Christmas lights, the wine, and his attention, Eleanor remembered being in love.

She looked down at her glass and saw that it was covered with black fingerprints. Wiping her hair out of her eyes, a gesture she did even when there was no hair falling, left a streak of ash across her forehead. Frantically, El began to brush her body, coal-like smudges appearing at each touch. She felt hot, like she was burning from the inside. And then relief. A cool splash, the cutting of bubbles off her body as she dove deeper into the pool. The dress changed from blue to red. As El swam, photographs of memories floated in the underwater world around her. It was blissful, sifting through the pages of her life under the cool weightlessness. El reached out to take hold of a picture, and as she touched it, she broke the surface of her dream and came sputtering back to reality, gasping for air like a fish cast to the dock.

Isabel, in the twin bed next to her sat up immediately.

"You ok?"

"Just a dream," El told herself.

"Wanna talk about it?"

"I need to call Walter."

"Now?"

"Now."

Somehow El had managed to carry a modicum of love that she used to feel for her husband back from her dream time. She knew if she didn't call Walter while she still had that in hand, she never would.

There were only three telephone numbers that Eleanor knew anymore—Isabel's, Jillian's, and Walter's. She had purposefully not programmed them into speed dial so that she would have to regularly test her memory. Before cell phones, she used to know so many—her neighbors, every ex-boyfriend, her nana, the pizza place the Page's ordered from every Saturday, the cab service in Seattle, and the Chinese delivery number she abused in grad school.

Eleanor dialed the ten-digit number slowly and pressed send. The phone rang one and a half times before Walter jumped on the line.

"El?" he answered, more urgent than angry.

"Hi."

"Are you ok? Where are you?"

"With Jillian at Grammy's."

"I'm …" his voice faltered for the first time since she'd known him. It was the faltering that gave away what he was about to say.

"I'm sorry, Nor. I've been the ass. I get it. I'll try harder. I will."

A long pause, one of those pauses that only married people can sit through.

"I love you, Eleanor."

Eleanor wanted him to suffer a little, but not so much that the meanness took over. She stretched the space between his words and hers out as far as it would go before responding.

"I know."

"Then you'll come home?"

"Here's the thing …" El said and then proceeded to tell him everything. El had never heard her husband cry. Not over Jillian, not over his father's grave, not over any argument they'd ever had. But he was crying now. ALS hadn't landed for him, but Lou Gehrig's had, so did "three-years tops," and "only treatment, no cure."

"I won't divorce you," El said. "I need your health insurance, but I don't want to be your wife anymore."

"But I want to be there for you. I want to help," Walter said earnestly.

"You can help by not arguing and by honoring this. I need your health insurance and a monthly budget. I want my own place. In exchange, I will do some public photo ops over the next six months but then I'm out. Out of the limelight, out of your campaign goals, out of the picture. No speaking engagements, period. From now on, my words are mine, not yours. And we need to change the wills. I also need a promise."

"Anything."

"You use this illness to raise money and awareness for the disease, not yourself. And when I'm gone, I don't want this to be a story you tell at parties and in tearful interviews."

"I'm not a total asshole, Nor."

El breathed dismissively into the phone. "And this. Face your daughter. Our daughter. She's amazing. Despite us both."

"Do you love me at all?" Walter said softly.

"I love you a little."

Eleanor hung up the phone and felt the acrid sting of tears. She squeezed her eyes tightly, bunched her covers into her mouth and bit down hard. Flashes of the dreams from earlier rose and then popped on the surface as quickly as they came. No more crying tonight. She couldn't take it. Isabel sat next to her on the bed, hand pressed heavily into her back.

"You did good, kid. You did good," Isabel said, stroking her hair.

El looked up to see a figure in the doorway. Exhausted, she imagined it was Grammy Doyle, or any of her better ancestors leaning into the door frame, holding up the house. Stepping into the light was Jillian. She had heard it all. Isabel rose to make room for Jill on the bed.

"Mom?" Jillian sniffled.

"It's ok, baby," Eleanor whispered as she took her daughter into her arms.

“It’s not ok,” Jillian said.

“No. But we will be,” Eleanor promised.

“I’m sorry I was so mean,” Jill sobbed again.

“You were perfect,” El said, and meant it.

“I’m still mad,” Jillian insisted, serious as ever.

“You should be,” El said, hugging her tight.

“I’ll take that handkerchief now,” Jillian said, saltwater running from her eyes and nose. El could have stayed there with her girl forever, hold this moment where forgiveness spoke louder than blame, but she knew they all needed rest before all that was to come.

“To bed, you. Go to that beauty of a woman. We’ll talk in the morning. I love you, kitten.”

Jillian rose at the command, “Open or closed?” she asked as she stood in the doorway.

“Open,” El replied. Definitely open.

Ajar

Not being married. She would get to not be married. Even if she wasn't divorced, not being married would be something. El had been good at being a wife, but there were domestic things that Eleanor just couldn't do. Or wouldn't do, as Walter liked to stress. Like screw on the lid of a bottle. It went against her nature to completely seal the aspirin or tightly twist the top of the salad dressing. Leaving the cap only ever so agape on the orange juice caused many a morning's upheaval, but for one reason or another, Eleanor could just not complete those domestic tasks. It wasn't intentional, but leaving things slightly open was just a part of her gestural life with objects. She never noticed the habit until Walter had pointed it out. She wondered if it was innate to her entire family. After one particularly angry row over ketchup and a new pinstripe, El retreated to her mother's house and checked the fridge. Lemon juice, one twist away from closed. Jam, slightly ajar. This inability to close appeared to be in the blood.

Mustard tops and Tupperware lids were not the only things outside El's domestic purview. She had never been one for cooking and often heard Walt slough off her culinary skills at dinner parties, saying with confidence, "The kitchen is not Nor's best room."

The joke always got a laugh, a knowing nod from the other men at the table, and a blush out of Eleanor. It was a relief that Walter liked to go out—more to be seen than to eat—and it saved her hours slaving over the stove. When she did cook, it warmed her that Jillian liked her simple fare—pasta, tuna melts, and the once-weekly breakfast for dinner.

As a child, El had always volunteered to do dishes, while Isabel clamored around their mother as she baked snicker doodles or prepped the holiday meal. Cooking was their special time and El was always happy to eat and clean up afterwards. It was no wonder that, when El called home from college to say she had gotten a holiday job in the housewares department of Bon Marché, the entire family was in hysterics. El recounted day one on the floor.

Her first customer, a vertical man with a list as long as he was, asked, "Where might I find your copper colanders?"

El had no idea what "her" copper colanders were, let alone where they might find them, but said, with a confident smile, "Follow me!" Walking through the long aisles of kitchenware, El scanned up and down, looking hard for the unknown. What a thing it was, she thought to herself, as she scanned high and low, *to wander in search of* with no idea what you are looking for. It gave her a wild pleasure, an Alice-like wonderment that might take her to anywhere. She suppressed a laugh as she got down on her knees to seriously inspect a stack of boxes that had not yet been put away. After about ten minutes the man pointed to the high shelf, "There!" El clapped her hands together once, "They must have moved them!" she exclaimed and climbed up the step stool to bring the object down.

"Strainer," she said to herself. "Bowl with holes." And rang the man up with a smile.

She could hear her entire family laughing on the other side of the line and imagined them, ears pressed to the phone, listening to her failure like fans to a radio program in the '30s.

A bowl with holes. What would that be like, Eleanor thought. Devastating? Liberating? It seemed to El that she wondered more about the affections of objects around her than what might please her personally. What if she treated her life with the kindness she showed her anthropomorphics? Perhaps if she left it ajar, some great mystery would seep in or some inanimate wisdom would leak out. Walter would think it all nonsense and say that she was one child-proof lid away from poisoning someone. But El was never one to be closed up too tightly. And now, not divorced but no longer a wife, she felt her lid at half spiral and delighted in the mess she might make if shaken.

Loss

I am trying to imagine myself without her. As The World, I am used to letting people go. It happens about 153,000 times per day. And it's not that I haven't grieved the loss of others before. I especially miss the feel of new feet upon my surface, and, even though I hadn't known them long, I still weep each time a child is snatched before they get a chance to take their first step. Let's see … there are others I've missed. There are the folks who did kind things for me—stopped over-fishing (I am very proud of my oceans, especially the blue whale, the shark, and the coral reef), planted new trees instead of cutting them down (I am prone to hot flashes lately and need the shade), and worked for alternative energy (Let me tell you about the constant defacement, all the picking and the pock-mark making at a more rapid rate than ever, and, oy, that fracking . . .). Then there are those I miss who don't so much do things for me but for others, those folks who just generally make me a much happier place to live. That's Eleanor—a recycler from the beginning and the way she always bought chocolate for her checkout girl. I love these things about her. But it isn't just her kindnesses to strangers. No, it is, for lack of a better word, her glow. I feel like I have a new fresh star of my own with Eleanor around. Somehow this one human person makes me feel better equipped, better . . . accessorized. Eleanor Darlene Page Murphy. That woman is . . . unique. And when my older, more enigmatic sisters—The Heavens—get her, I will feel a deep loss, and, quite frankly, a bit jealous. Fortunately, green is my color.

I do worry that, on that day that Eleanor moves out and moves on, the loss of this one, this precious human who is one of the best of them I've ever known, that this loss might cause such a sadness in me that I will flood a city or a nation again. But Eleanor wouldn't want that as part of her legacy. This I know. I will try my best to be contained, reserved. I am only 4.54 billion years old after all, mature for my age but still young for my solar system. I will do my best not to punish the rest of them with a crying jag. I will try, alongside the many others who will grieve upon my shores, to let her go without fury, without guilt, and imagine Eleanor happy, imagine her glow, somewhere out there in the universe, lighting up a new home.

Messy Business

A coven was quickly forming. The four women sat around the dining room table holding hands, leaning in as though to plan a battle or begin a séance. If any group could raise the dead, it would be this one. El felt their galvanized presence as she let them in on the details of the last few months. Steeling around her, El softened for the first time in ages. The relief was more delicious than she had expected.

"How have you been carrying this alone?" Melinda asked, a tear sliding down the side of her face. El wondered how much Jillian had told her in the middle of the night, or if Melinda was the sort of woman who knew things.

Eleanor shrugged. "I have carried a lot alone recently," she replied.

Jill stared at her mother with an intensity El had not seen before. At once furious, frightened, and in awe, Jill's gaze was a black hole, drawing every ounce of energy in the room toward her.

"I want to fucking kill him," Jillian seethed.

"He didn't know, honey," Eleanor replied softly, wondering why any part of her was still defending Walter.

"That's exactly why I want to rip his fucking head off," Jill said in a voice not entirely her own.

Melinda squeezed Jill's hand to settle her.

"We need his guilt and his money," Isabel said simply. "We also need his power. Eleanor will get the best treatment once he shines a light on this disease. Lots more people will. There's a lot of power in power."

"I still want to tear his frat boy face off," Jillian hissed. "He cheated on my mom while she was DYING? Seriously?!?! Are you fucking kidding me?! Aren't you mad? Aren't you fucking furious?"

"I stopped being mad years ago," El said, trying to soothe her daughter.

"Bullshit, mom," Jillian spat.

El could feel the pistol in her hand, the white powder on her eyelashes, the years destroyed one by one by one.

"I have been mad," El smiled.

"I'm serious, mom. I mean mad, like psycho crazy bitch mad," Jillian challenged.

The ceramic paperboy, the mother holding her newborn child, the little clown and his red balloon, the girl and her kitten. El could see their wide black eyes bursting into fragments. "I destroyed his collection," El's smile stretched devilishly. Jillian's mouth fell open.

"You what?! "How?"

"Firing squad."

Jillian smacked the table and jumped up, jubilant. "That's what I'm fucking talking about!" Laughing, she pulled El out of her chair and hugged her. Eleanor could feel her daughter's strong body shaking, and after a moment could sense the tempo shift as the laughter changed to silent sobs.

Melinda rose and wrapped her arms around Jillian, then Isabel stood and spread her arms around them all. Eleanor couldn't tell where her body ended and where the others began. Their sadness was heavy on her but lighter than the truth she had been carrying alone. After a while, the breath of the group slowed and the crying subsided.

"We're going to need a plan," Isabel said.

"We're in," Melinda replied. "No matter what."

"You're, we're, going to have to go back, mom," Jillian said practically.

"I know. Just not yet," El relented. "I have some things I would like to do before I go."

"I'm not leaving you," Jillian said.

"I know, baby," El smiled. "But I have a few more adventures in me. And then, I promise, I will let you all take over. Just not yet."

The quartet leaned in, heads together, snot running from their noses.

No one sniffled in subconscious solidarity with Eleanor, and like stalactites in the depths of a cave, the women let their sorrow drip and drain. This would be messy business—they could all see that now. It's funny how necessary dying is to know life, El thought. One thing was certain, they were definitely going to need more handkerchiefs.

By Going Where You Have to Go

On the long road for leaving, Death rides shotgun. There are no maps, no mile markers, just you and the road alone. Though El could have stayed in that house for days, she needed to get on with the going. Still well enough to be wild, she felt that, if she didn't get a move on and point her compass west, she might never get the chance.

After two days of planning, crying, plotting, crying, laughing, and crying, El was ready. A plan was argued and agreed upon—El would drive to the coast and look for Lee, her Holy Grail of a man. After one month—with or without him—she would return to Ohio and meet "The Coven," as the women had taken to calling themselves. Isabel would find the house, Walter would pay for it, and Jillian and Melinda would do the heavy lifting.

Isabel walked in and sat down next to El's duffel on the already made bed. Eleanor reached into her jeans pocket and produced a yellowed piece of their grandmother's stationary. On it, she had scrawled Dr. Bannon's number. She pressed it into Isabel's hand.

"Call him," El asked and only slightly demanded. "I don't want to hear 'No' right now. Call him, tell him I was too strong for you—that I tied you all up and escaped in the night. Tell him I'll need a prescription and I'll text the address. Tell him you will be in charge soon and that you are my primary contact. He needs to know who he's dealing with," El laughed. "And tell him not to worry. I will get back to the business of dying after I've found a life."

"Ok, I'll call." Isabel swallowed hard. They had both promised no tears today. Bel's eyes landed on a letter resting on the bedside table. "That looks ominous. Who's it for?"

"Not ominous at all—but it is something I feel bad about," El responded. "It's a letter to Riordon, my student back home. He starts middle school at the end of August, and I promised I would get him ready. I totally bailed."

"You can't worry about everyone else right now, El."

"I know, but this kid is magic. It can't be good juju to let down magic."

The letter had taken ten re-writes to get right. El had no idea how much she could tell an eleven-year-old. What would help him to understand and what would be too much to carry? She knew where it would eventually end, but the beginning nagged at her until this morning, when she settled on a stanza from Roethke's "The Waking."

> *We think by feeling. What is there to know?*
> *I hear my being dance from ear to ear.*
> *I wake to sleep, and take my waking slow.*

> Dearest Riordon,
>
> Do you know your name means, the "Royal Bard," that you are of the lineage of composers, singers, and declaimers of epic and heroic verse? You are. And you are perfectly named.
>
> This, I also know—that you think by feeling and that, like the voice in Roethke's poem, "The Waking," you also take your waking slow. This is a gift—this slow and thoughtful arrival to wonderment. It means that in action and in word, you experience each moment, taste each hue and savor of every consonant and vowel. You have helped me rub the sleep out of my eyes and see the talisman of a peach pit, to listen more softly and hear the music of the dashboard hula dancer. You may say I have helped you find your voice, but it is you who have helped me to listen.

> I am sorry I left without saying good-bye. I promise, I won't do that again. I have a big journey ahead of me, one that will require the strength and confidence of all of those whom I adore. You are in that fold. I will be gone until the middle of July. When I get back, we will work a little more and continue to help each other.
>
> Homework: I expect you to have all of "The Waking" memorized and ready for me for recitation. You will "learn by going where you have to go."
>
> Yours,
> Eleanor

El folded the letter and put it in the back pocket of her jeans. She would mail it on her way out of town. The smell of breakfast wafted between the sisters and carried them out of the room and down towards the kitchen. Though Eleanor would be able to swallow very little of it, she appreciated the care Mel took in creating the perfect olfactory palette. Even if she soon had to blend and drink her meals, she could close her eyes and imagine a four-course feast with Melinda in charge.

Jillian and Melinda were already seated at their spots around the kitchen table. Juice cups were filled, and the coffee was creamed and sugared, just as El liked it. Orange poppies smiled wide from her grandmother's blue-flecked pitcher. Eggs were portioned out on mismatched China—bacon for the others—and creamy cinnamon oatmeal filled delicate teacups, each hand-painted with a different wildflower of the region. It would have been a happy table if not for the looming goodbyes.

"Good morning," El said optimistically, hoping her spirit of adventure would infect the room. The foursome ate quickly. Breakfast was disappeared and dishes were cleared and rinsed and dried.

It's funny how we humans rush towards goodbyes, El mused, as the others seemed to almost push her towards the door—how the most difficult place for a person to sit is at the edge of THE END and not flip forward towards the last page. She remembered how eager she used to be for the end of long days, for that moment when she could turn off the light, and whisper goodnight to Jillian from the doorway. And even though she knew her little girl would not want to be tucked in and sung to forever, she still felt that gnawing impatience when it came to goodbyes. She sensed it now, all around them, the get-going and the get on with it. Plus, there was the pact not to cry.

"I will see you in thirty days, my loves," El slung her duffel over one shoulder as the four circled up for one last group hug. El tossed the bag into the passenger seat next to her, buckled her seatbelt and rolled down the window to wave.

They were beautiful, the three of them, standing like the Fates on the front porch of the prairie. There was Jillian, like Clotho, the spinner of the threads of life, Melinda, Lachesis, who measures those threads, and Isabel, Atropos, who would have the strength to cut them.

At the end of the drive, Eleanor slowed at the command of a lonely stop sign. There was not a car for miles, but she braked to look both ways. Before turning, she rummaged through her box of cassettes and pulled out a tarot card of a mixtape, *Music for Leaving*. She had no idea how any of this would go, but she leaned forward without fear. Eleanor plucked Jeremy, the hula dancer, from her spot, turned her around to face the road ahead, and hit the gas. Jeremy bobbled wildly. After a life of hindsight, she could finally see the future.

Hope

Just as I was ready to catch air and eat gravel, I was pressed back onto the altar of the dash and WOW, what a thing! I almost dropped my ukulele and ran to the glass.

The Future!

The Unknown!

It felt so foreign! So full of wonder! I had never seen anything like it. I had no idea I had been living in the past.

On the road of life, there are those who look forward and those who check their rear-view mirror again and again. To some, it might seem like safe driving. But from here, where I am now, it's a fearful gesture. Sure, there's a lot to learn from what's behind you, but to get stuck there, as I was—that's no way to hold this big and wondrous life.

I have only one ache from this new horizon—that I may never see her face again. Yes, as she squeegees the windshield, I might catch her smile for a moment across that liminal mud-streaked distance. But I will never lose myself in the mirrors of her eyes. It's her face I have looked to my entire existence. I have danced for her pleasure. Played my heart out for her laughter. Sung harmony to her dashboard blues. And now I face the future on my own. I will hear her, feel her, just there at my back, but it will take a careful conjuring to know she is with me. I want to believe that it is exactly this desire to see her that will return her to me. In every glorious detail. But I am new at missing her and can't yet be sure.

It's terrifying, this not knowing what's to come. I can already imagine Fear around every corner. The Unknown seems rife with it. But here, with this glorious new curiosity, is one thing bigger than all the plagues and dangers that could strike us down at any moment. Here in my chest, there is Hope. I can feel it inside Eleanor, too. Not the false hope that she will live forever or that Walter will change. But hope for what she has left while she has it. Hope for more sun on her face, to hear that one song one more time, to push off the wall and cut through water. Hope to hold hands again like she means it, to know herself without fear, to taste one last strawberry.

And like the thing with feathers, I will be right here, looking forward to the mess and the miles, trusting that the world will be made whole.

"Forward," by my aunt, Julie Bonasera (in her own punctuation and "voice" before her death from ALS, October 17, 2013)

Nothing is "all happy" or "all sad".....there's always a mixture of both. How do I start a forward...?

My niece, Erika, asked me to write a forward to her newly written book.

She's a very talented young lady and I felt honored that she would want to use my words. I've never done any writing before......

I knew that her main character in the novel would have several of the same health symptoms that I'd been struggling with for over a year and eventually the same diagnosis.

I'll never forget that day...! It just happened to be Valentine's

Day.....Feb. 14, 2012.

It had been nine months since my first symptom of slurred speech started on a vacation to another niece's H. S. Graduation in Portland, Oregon. After a myriad of other medical tests, my husband of forty-three years, Tom, sat next to me in the Neurologist's office. And after so many other Drs. repeatedly said the same thing....

Inconclusive, this Dr. didn't hesitate to give me the fatal news..... ALS, Lou Gehrig's Disease.

Of course, we held each other and cried for some time just thinking about my questionable future. My main thought was how long I would get to spend with my first two grandchildren, both due in the next June. But the story is not about the diagnosis, but what follows...?

We had dinner plans with friends that night, so on our drive home we talked about what we would do....Tom didn't want to go out and try to make small talk but I suddenly saw this decision as a forecast for the future. How would we handle these days ahead, sit at home and cry or keep enjoying the things we loved to do for as long as we can? So we decided right there and then to stay positive, not to whine, and have as much fun as we can with our family and friends!!

We didn't really tell friends until after babies in June. That was to be the focus for those few months.

So we didn't tell our friends that night. I remember nudging Tom under the table as he drifted off in thought to bring him back, but he was very gloomy...they probably thought he had just had a bad day at work..?! I can cover up for him pretty well.

Back at the very beginning...the more angry phase...I did yell at God several times "how bout cancer, at least I could fight that". And I thought "no, I would not say that and make my sister Susan's, or anyone's, fight any less heroic. And I always go back to kids with cancer... The worst!

Did they get to pick their own disease?

I've had several people ask me after my diagnosis, don't you ever ask yourself, "WHY ME?".......I've never even thought of that or would think of asking myself that....??

Instead I say to them and to myself..."Why NOT me?"

There are children who have cancer...!! There are young men dying everyday in war....!!

Those are so much worse than what I'm dealing with...!!

And look at my LIFE....!! It's been amazing...!! How can I regret how I'm leaving when my life has been SO blessed!? I was raised by terrific parents in such a happy household with six siblings!

Sure some of my siblings even complain about how they felt in such a big family...?? I don't get that...I thought it was terrific everyday...maybe I ONLY see the GOOD? But we were loved unconditionally everyday...!

Then I met my husband in college and we raised four awesome sons. I always wanted to be a teacher and was, but never realized how much I was made to be a Mother. I loved the years of staying home and raising our boys. They were the most rewarding days of my life! Each boy was so different and I thought it was the biggest challenge to let them be what they wanted to be and to encourage them in any way to get there. All that love I gave to them came back to me in so many ways. And now two of my sons are married and I finally have my "Girls"....my two daughters-in-law and my two grandsons..!! They give me so much Hope and Love that I feel like I could live forever.!

So it's not a matter of how you leave this world or when....But rather how you live your life or is it how you ENJOY the LIFE you are given...!

Gratitude

What a thing! To write a book and to finish it, even and especially after "failing" over 100 times. My Girl Friday, Megsie, could tell you the exact number of rejections from agents and editors, as she has charted them all and we have "cheers-ed" each and every one. But there, in my chest, was Hope. So on I pressed. … And so, too, did you, dear human reading this! Thank you for staying with me and with Eleanor to arrive here with us at *The End* and into this space of gratitude. Before anyone else, let me thank YOU! Thank you! Thank you! Thank you! Truly. I am so very grateful.

I am a lady blessed with a deep pocket full of beloveds. So many of you who have encouraged me to write down and share forward my thoughts in many forms throughout my life—Mikey, G, Marie, Buffy, Anna, Looney, Onye, Markas, Kevin, Sharon, Kate, Havi, Sam, KC, Beth Ann, Jess and Chris (The English and The American versions), Christopher, Shawn, the nares (Lauri, aka the prez, Lady Danger, and Carson), and and and … I am full-hearted in my love and gratitude for you. I also want to thank the dear humans who have championed my words, eagerly awaited this book, and made me want to finish—Katie and Tim, Jason, Lily, Jennifer, Wendy, René, Beth, Dougie, Bernadette, Jen Jen, Aunt Susan, Uncle Danny, Twila and Ron, and … oh I know I'm forgetting someone, and I don't want to mush you.

I could not have gotten here without my early readers, the six who read it in real-time back when it had a different title and didn't fully know itself. Sending a chapter each day kept me going as I wrote each morning before the baby got up, the email poured in, and the day got too busy to hear my own voice. Thank you to my sister, Ashley, who made me start this book and who shows up all over its pages and in the laugh lines of my heart. To db, who always believed in my writing and in this novel. Thank you, mister. To Miche, 2e, and mamakaty, thank you for the parades you threw for every paragraph and how you keep me afloat in this life. To my mama, Tink, who thought everything I did was brilliant—even when it wasn't—I am forever grateful. You laughed at every silly moment of my life. And stoked the dark side of my heart. I miss you every day.

A special thank you to Liana—I will never forget the time in the bungalow by the sea and how just imagining it made me keep going. Thanks to Marti Mihalyi for the words that inspired Eleanor's song in the Karlin Inn (page 62). Havilah sang these to me and Sam back in the day, and they hung on the wall of many homes we lived in together. Thank you to Kristen and her original "Jeremy" who stood watch over my Interlochen girls of summer—you all got me thinking in reverse so many years ago. And to Sammy—thank you for reading and embodying the words through our dances and films. All I had to do was see you in that red dress underwater, describe that moment, and it became real.

A forever thank you to my Aunt Julie, who was my advisor on the hard truths about ALS. Thank you for sharing your voice with me, just as you were losing yours to this terrible disease. Thank you, also, for lending me parts of you—swimming, teaching, and talking on the phone—and letting me make up the rest. You were blessed to be gifted a husband nothing like Walter, and I don't believe you lived one day in regret. Thank you for teaching me about gratitude and bravery, even and especially as you were fighting the battle of your life. If we had to lose you both, I'm so glad you and my mom are back together, now on the other side of the veil, talking and laughing as you always did.

Thank you to my brilliant editor, brain partner and reluctant friend, Tim Grassley. I knew I would win you over. I cannot thank you enough. This book would not be herself without you. Nor would I.

To my lightening in a bottle, my beloved kiddo, Ezra. Thank you for the first-hand research into the joy, panic, and failure of mothering and for the redemptive love that you offer me always. Thank you for getting me, your weirdo mom, and for saying, "Oh that's sad—in a good way," when I read parts out-loud. If ever you forget my voice, here it is, returned to you. You are the heart of my moon.

And then, there is Megan, my Girl Friday, my love, and my wife. At first, you were a friend who saw necessity in my words and in getting them out into the world. Thank you, dear one, for toiling tirelessly to try to get this baby in print. And then, after years of heartache and heart-opening and new discovery on every plane, you were still there, loving me and Eleanor. I can't believe how you see me. Thank you for encouraging me to self-publish, to hold hands again like I mean it, and to know myself without fear. It's you and me, all the way to the coast, babies.

Thank you for buying this book! A portion of the proceeds will go to support the Julie Bonasera Fund for ALS and neuromuscular disease.

Please visit and consider giving:

https://giveto.osu.edu/makeagift/details/315770

www.ingramcontent.com/pod-product-compliance
Lightning Source LLC
Chambersburg PA
CBHW020915310726
48980CB00011B/892/J

* 9 7 9 8 9 9 2 7 9 6 4 0 7 *